THE
MANOR

Parts of this book were previously published as *The Key of Greed.*

Cover Design by ambient studios

Print ISBN 978-1-957529-33-2

Ebook ISBN 978-1-957529-34-9

Library of Congress Control Number 2024942773

part one

MURDERS UNDER THE SUN
SEASON SIX; INTRO

MOLLY: Welcome to *Murders Under the Sun*, a podcast that explores a series of unusual crimes that have occurred in sunny Southern California.

I'm Molly Shure, your host. For the past five years I've worked as a journalist at a local news outlet. Stories of murder and mayhem come across my desk weekly, if not daily. However, one day last March, I noticed something startling.

There seemed to be a connection between several crimes that transpired over a five-year period—seven crimes to be precise. What connected them? Location for one. They all took place within a twenty-mile radius of each other, but that alone wasn't significant.

The thing that pinged in my brain was that many of the people at the center of these crimes knew each other. Not the criminals, which would be an obvious thread, but the victims. I know, I know, six degrees of separation. Didn't I already say the crimes took place in a twenty-mile radius? But we're not talking six degrees here. It's more like one degree.

You'll see if you stick with me for all seven seasons of the show, the crimes circle back around. The people you meet in the first season play a role in Season Seven's story.

Am I imagining things? Is the connection real? Is there one mastermind behind the crimes? Or are they linked by some kind of social, psychological or even spiritual force? I'm afraid that's something you'll have to decide for yourself.

Each season, I'll do a deep dive into just one

of these stories. You'll hear from the people who were victimized, and listen to transcripts of journal entries, memoirs, and letters from others who were involved—sometimes the criminals themselves—and behind the scenes information you can't get anywhere else.

So, get out your sunglasses. We're pulling back the curtains and letting the light shine on some of Orange County's darkest mysteries.

part two

MURDERS UNDER THE SUN
SEASON SIX; EPISODE ONE

MOLLY: Welcome to Season Six of *Murders Under the Sun*. This is Molly Shure, your host.

I have to say this season, which I've entitled *The Manor*, may be the most compelling or unsettling or fascinating yet. I'm not sure which adjective fits best. Maybe all of them. I was absolutely riveted by Willow's story.

When we wrapped up last season, we learned that she was dating a man named Jonathan. He seemed perfect. He was handsome, fun, had a good career, came from a wealthy family, and liked to cook. Even Booker, Willow's dad, liked him.

As this season opens, we discover that Willow is pregnant with Jonathan's child. Their relationship went from casual to serious in a matter of months. We also discover that his father has died, which may require Jonathan to get more involved in his family's affairs.

As long time listeners know, in every season I interview the person impacted most by the crimes. In this case, it's Willow. I then take my notes and create a third person narrative in which I attempt to put you, the listener, into their mind, so you see what they see and feel what they feel. This script goes through several edits. It bounces back and forth between me and the individual until we're both happy with it. So, I can safely say you will experience the story as close to the way they experienced it as is possible.

Each season, I also include missives from another character that reveal things that have happened behind the scenes. Listeners often don't know who that individual is until our hero knows.

In *The Manor*, I've included entries from a journal Willow finds in Episode Four. She won't know who the writer of the journal is until the very end, however, so neither will we. The diary is hard to hear in spots, but it becomes very important as the story unfolds. It provides clues that help Willow—and us—uncover the who and why behind the crimes.

I decided to start off today with a short journal entry. The style it's written in is very different from Willow's matter-of-fact communication. It's a little poetic, and definitely imaginative and evocative. I feel like this first entry sets the tone for the entire season.

JUNE 3

My cage is gilded. Like the proverbial songbird, I have everything I could ever want except freedom. The meals I'm served are delicious. The pictures on my walls, expensive. Even my bedding is the highest thread count money can buy. I don't care. All I want is out.

If that's going to happen, I'm going to have to engineer it, cleverly, creatively, because they don't want me to leave. They believe, wrongly, that I'm too valuable.

I've always thought being a commodity was something to be aspired to. Who doesn't wish to be treasured? I now know that coin has two sides, heads and tails. Heads is the winning side of the equation, the only side most of us have ever imagined. It's the only side I'd ever considered.

Coins can be spent, or they can be hoarded. When they're spent, they circulate, moving from admiring hand to admiring hand. When they're hoarded, they're locked in a secret place, held for some future event—real or imagined. Heads, I win. Tails, I lose. Tails has become my life.

MOLLY: The writer's words make me feel so claustrophobic. Did I mention in past seasons that I don't like close spaces? Maybe that's why this season impacted me so personally, but enough about me. Let's get into Willow's narrative.

6.1.2

EVERYONE WORE BLACK BUT WILLOW. How stupid could she be? Even the universe seemed to understand the need for adherence to tradition. The day wore gloom like a shroud, the priest's white collar neon against its leaden sky. She tugged her green blazer tighter around herself, hoping to cover more of her cream silk blouse.

Willow cast a glance at Jonathan, who stood granite still next to her. His blue eyes, almost iridescent in the colorless surroundings, were dry, his square jaw tense. Only the pallor of his face gave any indication of his emotion.

Her gaze roamed the rest of the group gathered at the grave. They were as somber as their clothing, each appearing deep in their own dark thoughts, expressions unreadable. Not even Hamish's widow or daughter shed a tear. *Note to self—the wealthy do their crying in private.*

She'd expected this event to be well attended. Hamish Lauder was rich if not loved, and well-known with Orange County's elite, but his funeral was as tight-fisted as the man had been. She squeezed Jonathan's arm in sympathy.

The priest nodded his head toward Gerry, Hamish's widow. Jonathan tugged Willow's hand, dropped it, then hurried to his mother's side. Gerry and Jonathan walked together toward the yawning hole in the otherwise perfectly groomed lawn. Was Willow supposed to follow?

She stood still, wishing she'd worn something more appropriate, wishing she knew what to do. Gerry plucked a white rose from a vase balanced in the grass and let it fall into the abyss. Jonathan glanced at Willow over his shoulder and widened his eyes meaningfully before doing the same, and after a quiet moment the two resumed their places.

He leaned toward Willow when he reached her side and lowered his voice. "Why didn't you come with me?"

Her answer was a small shake of her head. She didn't go because she'd have felt like a Protestant taking communion at a Catholic Mass. This wasn't her clan, her people. They'd had this discussion before, and he hadn't understood her feelings then. Now wasn't the time to tackle the topic again.

A rustle of fabric drew Willow's attention. Chloe, Jonathan's beautiful twin, and her fiancé walked up the grassy aisle to the grave. Mat and Chloe had only been engaged a month and a half longer than Willow and Jonathan, but he seemed perfectly at ease with the Lauders.

Of course, he came from money. Mateo Avila was a pediatrician. He was also descended from one of the first Spanish families of Southern California. Willow was descended from a Kentucky firefighter and a chef who specialized in Southern-French fusion food.

Mat's suit probably cost more than she paid for three months' rent, and Chloe's outfit—a flowing, black dress with an edge of lace peeking from the hem—more than Willow's annual grocery budget. They looked cool, sophisticated, and elegant. Willow shifted her weight until her pilling gray wool slacks were halfway hidden behind Jonathan.

After Chloe and Mat paid their respects, Hamish's brother, his rabbit-faced wife, and his pale daughter each threw a rose into the dark hole. Willow had met them briefly at Sunset House the month before. The daughter's name was Ophelia. Willow remembered it because the Shakespearean association was so apt. According to Jonathan, Ophelia was the crazy cousin every family had and tried to hide.

The final flower was tossed into the grave by an olive-skinned, hollow-eyed woman of about Willow's age. The priest stood, gave a short homily, prayed, then announced the reception following at Sunset House. Nobody gave a eulogy.

Months ago, when Willow's father, Booker, was in the hospital, fear had painted visions of his death and burial in her mind. If her father had died—thank God he hadn't—she was sure the entire fire department would have turned out for the funeral, along with the neighborhood and the entire large, unruly, extended Wells family. Eulogies would go on for hours amid tears and laughter and toasts to his memory.

Hamish's family turned away from the gravesite without a backwards glance. Everyone made their way toward the cars parked along the cemetery's narrow streets. The clicking of their hard-soled shoes echoed in the holy hush. Willow gripped Jonathan's arm. She'd been a bit off-balance lately, and her kitten heels weren't helping. "How are you doing?" she asked under her breath.

Jonathan inhaled deeply as if he were going to speak then tightened his lips. He'd been opaque since his father's death. A neutral veil had slid over his face, masking his emotions. The death had been a surprise, but not a shock. After Hamish's first stroke, the doctor had warned the family another could come at any time. Willow had assumed Jonathan was ready for this eventuality, but now she wasn't sure. Grief, anger, denial, whatever he was feeling was a mystery to her. He wasn't sharing.

"I think I should call an Uber," Willow said.

Jonathan stopped walking and stared at her. "Why on earth would you do that?"

"I don't belong in the limo."

"Of course you do. You're my fiancée."

"I'm not family yet."

He placed his free hand on the small bump hidden beneath her blazer. "You're carrying family. That's more than Mat can say." He removed his hand quickly, tugged her arm, and began walking again. Willow tumbled forward, righted herself, and hurried along beside him.

She might be carrying Hamish's grandchild, but nobody knew it. They'd planned to break the news to Jonathan's parents when Hamish recovered from his first stroke. He'd died before they'd had the chance, and it didn't seem appropriate to bring it up now.

They reached the limo after Gerry, Chloe, and Mat had been seated.

As Willow slid inside, she noticed the woman who'd thrown the last rose unlocking a car across the narrow road. Tears streaked her face. Someone had loved Hamish, then. Who was she?

The fifteen-minute ride from San Juan Capistrano to San Clemente was silent and awkward. It was a relief when the wrought iron gates of Sunset House opened and the parade of vehicles processed through. A staff of four, all dressed in somber black uniforms, met them at the top of the circular drive. It looked like a scene from *Downton Abbey*.

The first time Willow had visited Sunset House, she'd been in awe. She hadn't been raised in poverty, far from it. Her upbringing was very middle class. She hadn't had everything she'd wanted, but she'd had everything she'd needed. Sunset House was a fairy tale. It was full of things you never knew you should want until you saw them.

House was a misnomer, though. It was an estate, a manor. Behind its high walls and locked gates were several buildings. The main house, or *hacienda*, was horseshoe shaped—a two story building encircling a courtyard of fountains and flowers. There was also a botanical conservatory, two unattached garages that housed six to ten cars each, a pool house, a garden shed that could sleep a family of five, and a library. The property bordered the Pacific Ocean, hence its name. The sunset view was breathtaking.

"What can I do to help?" she asked Jonathan after they dropped their coats into the arms of a dark-haired maid.

He tipped his head to one side, a quizzical expression on his perfectly proportioned face. "We have plenty of help."

She thought she heard condescension in his tone and felt her own face redden. This new Jonathan, the man he became when he was with his family, was foreign to her. Where was the fun foodie she'd sampled beer with in San Diego? Where was the man who'd been nervous about barbecuing ribs for her parents? "I, I know, but—"

He squeezed her shoulders. "You're very thoughtful, babe, but mother has it covered. It's what she does. Just be your beautiful self."

Willow decided not to interpret that comment to mean she wasn't good for anything but being attractive. She gave Jonathan an anemic smile and followed him from the front hall into the great room.

If the group of mourners seemed small at the gravesite, it appeared minuscule in the cavernous space. The ceiling was low, but the room went on for miles. A fire crackled at its far end. Long tables festooned with overflowing vases of flowers were filled with enough food for fifteen times the number of guests. Heavy, antique Spanish furniture beckoned the weary into their deeply cushioned embrace. Gerry Lauder had handled things beautifully, Jonathan was correct.

"Jonathan. Willow." Ophelia floated toward them under a cloud of platinum hair. "How are you holding up? It was a lovely ceremony, don't you think? Uncle Ham would have approved." She gave Jonathan a tight smile, then kissed Willow's cheeks with featherlight kisses.

Lovely wasn't how Willow would have described the funeral. Distinguished, staid, stoic, all seemed more appropriate. She didn't argue, however. Ophelia had already moved on to other topics.

"I'm sure Gerry appreciates you staying at the house. Chloe means well, but she's—"

Willow watched as Jonathan's sister glided up behind Ophelia and wondered if she should somehow warn his cousin.

"I'm what?" Chloe said.

Ophelia didn't turn, didn't blink, didn't miss a beat. "Practical and unemotional, which has its place, but a grieving widow needs compassion."

Chloe closed her eyes for a long beat. When she opened them, they held a combination of frustration, irritation, and humor. Willow had seen the same look play across Jonathan's features when he talked about his cousin. "I hope you don't run away in horror after this exposure to the family, Willow," she said.

"Not at all. I think everyone is handling the day well, considering," Willow said.

A bubble of laughter popped from Ophelia's lips. She fluttered a hand to her mouth as if trying to cork it. "Handling it well is an understatement. Zero drama is closer to the truth."

Chloe turned ninety degrees to face her cousin. "And what should we do? Weep, wail, gnash our teeth?"

"Any of the above would be more human."

"That's your role in the family."

Ophelia licked her teeth before baring them. "One of us must represent the human race."

Chloe's lip twitched with a retort, but before she could voice it, Jonathan intervened. "Can we save this for another day?"

"Absolutely," Ophelia said. "Let's pick it up at the reading of the will." She turned her faded blue eyes on Willow. "You'll be there, won't you?"

Willow was startled. She hadn't known there was such a date and wouldn't go if she had.

"She's a busy woman, Lia." Jonathan answered for her.

Ophelia's gaze flitted to Willow's abdomen and lingered for a beat too long. "I guess you'll have to watch out for her interests," Ophelia said.

"I don't have any interests." The words exploded from Willow. The last thing she wanted was Jonathan, Chloe, or anybody else in the family to think that she was marrying for the money. As far as she was concerned, Jonathan's wealth was a liability, not an asset. It came between them like a physical thing at times.

Chloe looked back and forth between them, confusion in her eyes. Jonathan stared at his shoes, cheeks reddening. After a hesitation, Ophelia pivoted on her expensive heel and walked away.

"Is there something I don't know about?" Chloe asked.

Jonathan watched Ophelia cross the room. "No."

"Has she done it—" Chloe looked at her brother.

"Again? You know I don't—"

"Believe in that." Chloe finished his sentence, just as he'd finished hers. "It doesn't matter what you or I believe. She knows something."

Jonathan locked eyes with his sister, their faces suddenly so similar. "No," he said again.

Neither spoke for a long moment, but that didn't mean communication had stopped. The twins had a language all their own, and sometimes it was non-verbal.

Chloe broke the tension. "I'd better find Mat."

Willow grabbed Jonathan's arm after she walked away. "Did you tell Ophelia about the baby? Shouldn't we tell your mother first? I thought we were going to wait?"

"I did not say a thing." His voice was tired.

"Then how does Ophelia know?"

He inhaled and exhaled slowly. "She's fishing. Lia fancies herself a psychic. Oh, she doesn't use that word. She says she has dreams. I think she's just good at reading people."

"Dreams?"

"Yes, dreams that appear to come true." He wagged a hand in the air as if he were playing a tambourine.

"That's... " Willow let her sentence trail off for want of an adjective. Crazy was the one that came to mind, but she didn't say it. She'd never liked the use of the word in conjunction with Ophelia's name. She'd always felt it was unkind, demeaning.

"Crazy," Jonathan said for her. "Now you know why we say it. The dreams are only the tip of the delusional iceberg."

"Jonathan. Willow." Gerry's voice carried across the room. "Come and eat. There's too much food, as usual."

Jonathan kissed Willow lightly on the lips. "We'd better go."

She followed him to a buffet table and perused the shrimp and caviar mounded there. She craved macaroni and cheese, but didn't see anything even closely resembling it. She picked up a plate and spooned a bit of salad onto it.

Jonathan's inheritance had advantages, but it also complicated her life. It drew her and repelled her like a moth to a citronella candle. If she hadn't been so crazy in love with him, and if she hadn't been pregnant, she'd have asked him to wait on the engagement. Easing into their joined life would have been more comfortable.

At least, they wouldn't have to worry about the bulk of the estate until Gerry died, and that would be years from now.

6.1.3

WILLOW FINISHED the salad but couldn't stomach anything else. She'd been told that after the first three months of pregnancy, morning sickness, sensitivity to smells, and all-day queasiness would fade away. She'd passed the three-month mark a week ago, but the magic hadn't happened. It had better happen soon. It couldn't be good for her growing child to subsist on crackers, macaroni and cheese, and the occasional bowl of vegetarian pho.

She stood near the fireplace, pushed an olive around her plate with a fork, and tried to maintain a fascinated expression while Ophelia's father regaled her with sailing stories. She felt, rather than saw, Jonathan come up beside her—her gaze being fixed on Bob. Or was it Rob?

"Can I borrow my fiancée, Uncle Cob?"

Cob, that was it. What was Cob short for? Coben, like Harlan? But Coben was Harlan's last name. Jacob, maybe?

Cob's words interrupted her musings. "Of course. I think I was boring her anyway."

"I'm sure you weren't," Jonathan said.

"I was telling her about the time Alan and I almost won the first race of the Spring Series out of San Diego Harbor. You remember that story don't you, Jonathan?"

Jonathan latched onto Willow's elbow and began to drag her

toward the French doors that opened onto the courtyard. "How could I forget?"

"The sea was angry that day... " Cob called after them.

Jonathan continued their walk toward the door, lobbing words over his shoulder. "It's a miracle you didn't capsize."

"It was a close—" The end of Cob's sentence was cut off by the closing of the glass door behind them.

"Sorry about that," Jonathan said. "Uncle Cob has had one adventure in his life, and he wants everyone to know about it."

"Didn't George Costanza say that?"

"What? That Uncle Cob only had one adventure in his life?"

"No." She slapped his arm lightly. "*The sea was angry that day, my friend—like an old man trying to send soup back in a deli. It's from Seinfeld.*" Jonathan's brow furrowed. "Don't tell me you've never seen *Seinfeld*?"

One side of his mouth raised in chagrin. "Okay. I won't."

Willow shook her head. "I don't know how this relationship is going to work."

"I'll watch it. I promise." He drew her across the paved courtyard. "But I want to show you something first."

The damp evening air was scented with jasmine and orange blossoms. The flower beds shone in the dying day. Willow wanted to slow down and take in her surroundings, but he hurried her forward. They walked through an opening in the hedge and onto a broad lawn. She stopped short.

An ocean vista opened before her. The gloom of the day had lifted like a stage curtain to reveal a breathtaking show. Golden wisps of clouds danced with slashes of deep purple against a crimson background. "Oh." It was the only word she could manage.

Jonathan slowed his pace. "It's beautiful, but it isn't what I wanted to show you."

"What could be better than this?"

"You'll see." He took her hand and gave her a tug. Willow walked with him, but craned her neck to watch the sunset. He dragged her past another hedge and onto a path lined with paving stones where she was forced to turn her gaze forward so she wouldn't stumble. The path ended at a stucco building she knew was the library although she'd never been inside.

Its windows were dark and empty and uninviting. She wished they'd have stayed at the cliff, but Jonathan had already pulled a key from his pocket and was opening the front door. He shot her a bright smile then disappeared into the black doorway. Willow hesitated for a second, then followed.

She smelled the library before she saw it. Jonathan snapped on lights to reveal a small foyer that narrowed into a hallway. The scents of old leather, furniture polish and something else, something she associated with orchestra pits, surrounded her. She closed her eyes and sniffed. Rosin, that was it. Pleasure coursed through her.

She was at school, in the orchestra pit, tuning her violin and waiting for the first downbeat of the conductor's baton. She hadn't realized how deeply she missed it until she'd smelled this smell. Pounding on the upright piano in her classroom to accompany children as they sang *My Bonnie Lies Over the Ocean* wasn't the same.

When she opened her eyes, she was alone in the foyer, but a patch of light that hadn't been there before shone from an open doorway down the hall. She walked toward it and came to the source of the wonderful perfume, Hamish's office.

Jonathan gestured for her to close the door. She did, and moved into the center of the room. All around her were floor to ceiling bookshelves lined with volumes. Breaking up the front wall was a huge stone fireplace flanked by tall windows. Light shone through them, creating mauve rectangles on an ancient Persian carpet. It only took a second for her to take all this in before her gaze was drawn to a violin stand next to one of the windows. A violin more beautiful than any she'd ever seen rested on it.

Without realizing how she'd gotten there, she found herself standing beside it, her hand stroking the gleaming wood. "Is this a Romeo Antoniazzi?" she asked. They were priced in the tens of thousands. Willow still played the Jay Haide her parents had purchased for her when she went to college. It was a good instrument for its price range, but it couldn't compare to the Antoniazzi.

"It is," Jonathan said.

"I didn't know your father played."

"He did. Not nearly as well as you do, but it was something he loved."

"It's amazing."

"Play it."

"I couldn't."

Jonathan strode to the violin, lifted it and its bow from the stand, and handed them to her. "Please."

Willow drew the bow across the strings, and shivered. The notes were deep and mellow and pure, but out of tune. She plucked strings and turned pegs until she was happy, then played the opening measures of Amy Beach's *Violin Sonata*.

Jonathan applauded as the last notes reverberated through the grand space. "No, Dad didn't play anything like you do. That was beautiful."

Willow replaced the instrument on its stand. "I'm surprised he didn't keep it in its case."

"The room is temperature and humidity controlled because of the books." He waved a hand at the shelves. "The violin isn't the most expensive thing in here."

Her gaze roamed the shelves. She saw many titles she'd never heard of, but there were also books by authors she loved, like Twain, Du Maurier, and Tolkien. Shakespeare, including five volumes with narrow spines labeled *Macbeth*, took an entire shelf. Based on the number of tooled leather covers, she guessed many were either early or first editions.

Jonathan walked to the back of the room and opened the drawer of a mammoth desk that sat in the far corner. "My mother had the run of the house, but the library was Dad's domain." He removed a pair of white gloves and slipped them on.

There was a glass-fronted cabinet on the wall near the desk. Jonathan pulled a ring from his pocket, inserted a key into one of its doors, turned and opened it. He reached inside with gloved hands and removed a stack of volumes. "Come see." He placed them on the desk.

Willow wandered over. What other wonders had Hamish possessed? When she saw these, she gasped. Spread across the desktop was sheet music spanning the alphabet from Beethoven to Vivaldi, every book old and brittle.

"His sheet music is worth a small fortune. Some of the scores have composer's markings. Some were used and signed by famous musicians," Jonathan said.

"I didn't realize your father was such a collector."

He gave her a half smile. "When you have more money than you need, you have to do something with it."

Willow didn't touch the music since she wasn't wearing gloves, but Jonathan leafed through the books showing her the highlights. He returned them, and as he locked the cupboard doors again, he said, "Now for the *pièce de résistance.*"

She laughed. "I don't think I can take anymore."

"Seriously, look at this." He led her to a frame on the wall. Beneath the glass was a fragment of music, yellowed with age. Words were written beneath the notes. It was a vocal piece. She squinted in an attempt to read them.

Let's have a dance upon the heath. "Is this from Davenant's *Macbeth*?"

"Very good. Yes, it's Lock's song for the weird sisters, or the three witches, as they're more commonly known."

"How old is it?"

"Very. It's not original, but probably from the early 1800s. Davenant's *Macbeth* went out of style before the middle of the century. My father was somewhat obsessed with *Macbeth*."

"I saw five versions on the shelf." Willow waved to the wall where the Shakespeare was kept.

Jonathan took the hand she waved and pulled her into a hug. "Despite the way it may appear, I didn't bring you here to show off."

She gazed up at him. "No? Because I'm impressed. You had me at the Antoniazzi."

"I want to get married, soon."

She pulled away from him. "We talked about this. We decided to wait until after the baby is born so I can enjoy a glass of champagne at my wedding."

"We can have a wedding, a reception, anything you want after the baby comes. I want to elope now."

"Elope?" This was a new idea.

Jonathan broke into the kind of smile she hadn't seen since his father passed away. His face, always handsome, was fine art when he smiled. "We can go to the Central Coast. A family friend owns a vineyard there. We can marry under his vines and stay in the guest house for the weekend. We'll have a real honeymoon later, but it would be romantic, don't you think? Just you and me and the grapes?"

Willow couldn't help herself. She felt her face break into a grin to match his. "It does sound romantic, but I wanted to live together after we got married."

"So, we'll live together."

"But my apartment... I was going to hold on to it until I found a job in Orange County."

He hit his forehead with the heel of his hand. "Sorry, I wasn't clear. This is your job. Or it could be your job."

"This?"

"The collection. Someone needs to catalog it."

Confusion flushed her face. "I'm not an antiques expert."

"No, but you're so good at research, and you definitely know more about the music than the rest of us."

"There are professionals—"

He cut her off. "And we'll hire one when we get ready to sell what we don't want to keep. We still need someone in the family to work with them, someone who knows what we've got here. Dad was very organized about business, but not about his hobbies."

Willow turned slowly and surveyed her surroundings. It would be amazing to spend time in this room, researching and poring over its contents.

"You can practice on the violin. Maybe after the baby comes, you could audition for a local orchestra, the Pacific Symphony even. Instead of teaching music, you could perform." He said the last word as if it were holy.

A thrill of pleasure bubbled inside her. "I don't know."

"Why not?"

Willow couldn't say why not. She wasn't sure. It was tempting. This room, the violin, they were tempting. She hated being away from Jonathan when she was in San Diego and he was here. Her mother would be happy if the baby were born on the right side of the sheets. There were so many reasons to say yes. "I have two more weeks of school. Why don't we think about it?"

The light in Jonathan's eyes faded. "What's to think about?"

"It's a big decision."

"You're wearing my ring."

"I know, but I thought we were going to get a place together after we married, not move in with your mother."

His eyebrows lifted. "Is that all? Then we'll find a place in San Clemente, or Dana Point, or wherever you want."

She placed a hand on her growing abdomen. She wouldn't waddle down the aisle. She'd decided that when she'd discovered she was pregnant. It was now, or a year from now. Jonathan's Mediterranean-blue eyes lured her like a tropical vacation. "I love teaching."

"You can find another teaching job when the baby is older."

"It's hard to get back in when you've taken time off."

He lifted a shoulder and let it drop. "You're a Lauder, or you will be. My family has connections."

Willow's jaw tightened, and the happy bubble inside her burst. There it was again—the push and pull. Money was lovely when it provided world-class violins, not as lovely when it bought you favors.

She'd been taught that level playing fields were the fair ones, that earning her own way in the world was something to be proud of. She wanted to raise her child, their child, with the same values. She broke away and walked toward the door, her movements stiff. "I'll give you an answer before school is out."

6.1.4

THE WHITE BENGAL TIGER YAWNED, displaying teeth longer than Willow's fingers. The animal stood and rubbed its side languidly against the bars of the enclosure. "She seems healthy, but I can't help feeling sorry for her," Honey said.

"I know." Willow turned away from the cage and walked along the dusty path to view the other animals. She should have realized taking her mother to Rancho Las Lomas—taking Honey to any kind of zoo or animal sanctuary—was a bad idea. "She can't live in the wild. That's what the handler said. Her coloring would make her a target."

Honey paused at another enclosure to watch a pair of raccoons snoozing in the shade. "She's always lived in captivity. So, I guess, she wouldn't know what to do with herself if she was released. She'd probably starve to death. It just seems sad. An animal that can run thirty miles an hour stuck in a cage."

Irritation, hot and itchy, crept up Willow's neck. "I didn't bring you here to bum you out, Mom. I was trying to do something nice."

Honey hugged her daughter. "I'm sorry. This is nice. So nice. It's beautiful here. I'm just a worrywart when it comes to critters—you know that."

Willow returned the hug, then broke away. "Let's eat. I'll get you a flight of wine at the barn if you set up the picnic."

"I don't need any wine. Bubbly water is great for me."

Bubbly water was never great for Honey. She was trying to be supportive because Willow couldn't drink. It was sweet of her. They made their way over the uneven terrain past enclosures of exotic birds and animals to the "booze barn," as Booker called it. "I wish Dad had come," Willow said.

Honey lowered herself onto the blanket Willow had spread on the grass earlier. "It's Mother's Day. I wanted you to myself."

"If Ash had been able to get away, Dad would be here." Willow's brother was a Marine stationed at Camp Pendleton. His schedule was controlled by the military.

"But he couldn't, and Book thought we'd like time to ourselves. It was very thoughtful of him." Honey unzipped the thermal bag Willow had packed and began removing its contents.

A lump formed in Willow's throat. Her father always seemed to have time for everybody but her. The thought was petty and probably untrue. If she voiced it, Honey would tell her how much her father loved her, and that she was being ridiculous. It felt true, though.

"Oh, you brought Brie." Honey almost groaned. "I guess I have to have a glass of wine. It's mandatory with Brie."

"I'll get it." Willow rose and wandered into line at the barn. By the time she returned, Honey had laid out the food and somehow managed to make the simple offering look like the cover of *Food & Wine* magazine. "How do you do that?"

Honey watched as Willow dropped onto the blanket. "You're starting to show," she said, ignoring the question.

"You think?"

"If I didn't know how skinny you usually are, I wouldn't notice. But I do, and I can see my grandbaby."

Willow reached for a piece of bread Honey had topped with a slice of hard cheese—no Brie for baby. Eating gave her a minute to collect her thoughts. She knew her parents were torn about her decision to wait on the wedding. On the one hand, they were old-fashioned enough to want their grandchild to be born inside of marriage. On the other, they didn't want her to rush into anything. Willow and Jonathan had only been dating for a little over a month when she got pregnant. And they'd met through an online dating site, another thing her parents weren't crazy about.

Jonathan had wined her and dined her, and Willow had wound up in bed with him after only a handful of dates. It wasn't her normal MO, which made the pregnancy seem even more unfair. She'd only had two other boyfriends in her life: Carl Sanderson, who'd taken her to prom, and Drake.

She'd been sure she was going to marry Drake. They'd dated all through college. After graduation he moved to San Diego to take a journalism job. She immediately started applying for teaching positions in the area. By the time she found one and moved south, Drake was living with another girl. Willow had been heartbroken.

Maybe she had rushed into things with Jonathan, but he was wonderful. When she was with him, she felt like the most valuable thing in his world. She'd been worried when she saw the little line on the pregnancy test, and had expected him to break up with her, accuse her of trying to trap him for his money.

He'd been delighted. So delighted that a week later he'd dropped onto one knee with a ring. Which brought her to her current dilemma. Why was she dragging her feet about marrying now?

Honey reached a hand toward Willow's face and brushed a hair from her eyes. "You're awfully pensive."

"Jonathan wants to elope." Willow blurted out the words.

Her mother's eyebrows disappeared under her highlighted bangs. She hesitated for several seconds then said, "And how do you feel about that?"

Willow pulled a grape off the bunch resting next to a wedge of cheddar and rolled it between her fingers. "I don't know."

"I thought you wanted a big wedding?"

"I do. He said we can still have one after the baby comes, like we'd planned, but this way we could make things official now."

Willow could see her mother weighing her words. Honey knew how important independence was to her daughter and tried very hard to give it to her. "He does have a point," she finally said.

"I knew you'd say that." Willow's words came out more harshly than she'd intended. Before Honey could defend herself or backpedal,

Willow added, "I didn't mean that the way it sounded. I know how you and Dad feel about us being married before the baby comes. It's not wrong. In fact, I agree. Theoretically. If you'd have told me a year ago I was going to be pregnant before I was hitched, I'd have laughed at you. But now that I am, I have to weigh my options."

Honey lifted her face to the sun before responding. She looked beautiful. She'd come through the terrible experiences of four months ago a changed woman. It wasn't only that she'd shed the stress and the weight she'd been burdened with for years. She'd also gained a kind of radiance. Facing death destroys some people, but others go through the crucible and are refined by it. Honey was one of the latter, and Willow was proud of her.

"I think I know what my problem is," Willow said.

Honey dropped her face and gazed at her daughter. "Yeah?"

"Jonathan is rich."

"That's not a news flash."

Willow held up a hand. "It's different now. His father has died, and he stands to inherit a lot of money."

"Money is a bad thing?" Honey's eyebrows knit together.

"No, but it makes me nervous. It's kind of like that tiger." She waved her hand in the general direction of the enclosure. "If you have everything you need handed to you, it can make you weak. After a while, you can't survive on your own."

"That's true, but wealth can also be a tool for good. You can be in charge of it, or it can be in charge of you. You're tough, baby. My money, no pun intended, is on you."

"So you think we should elope?"

"I think Jonathan is the father of your child whether you elope or not."

Willow acknowledged the truth of that statement with a nod, but she no longer wanted to talk about it. "Did Ash call you this morning?"

"He did. He wished me a happy Mother's Day."

The conversation shifted to the latest news from Willow's brother then wandered to funny stories from Honey's shop—Sweeter than Honey Gourmet Cooking Supplies. Forty-five minutes or so later, a breeze kicked up, and goosebumps pimpled Willow's arms. "You ready to go?"

"Yes." Honey's voice was heavy with regret. "I guess we should. Tomorrow is Monday. We both have to work, and you have a drive ahead of you."

As they packed the leftover food, Willow's phone buzzed from somewhere deep in her purse. She fished it out just in time to catch the call before it went to voice mail.

"Hey, Will." Jonathan's voice sounded strained.

"Hey, baby." *It's Jonathan*, she mouthed to her mother.

"I have bad news."

"What?" Worry raised the hair on her already chilled arms.

"Mother collapsed. I'm here at the house waiting for Mat. He's going to check her out. I don't think I'll be able to do dinner tonight." They had planned to go out for Willow's first Mother's Day before she headed to San Diego.

"Oh, no. I can be there in—"

"You don't have to come," he cut her off. "Chloe's with me."

A stab of jealousy poked at Willow. "If you're sure... "

"I'm sure. You get home safe. I'll call you tomorrow."

She disconnected the call and stared at her phone for a long moment.

"What happened?" Honey's forehead creased with concern.

Willow filled her in on the call as they cleaned up their lunch. "I offered to go to the house, but he said he was with Chloe." She bit off the end of the sentence.

They stood and began the trudge to the parking lot in silence. When it became obvious Willow wasn't going to say more, her mother spoke. "They are twins, darlin'."

"And?"

"Twins are, well, they're different than regular brothers and sisters. Poppy and Reed were inseparable as kids." Two of Honey's siblings were twins.

Willow's Honda came in sight, and she clicked the key fob. "Yeah, but they aren't inseparable now. Not as adults."

Honey walked around the passenger side of the car but paused before getting inside. "They still read each other's mind. Your uncle Fitz told me Reed called Poppy after her car accident."

"I'd call Ash if I heard he was in a car accident."

"That's what I'm saying. Nobody told Reed she had an accident. It had only happened an hour or two earlier. The family gossip chain hadn't been activated yet."

Willow pulled the rear door open and tossed the soft cooler onto the seat. "Maybe Uncle Reed was just calling to say hello, and he could tell Aunt Poppy was upset by the tone of her voice."

"At midnight?"

Willow dropped into the driver's seat. She hated these conversations. Her mother was a spiritual person. She wasn't. People always thought musicians were intuitive and ethereal, but it wasn't true. Most of the students in Willow's performing arts program were like her, logical.

Music is math, as her Theory One teacher used to say. Notes had measurable values. Even a *demisemihemidemisemiquaver*, a note so brief it was difficult to hear, had a number attached.

Honey patted the roof of Willow's car before entering. "Not everything fits neatly under a heading on one of your spreadsheets."

"Well, it should." Willow started the engine.

6.1.5

AS SOON AS the last choir member pushed through the swinging doors of the auditorium the next day, Willow gathered her music and headed after them. She shoved open the door with her shoulder, slid into the hallway, and ran right into Jaiden.

The woman backpedaled, a look of alarm on her pretty face. "Girl, where're you going in such a hurry?"

Willow hugged her stack of books to her chest. "Sorry, I'm headed to karate. I have a 4:30 class."

"Your dojo has adult classes at 4:30?"

"No." Half of Willow's mouth tipped into an ironic smile. "I can't stay awake after 8:00, so the 6:30 classes are out for me. I go to the teen classes."

"I guess that means you don't want to go out tonight?" Jaiden raised her eyebrows hopefully.

Willow opened her mouth to say no, but before she did, Jaiden said, "Michael's band is playing at that new wine bar. I think he was nervous to ask you because of your music background and all, but I know he wants you there. A group of us are going."

Michael was a sixth-grade teacher and a very talented guitarist. He also had a crush on Willow. At least, that's what Jaiden thought.

"I can't." Willow shifted her load of books. "I have karate."

Jaiden flipped a black ringlet over her shoulder and stuck out a trim hip. "At 4:30. Michael isn't on until 9:00."

"I know, but... " Willow wasn't sure how to end the sentence without sounding like a little old lady. She hadn't told anybody but her family that she was pregnant. She didn't want people to think that was why she and Jonathan had gotten engaged so quickly, even though it was.

Jaiden wagged a finger at her. "You know, ever since you started going out with that blue-eyed man, you haven't been any fun at all."

"I've just been busy."

Jaiden tipped her chin and looked at Willow through her eyelashes. "Doing what?"

Willow gazed at the ceiling. She couldn't keep her pregnancy a secret forever. According to her mother, she was starting to show. "Growing a baby."

Jaiden's eyes widened until white surrounded her iris. "No, sh—"

Willow hoisted her books under one arm, grabbed Jaiden with the other, and dragged her into the auditorium. The door closed behind them with a thud. "I haven't told anybody. I mean, hardly anybody. My parents and my brother know, but even Jonathan's family doesn't know yet."

"So, that's why you and Jonathan got... " she gestured to the rock on Willow's hand.

Willow licked her lips. "Well, not only that. I love him, of course."

"Of course."

"Don't say it like that."

"Like what? I said 'of course'. I'm agreeing with you."

"It doesn't sound like it."

Jaiden peered into Willow's eyes like she was searching for something there. "If you're happy, I'm happy for you."

"I'm happy."

"Okay."

"I'd better go."

"Karate. Right."

Jaiden followed Willow down the hall to the teacher's lounge, chattering about her students' essays on the topic she'd assigned, "My Favorite Pet." Willow laughed in all the right places.

Jaiden opened her locker. "Ryan Fitzroy has a snake. Did you know that?"

"Ugh." Willow grabbed her gym bag from her own locker.

"I mean, most of the kids have cats and dogs and guinea pigs and fish. Who would get a ten-year-old a snake?" Jaiden hefted a tote bag full of books over her shoulder.

"Especially one like Ryan Fitzroy."

"Right? It explains a lot, doesn't it?"

They left the lounge and headed into the hallway again. When they reached the parking lot, they both stopped at Willow's car.

Jaiden touched her arm. "I won't say anything about the baby."

"I appreciate that," Willow said.

"But it's nothing to be ashamed of. You're going to have a sweet, little person in your life soon. That's something to celebrate."

Willow was taken aback. *A sweet, little person.* Was that what she was carrying? She'd been thinking about pregnancy as a condition, not a person. She opened her car door. "Tell Michael to break a leg."

Grunts and cries and the overpowering smell of disinfected rubber mats assaulted Willow when she entered the karate dojo. She crossed the large room, dodged a tangle of white-robed students, and entered the bathroom at the rear of the building.

After closing herself into one of the stalls, she grabbed the zipper tab of her conservative, school-teacher skirt and tugged. An ecstatic moan escaped her lips. Release and relief. When had it gotten so tight?

I can see my grandbaby. Her mother's words played on the turntable in her mind. The next lyrics were Jaiden's, *a sweet, little person.* But the song seemed to have been written for someone else, not her.

Willow pulled on her gi and decided right then and there she would wear it everywhere—to school, on dates with Jonathan, grocery shopping, everywhere. It was so comfortable.

As she opened the stall door, the diamond on her finger caught the overhead light. She paused, admiring the prisms of color in its depths. Her stone was white. That's what the jeweler had said when she'd taken it in to get it sized, but a rainbow of hues was hidden inside.

It was a contradiction. Normally, Willow didn't like contradictions. She liked life to line up like the notes in a musical score, the highs in the treble clef, the lows in the bass. Rhythms were stated in the time signature at the beginning of a piece and obeyed. One of the reasons she didn't play jazz was that, often, it didn't obey the rules.

She did love her ring, however. She removed it and stowed it in her wallet. No jewelry in class. That was a dojo rule. Rules were good. She liked rules. So why did her life seem more like a jazz riff every day?

She re-entered the dojo and moved toward the group of students at the mirror, but hesitated before taking her place. Willow was a black belt and always one of the oldest people in the afternoon classes, which meant she should take a senior position.

Today, however, she saw a handful of women her age and older. She glanced at their belts. They were white, which meant either they were less experienced than she or they were visitors. She took a place to their left. Karate was built on a comforting foundation of etiquette and decorum. She always knew where she stood in a karate class.

The sensei walked to the front of the room, and the students came to attention. "We have guests." He gestured to the women standing next to Willow. "They're here from a YMCA self-defense class to learn some of our techniques."

The next half hour was spent perfecting a guard stance and various strikes and kicks to use against attackers. None of it was new to Willow.

She'd been doing martial arts since Ash turned eleven, had a growth spurt, and passed her up in height. That's when she discovered little brothers were fun to abuse—until they got bigger than you. Then watch out. Especially watch out for little brothers who were obsessed with the military.

Ash had ambushed her, staged frontal attacks, bombed her from his top bunk, and basically made her life miserable until their mother enrolled them both in karate classes.

When the Sensei was satisfied the group had learned the basics, he divided them into duos to practice on each other. Willow was paired with a boy named Roger. He was only a few inches shorter than her but probably weighed twenty pounds less. She bet his mother sent him to karate because of problems at school. He looked like bully bait.

Roger played the villain first. He moved toward her with a wicked grin on his pimply face. Willow advanced, one hand forward, wrist flexed, and aimed a strike near his jaw. The first blow was intended to surprise him and block his line of vision so he couldn't see what was coming next. In real life she would make contact, but this wasn't real life. She stopped short of hitting him.

She then tightened her abdominal muscles, rotated her hips, and pushed off her back leg for a maximum power strike to the nose with her other hand. This would be the fatal blow in an actual attack. Her teenage opponent feigned a fall to the floor, and she sprinted away.

Then it was Roger's turn to defend. Willow advanced. Roger's palm whisked toward her face. Too close. Too fast. She had to leap backward to avoid impact. Her foot caught the edge of the mat. She teetered and fell hard onto the wood floor.

Panic erupted in her chest. The baby. What had she been thinking? What if she'd hurt the baby? The sweet, little person. She lay there for a long moment, panting, tears welling in her eyes.

"Gosh, I'm sorry." A worried Roger was at her side.

"It's okay. I'm not hurt."

His forehead furrowed in confusion. Falling wasn't uncommon in class. Even a fall off the mat onto the boards happened occasionally. What didn't happen was tears, at least not from her.

Willow pushed onto her elbows then sat up slowly, wrapping a protective arm around her middle. Roger stuck out a hand to help her, but she refused it. "Really, I'm okay. It's just been a long day."

Actually, it had been a long three months.

6.1.6

WHEN WILLOW GOT HOME, she dropped her bags on the floor by the front door, crossed her tiny living room in four long strides and entered the bathroom. She pulled off her gi and panties and relief coursed through her. No blood. She wasn't spotting. That didn't mean there wouldn't be complications later, however.

A shower calmed her nerves a little. As the hot water sluiced over her tired body, she made a decision. She'd call her doctor's office as soon as she got out. After drying off and dressing in pajamas as quickly as she could, she punched in the number with shaking hands.

A recording. Of course, it would be a recording. It was 7:00. The office closed at 5:00. She was directed to the number for the on-call doctor, dialed that and got another recording. She left a message requesting a call back and slumped onto the couch.

Willow stared at the phone in her hand for several long seconds, but it didn't help. The doctor couldn't feel her willing him to return her call.

Her father. She'd call her father.

She counted the rings: one, two, three, four—tears threatened to spill from her eyes again. "Dad, please answer."

Five, six. "Hey, sweetheart. This is a pleasant surprise."

"Dad." Willow's voice broke, and the tears fell.

"What is it?" His lighthearted tone darkened. "What's going on?"

It took a moment for Willow to get the words past her constricted throat, but she managed to tell him about the incident in the dojo.

Suddenly he was all business. Booker had been a paramedic before joining the fire department and kept up on all his certifications. "How hard did you fall?"

"Not that hard. My foot caught on the mat, and I went down backwards." She sniffled.

"On your butt?"

"Yeah."

"At fourteen weeks, your little guy is only about the size of a peach. He, or she, is pretty well protected. I don't think you have anything to worry about. Call your doctor, but I think they'll tell you to rest, keep your feet up, and not to worry."

A peach. A tiny form, a baby nestled in a basket of leaves and peach blossoms like the Thumbelina illustration from one of her childhood books, filled her mind.

Willow drew in a shaky breath. "I'd feel so guilty if anything happened."

"Now don't go there. We all do stupid things." He paused. "You do realize karate classes when you're pregnant is probably stupid?"

"The doctor said exercise was good."

"Right. Walking—fine. Shadow boxing—fine. I'd stay away from hand-to-hand combat."

Willow ran a finger under her nose. "Yeah. I think I figured that out."

"Try yoga."

Willow gave a small laugh. "I don't like yoga."

"Learn."

"Okay, Dad."

They said goodbye. Willow was about to hang up when her father's voice stopped her. "Will?"

"Yeah?"

"Take care of yourself, okay?"

She felt her heart harden. Why did he always assume she needed to be reminded? Why didn't he have confidence in her? A vision of her on the dojo floor popped into her mind, and she flushed. She searched for a response.

He spoke before she could think of one. "I love you."

His words wrapped around her like a blanket. She softened. "I love you, too, Dad."

Her relationship with her father was complicated, but she was grateful he was in her life. As difficult and sometimes overbearing as he was, she'd always felt sorry for her friends who'd been raised by harried, busy, single mothers and weekend-only dads. They loved their children, and they tried, but their separation made life difficult for everyone. "Hug Mom for me."

"Will do." He hung up.

Willow basked for a moment in the warmth of the phone call. Family, with all of its ups and downs, meant security. Knowing her parents, her brother, and the big extended Kentucky clan were there was what gave her the courage to leap into her own life.

When she was a child, they'd had a trampoline in the backyard until one of the springs broke. She'd loved the sensation of flying she had when jumping. When she got off, she'd felt heavy and awkward.

Family was like that trampoline. The tension, the pull between opposite poles, gave her life bounce. She wanted that for The Peach. And Jonathan wanted her and his child. He was a good man, and she believed he'd be a good father. They had differences to work out, but wasn't tension necessary for a trampoline to function?

The phone rang and jangled Willow from her thoughts. It was the on-call doctor. She explained what had happened, and he echoed Booker's words. Willow should take it easy for a couple of days. If she started spotting, cramping, had pain, dizziness or discomfort of any kind, call and go to the emergency room. And no more karate.

Willow made her way into the kitchen and rummaged through the fridge. There was a half order of vegetarian pho from the Vietnamese place around the corner, some wilted lettuce, and three pieces of whole-grain bread. She really had to start eating better.

She pulled the pho and the bread from the fridge, set them on the counter, and had a realization. She'd been resisting the pregnancy. It was out of order in her playbook. It should have come after a year of dating, a long engagement, and a trip down the aisle in a floor-length white dress.

She poured the soup into a bowl and watched it turn in circles inside her microwave. It, however, was here and now. And despite only being the size of a peach, it wasn't an it. It was a someone. The fall at the dojo had shocked her into reality. She had a person on board. A person she was responsible for. A person she now knew she loved.

Willow balanced a piece of stale toast on the side of her bowl, took her dinner to the couch, picked up the remote, and turned on *The Great British Baking Show*. She needed to turn off her brain. Cooking was her mother's domain, not hers, but it was comforting to watch other people do it.

The episode ended, and she found herself alone in her own cramped apartment again. It was true what they said, it was no use running from yourself because, wherever you went, there you were. She had decisions to make.

She eyed her dirty dish. Fatigue made rinsing it and throwing it in the dishwasher seem a monumental task. She swung her legs off the coffee table, reached for the bowl, and was saved by the bell. Her cell played Jonathan's seaside ringtone. The first of her big decisions was on the line. "Hey, babe," she said.

"Hey to you."

"How's your mom?" Willow felt a jab of guilt. She should have called him on her way to karate class to ask about her. Mat had insisted Gerry go to the emergency room where they'd done a battery of tests. The results hadn't yet come in when Willow had spoken with Jonathan before work that morning.

"Contrite."

Willow replaced her feet on the table and settled into the couch cushions again. "Why contrite?"

"Apparently her collapse came from lack of food and too much wine."

Compassion broke through a thin layer of ice inside Willow. Gerry wasn't her favorite person. She was cold and proper, never a gray hair loose in her tight chignon. Hearing that the dignified Mrs. Lauder messed up, didn't eat, and drank too much made her seem human. "She's grieving."

"She is." Jonathan's voice softened. "Chloe is going to stay for an extra three days, and I postponed a business trip so we can keep an eye on her. How are you feeling? Nausea any better?"

"A little." Willow paused. She ought to tell him about the fall, but Jonathan had enough to worry about without having to worry about her and The Peach. She wanted to be a support like Chloe. Not a burden.

"But?"

"I've been thinking about your proposal," she said instead.

"To run away to the vineyard?"

He sounded so hopeful, she laughed. "Yes, to run away to the vineyard."

"And?"

"Yes."

"Yes, you'll do it?"

"Yes, I'll do it. I want our baby to be *our* baby when he or she comes."

Jonathan was silent for so long, Willow wondered if the call had disconnected. "Jonathan?"

"Yeah, sorry. I'm just so happy." His voice cracked. "I'll come down tomorrow, and we can get the license."

They made plans for the following day, made kissing noises into the phone, and hung up.

She'd done it.

She'd made the decision she'd been hemming and hawing about. She was getting married. A list of all the other things she needed to do began forming in her mind. No longer tired, Willow rose, rinsed her bowl, and grabbed a pad of paper and a pen from her kitchen drawer.

She had to give her notice to the landlord. Finish correcting the last music appreciation papers and hand in final grades. Shop for something pretty to wear. It didn't have to be white, but Honey always said white looked good with her olive complexion. Willow began to write.

Ten minutes later, she put down her pen, shut off the kitchen lights, made her way into the bathroom, and brushed her teeth with more energy than she'd had in a week. She tumbled into bed and tried to relax. After several minutes of tossing about, she kicked off the covers.

Pregnancy raised her temperature, but tonight it was worse than usual. Nerves. That's what caused the extra adrenaline. She was riffing, improvising. It made her nervous.

Riffing made her think about jazz. And jazz made her think about breaking rules, which made her think about contradictions, which made her think about her diamond. She lifted a thumb to straighten her ring, a habit she'd acquired along with the gem. It found nothing. Her finger was bare.

Willow bolted from bed, heart thumping. She jogged to the living room, pulled her wallet from her purse, and snapped it open. There it was, nestled between the pennies and dimes in the change section. She slipped it on her finger and turned it until it caught the light from the overhead lamp. Until she could see the prisms inside.

She was getting married. Six months ago, she was crying over Drake. Tomorrow she was getting a marriage license with Jonathan. Life had changed keys on her, but a good musician knows her flats and sharps. She'd transition.

MOLLY: A lot has changed in Willow's life in a short time. She's struggling to adjust. Not only is she in a new relationship, engaged, and pregnant, but Jonathan's lifestyle is very different than the one she's used to.

I think she said it best when she compared her childhood with the world of Sunset House:

"She hadn't had everything she'd wanted, but she'd had everything she'd needed. Sunset House was a fairy tale. It was full of things you never knew you should want until you saw them."

If you listened to last season, you've already heard my diatribe about fairy tales, so I won't bore you with it again. Just suffice to say, a fairy tale may be a better metaphor than Willow realized at the time.

Okay, I have one more journal entry to read before I wrap up the episode with a question of the week.

JUNE 4

My doctor thought it would be good for me to keep a journal. I don't know why. Nothing happens here. I see the same few people, day after day. I'm never allowed out except for a turn around the garden with supervision.

They're worried about me. That's what they say. But they're the ones who are driving me out of my mind. I wasn't a danger to myself, regardless of what they've been told, but I could become one. If I do, it will be their fault.

My room is on the second floor. I'm so desperate to get out of here, I've thought about jumping. But if I jump, I don't think the hydrangea bush under the window will break my fall. I've spent hours gazing at the vines plastered to the outside walls and the drainpipe that is just out of reach.

I pulled a length of vine off the stucco yesterday and tugged on it with all my strength. It tore. I landed on my butt on the Aubusson rug, then raced to my bed and pretended to sleep, worried someone would hear the thump and come investigate. No one did.

I thought about yelling to the gardeners this morning, but they're on the payroll and have probably been fed lies. It would be useless.

The window is a tease. I should stop looking through it. It's a reminder of the world outside my prison, but no help at all. The only thing it's good for is dumping the contents of my evening cup of tea, which I no longer trust.

The hydrangea is blooming. The flowers are big and blue. Whatever is in the tea must agree with it.

The point is, if I were truly a danger to myself, I wouldn't worry about whether or not the hydrangea flowers were thriving or whether or not the bush would break my fall. Would I? I'd jump and say the hell with it. But I haven't. I want to leave here in one piece. There are things I need to do.

MOLLY: Interesting. I wonder what the things she needs to do are, and if she ever got to do them.

Which brings me to my question for you. I forgot to mention in the intro to the season, that there is a *Murders Under the Sun* Facebook group. We have rollicking discussions—sometimes arguments—about murder, psychology, personal experiences, justice, you name it. It's a great community.

We're even in the middle of a separate mystery that has nothing to do with the ones we're exploring here on the podcast. At least, I don't think it does. Something happened last season that makes me wonder. However, I'm out of time. The mystery behind the podcast mysteries will have to wait until next episode.

Meanwhile, what do you think about Sunset House? Does it sound like your dream home, or a nightmare? Would you love to experience the lifestyles of the rich and famous? Or are you content to live in a humble abode as long as your needs are met? The link to the Facebook page is in the show notes. Hop on and let me know what you think.

Join me next time for more *Murders Under the Sun*.

(cue music)

VO: If you enjoyed this episode, please leave us a five-star review on your favorite podcast service—it really helps. *Murders Under the Sun* is edited by Jim Wilbourne, theme music is by Eclectic Blends, and I'm your host, Molly Shure.

part three

MURDERS UNDER THE SUN
SEASON SIX; EPISODE TWO

MOLLY: Welcome back to *Murders Under the Sun*. I'm Molly Shure, your host.

Before we get into today's episode, there were a ton of comments on the Facebook page about the personal mystery that I mentioned last week. More of you asked about that than answered my question of the week. So, I'll give those who are just joining the podcast a summary.

I got my degree at Cal State-Fullerton about twenty years ago. While I was in school, my roommate disappeared. Melissa went out one night and never came back.

I mentioned to the listeners that this event changed my career trajectory. I did what little research I could at the time. It didn't lead me to Melissa, but it did lead me into changing my major to investigative journalism.

When I shared that story, listeners got involved. Some knew other students who disappeared at that time. They began emailing and commenting on Facebook. The community reached out to friends who'd attended Cal State-Fullerton around that time to find out what they knew, if anything.

Information starting drizzling in. It turns out that two other students went missing at the same time Melissa did. Raphael Jimenez, a TV and Film major, and Ariana Blackstone, a Drama major.

If you want the full story, I suggest going back to *The Cliff House* and listening to each season of the podcast. I've commented here and

there between episodes about what I've learned
so far.

I'll fill you in on as much of the backstory as
I can as I share new discoveries. If this evolves
into a full blown story, I may have to start
another podcast. We'll see.

But meanwhile, today is about Willow. When we
left her last week, she'd said, "Yes," to
Jonathan's proposal.

Two weeks later, Willow said goodbye to the principal of Cranston Academy, and she and Jonathan drove up the coast to Siren Vineyard. They married next to the zinfandel grapes at sunset. It was impossibly beautiful and romantic. Willow was happy. She wished they could stay forever.

She tried not to think about home and the decisions waiting for them there. When she did, the fizz of joy running through her began to flatten like old champagne. Instead of thinking, she dragged Jonathan to Hearst Castle, the galleries in Cambria and the seafood restaurants in Morro Bay.

On their final morning, thoughts of home hovered like a summer storm coloring the atmosphere in gray heat. As she packed the few things she'd brought, she heard Jonathan's voice from the sitting room of their suite. "We should be there by dinnertime."

Willow paused to listen.

He laughed lightly. "We'll fill you in when we get there."

She could hear Gerry's voice, thin and reedy, through the phone but couldn't make out the words. Jonathan responded. "What do you mean, who? Willow and me, of course."

The silk nightgown she'd been holding slipped through her fingers forming a white puddle in her suitcase.

"Look, Mom, I've got to go. We'll see you tonight. I have a surprise." Another laugh. "A *surprise*." He emphasized the word as if speaking to a child caught breaking into her Christmas presents early. A moment later Jonathan appeared in the bedroom doorway. "Almost ready?"

Willow snatched up the silk and rolled it into a clumsy ball. "Almost."

"I'll go pick up the wine and bring the car around." He moved across the room, grabbed her by the shoulders and kissed her before leaving.

They'd bought two cases of the vineyard's famous blend, Red Ravish. Willow had laughed aloud when she'd discovered this was the winery that produced Honey's favorite wine and, small world, it was Gerry's favorite as well. They'd purchased a case for each side of the family as a peace offering. Neither mother would be happy when they found out Willow and Jonathan had married without them there to witness the nuptials.

Willow swallowed the sense of dread that had woken her before the sun that morning and finished packing. They had to face the music sometime.

Jonathan must have sensed Willow's mood. He regaled her with funny stories from his childhood all the way from San Luis Obispo to Los Angeles. Twins pull crazy pranks, apparently.

She must not have laughed enough, because when they hit their first bank of brake lights, his face grew serious. "It's going to be okay, Will. They'll be a little upset, but they'll get over it."

"It's not only that."

"What is it then?"

She traced the leather seam of the car seat with her fingernail. "The uncertainties. I'm not good at uncertainty."

He stared ahead, navigating the traffic for a long beat. "You sorry we got married?"

She sat up straighter. "No. Absolutely not. It's... I don't have an apartment anymore, and we don't know where we're going to live, and I don't have a job and... Everything."

"You do have a job. It may not be your dream job, but it'll keep you busy until the baby comes."

She gave him a noncommittal grunt. She was looking forward to digging into the treasures in Hamish's office; she just didn't think of it as a job. Not a real one anyway.

"And I thought we decided to stay at Sunset House until we found our own place?" he continued.

"We did, but I don't want to impose on your mother." *And, I don't think she wants me there,* she thought but didn't say.

"There are so many spare rooms at Sunset House we could sleep in a different one every night for a week and a half. We're not imposing. She's excited we're staying."

"She's excited you're staying."

He took his hand from the wheel and grabbed hers. "We're a package deal now."

"I guess."

He squeezed her hand before releasing it. "Don't worry. She'll be thrilled we're married, especially when she finds out about the baby. She and Dad started talking about grandkids as soon as Chloe and I hit puberty."

"You're sure?"

"I'm sure."

The dread lifted, and, by the time they drove through the gates of Sunset House, Willow was almost looking forward to breaking the news to Gerry. Her good spirits were short lived, however.

The moment Willow and Jonathan pulled onto the circular drive, Chloe, her golden-brown hair wild, burst from the front doors waving her arms. "Jonathan. Thank god, you're here. I was just going to call you."

Jonathan leaped from the car. "Why, what's happening?"

"It's Mom. She went down for a nap a couple of hours ago. She told me to wake her before dinner. I went in, and she's throwing up every-where. It's awful."

"Did you call someone?" He jogged toward the house.

She spun and followed him. "Yes, of course."

The two disappeared inside. Willow stared through the windshield at the space they'd just vacated, paralyzed with indecision. Should she follow them? Technically, she was family now. Or, should she park the car and let them handle their mother on their own?

If Honey were upchucking, she wouldn't want her brand new son-in-law in the room. And Willow was so sensitive to smells at the moment. She imagined the scene upstairs, shuddered, and slid into the driver's seat.

She steered the car around the circle and up the gravel drive toward the garage. The building was long and low, shaped more like a horse barn than a garage. At its closest end was a roll up door wide enough for a Hummer. Willow stopped in front of it and bit her lip.

How did it open? Jonathan had an app on his phone that controlled everything at the house, but she didn't.

She checked the sun visor first. That's where she kept her remote when she lived at her parents' house. There was nothing there.

The whole thing was doubly annoying because her own car was parked in the garage. Not having access to it gave her a pinch of claustrophobia. She exhaled slowly.

Maybe the glove compartment? She leaned forward and popped it open. It was filled with the usual paperwork, but no opener.

The only other place something like a garage door opener could hide was the center console. She lifted its lid and began rifling through. Her fingers touched something cold. She grabbed it and pulled it into the waning light.

Not a garage door opener. A gun.

It was small, what her father would call a lady's handgun. Despite its diminutive size, a shock ran from the weapon all the way up her arm.

Her shock wasn't due to fear. She'd grown up around firearms. Booker had many friends in law enforcement who carried, and all her uncles and lots of her cousins in Kentucky hunted. Her father had made sure she and Ash were gun-safe at a young age. He'd taught them to respect weapons, not to fear them.

She was shocked Jonathan owned a gun. She would have sworn, based on his political opinions, that he was opposed to them. Why would he have one?

She replaced it carefully. There were so many things she didn't know about her husband. Like—she snapped the console lid shut—where he kept the garage door opener.

She wouldn't bother putting the car away tonight. Jonathan could do it tomorrow. Instead, she pulled alongside the building, turned off the ignition, and trudged toward the house.

The front doors loomed large before her. This wasn't how she'd expected their homecoming to be. She'd thought there would be tension, maybe even hurt feelings, but she'd assumed she and Jonathan would face them together.

She entered the silent foyer alone and paused. What should she do? She wanted to be helpful but not to insert herself where she wasn't welcome.

The sound of a car crunching on the gravel outside pushed her into action. It must be a doctor, or an ambulance. She'd meet them and lead them to Gerry's room. She wasn't sure where Gerry's room was, but she'd find it.

A black suited figure met her on the porch. It was Mat. She'd forgotten Chloe's fiancé was a doctor. He glanced at her as he pushed past her. "Willow." He sounded surprised to see her. She opened her mouth to return the greeting, but he bolted up the stairs before she had a chance.

Twenty minutes later Jonathan found her sitting in an armchair near the cold fireplace in the darkening great room. "There you are. I was looking for you." He perched on the arm of her chair and ran a hand through her hair. "Chloe and I are going to take shifts sitting with Mom. I'm afraid I have first shift."

"How is she?" Willow asked.

"Not good. She's very ill. Mat thinks it may be food poisoning. He's given her something to help her with the nausea, and to help her sleep."

Willow stood and reached for her jacket and purse. Jonathan placed a hand on her arm. "Where are you going?"

"I'm coming upstairs. She's my mother now, too."

He gave her a half smile. "I'll be there for hours. You stay here. Dun will get you some dinner. I think she made up a bed for us."

Willow was surprised. She knew Lauder rules hadn't permitted them to sleep in the house together before marriage, and they hadn't told Gerry about the elopement yet. "She knows we're married?"

"You can't get anything past Dun."

Willow wasn't sure how to react to that. There were so many things she didn't understand about this household. All her questions would be answered in time, she was sure, but now wasn't the time to start asking them. "I think I should come sit with you."

"No, honestly, I'd just worry about you." He patted her head as if she was a family pet. "I'll make it up to you."

She stood. "There's nothing to make up."

"This isn't how I wanted to start our married life."

"I know that. You go take care of your mom. I'll be fine." She kissed him and gave him a little shove toward the stairs.

As he walked away, a bereft feeling she hadn't had since childhood stole over her. It took her a moment to identify it. It was homesickness. She wanted more than anything to race out the front doors, get in Jonathan's car, and drive up the 5 Freeway to her parents' house in Laguna Niguel. It was only half an hour away, if that. She could sleep in her old bedroom tonight.

The impulse was so strong she would have given in to it if Ms. Dunfrey hadn't appeared beside her like an apparition. "The cook made bœuf bourguignon. Would you like to eat by the fire?"

Willow stared at her own feet and willed them to stay in place. She was a married woman now, not a child. How would it look if she ran home to mother at the first sign of trouble? She shifted her gaze to Ms. Dunfrey. "That would be lovely."

And it was. The fire warmed the room. The food and herbal tea warmed her belly. A contented sleepiness wrapped around her, and her eyelids drooped.

The next thing she heard was a throat clearing. Her eyes sprang open. Ms. Dunfrey had snuck up on her again. Willow wished she'd stop doing that. Between the sheer size of the almost empty house surrounding her and its heavy antiques, all this stealthy appearing and disappearing felt like something from a Gothic novel.

"You look exhausted." Ms. Dunfrey smiled, revealing a mouth full of discolored teeth. Tetracycline, maybe. She was old enough to have taken it before the medical community understood the side effects on forming teeth. "I can take you to Johnny's room."

Johnny? Willow had never heard anyone call him Johnny, not even his parents or Chloe. "That would be great." She pushed herself off the couch. "I have to get my suitcase from the car first."

"It's in your room already."

Willow's cheeks flushed. Of course, it was. Things, like people, in Sunset House seemed to magically appear when needed. She wondered if they also disappeared when the family was done with them.

She followed Ms. Dunfrey down a hall, through a doorway, and up a narrow flight of stairs.

"I hope you don't mind taking the back stairs. They're closer to your room." She sounded apologetic.

"Closer is great. I'm dead on my feet."

"I can give you a full tour tomorrow."

Tomorrow, Willow planned to look at rentals. She'd agreed to stay at Sunset House until they found their own place. She wasn't going to drag her feet on that. An unexpected longing for her 600-square-foot studio, with its leaky kitchen faucet and noisy upstairs neighbors, filled her. Be it ever so humble, at least she'd known the rules.

6.2.2

WILLOW WOKE but didn't open her eyes. She'd dreamed a wonderful dream about a sunlight-filled apartment overlooking the Dana Point harbor. A tall, auburn-haired real estate agent had just presented her with a rental agreement. Willow wanted to sign it before she was fully awake.

Despite the soft bed and crisp sheets, her mind wouldn't cooperate. The wheels had begun to turn, and her day had started whether she wanted it to or not. She opened her eyes.

Jonathan's old room, at least she assumed that's what it was, must have been redecorated since his boyhood days. It now resembled a very posh hotel room. The furniture, like that in the rest of the house, appeared to be antique. Unlike the rest of the house, she was fairly sure these pieces were replicas. Everything from the wall color to the textiles were soft and heavy and luxurious.

She turned her head to the left to watch Jonathan sleep. She hadn't heard him come to bed, but knew it had been late. She'd gotten up at 2:00 for one of her nightly trips to the bathroom—since she'd become pregnant, she had to pee every time she rolled over—and his side had been empty.

She slipped out from between the sheets, and padded across the dim room to the window swathed in heavy draperies. She pulled back the curtains, and the sun almost blinded her. She'd assumed the day was dreary.

When her eyes adjusted, she gazed through the panes at the beautiful day outside. Their room overlooked the section of the grounds that housed the pool and the pool house. He'd mentioned they had one, but had neglected to mention it was an Olympic-length lap pool surrounded by Queen Anne palms and flanked by his and her shower rooms. It looked like a resort, a very expensive resort.

There was a lone figure slicing through the clear blue water below with sure strokes. The swimmer, a female, executed a professional flip turn and headed back the way she'd come. Swimming was probably a better form of exercise than karate for Willow at the moment. She didn't love it, but she was proficient at it. Not as proficient as the woman in the water, but her freestyle wasn't bad. Her father, having been called to one too many drowning accidents, had insisted both his children learn to swim when they were young.

Willow watched the woman do three more laps and felt a rumble in her stomach. She'd better put something in it, or she'd be gagging in the elegantly appointed bathroom attached to the bedroom. Morning sickness was only soothed by food, which seemed an odd way to cure nausea, but it worked.

She'd noticed her robe hanging on the back of the bathroom door last night when she'd brushed her teeth and went to retrieve it. Ms. Dunfrey had told her the bags would be in the room; she hadn't mentioned they'd be unpacked.

She'd had an uncomfortable moment when she'd opened the bureau drawers and found her underwear neatly deposited into square dividers and the t-shirt she wore to sleep in rolled Marie Kondo-style next to them. Her jeans and blouses had been hung on hangers in the closet, where she also found her moccasin slippers.

She didn't want to wake Jonathan so, rather than dressing for the day, she pulled on the robe, stuck her feet into the moccasins, and left, closing the door softly behind her. She was grateful for the narrow stairway only yards from her door. The last thing she wanted to do was descend the grand central staircase in her old terrycloth robe.

When she reached the ground floor, she paused. She'd never been in the kitchen of Sunset House. Which way? Should she go right, or left? In the end, she followed her nose. The scent of something delicious drew her toward a door at the end of a long hall. She pushed through it and was greeted by the sound of an acoustic guitar. A deep bass rumble accompanied the soprano tones of Taylor Swift. They sang about swinging screen doors and oblivious mothers.

Willow rounded an industrial-sized refrigerator and saw a large, Black man in a very white chef's jacket. His back was to her, and she watched him work for a moment. He lifted a kettle onto the biggest stove she'd ever seen and lit a flame under it, hips and shoulders moving in time with the beat.

"Ah, good morning." She raised her voice to be heard over the music. His massive head swung around.

"To you, too." He wiped his hands on a towel and held one out to her. "You must be Willow. Jonathan's bride. They call me Cookie."

She offered her hand which was immediately enveloped in a warm floury embrace. "How does everybody know we eloped? We thought it would be a big surprise."

He grinned. "Not a lot gets by Dun." Exactly what Jonathan had said. Apparently, if she wanted to keep a secret, Dun was the one to hide it from. "What can I get you?"

"I was hoping for some mint tea. I can make it myself, though."

"Not in my kitchen."

Willow laughed. "You're just like my mother."

Cookie's face collapsed into comical confusion. "That's the first time anyone's ever said that to me."

"I mean, she's a chef too. She hates it when people mess around in her kitchen. Very possessive of her pots and pans."

"Sounds like a wise woman. The messes I find in the morning, or worse, after my days off, well... It's enough to make me want to camp out right here." He gestured to an island so large he probably could sleep on it.

Willow settled herself onto a tall chair opposite his workstation. "What smells so wonderful?"

"Hot cross buns. I always make them this time of year. Ms. Lauder loves them. When I heard about her upset stomach, I thought she just might be able to hold one down." A timer dinged. He donned a pair of kitchen mitts the size of baseball gloves and lifted the buns from the oven. The smell was heavenly, and Willow thought she might be able to hold one down as well.

As the bread cooled, she and Cookie swapped histories. She discovered he'd once played sax with a traveling jazz band. He was duly impressed by her music degree. He set out two small plates. "Maybe we can jam sometime."

"I'm not very good at improvising."

"It's easy if you know your keys, and I'm assuming you know your keys."

Willow nodded. "I had to memorize the circle of fifths my first year."

"Well, then, you won't have any trouble. You just got to relax and trust yourself."

Relax and trust herself? That was easier said than done. Cookie handed her a bun, butter, and a steaming cup of mint tea. "It's kind of like cooking. Recipes are a great place to start, but if you want to make something really special, you gotta fly by instinct. Ask your mama. She'll tell you I'm right."

Throughout Willow's childhood, her father had constantly pointed out the dangers surrounding her. She'd learned to be cautious, to evaluate every possibility before committing herself to a course of action. Consequently, her instinct was to distrust her instinct.

The bun exploded with flavor in her mouth. She tasted clove and orange peel and cinnamon. "This is amazing," she mumbled through the food. "My mother needs this recipe."

"Tit for tat. She'll have to give me one of hers."

Willow pondered which of Honey's many recipes she would recommend to Cookie, but before she'd decided between the Christmas cinnamon buns and the flourless chocolate cake, the door swung open. "Hey, Cookie. What is that amazing smell?" Ophelia appeared around the fridge. Her eyes widened when she saw Willow. "Oh, good morning. I'd heard you were back in town." Cookie slid a plate with a bun on it across the island. Ophelia caught it.

"We got back last night," Willow said.

"Seriously dreary homecoming." Ophelia shook her head. "Better get used to it."

"Lia." Cookie's deep voice dropped even deeper, a warning growl.

She picked up the bun, took a bite, chewed, then swallowed. "So, I heard that Aunt Gerry is sick. What's wrong with her?"

"The flu." A new voice rang behind them. Willow spun around on her chair. Chloe glared at the back of Ophelia's head, pink satin arms folded across her pink satin chest. The color matched the blush of her cheeks and lips. Her hair was perfectly mussed. It looked as if a team of beauticians had gotten her ready for a photo shoot for a mattress ad.

Willow adjusted her robe to cover her father's old fire department t-shirt. She'd bought new lingerie for her wedding trip—the white silk negligee and a few other things—but had wanted the comfort of her old sleep shirt last night. Now she wished she'd worn the silk.

"Mat thinks she picked up a stomach bug, but you know Mother. Every headache could be a brain tumor, every stomachache, pancreatic cancer. She's sleeping now, so I thought I'd come down."

"She has been sick a lot since Uncle Ham died," Ophelia said.

"She's grieving." Chloe walked to the end of the island. "What are you doing here, anyway?" She addressed the question to Ophelia.

"I lent Uncle Ham a book a few months ago. I wanted to check the library, see if I could find it."

"Jonathan has the keys. I could get them for you," Willow said.

Chloe looked back and forth between Willow and Ophelia, her expression difficult to read.

"Hot cross bun?" Cookie waved a plate at her temptingly.

"I'm not hungry, but I'd kill for a cup of coffee."

Not hungry? Who needed to be hungry to eat one of these delectable treats? Willow had been going to ask for another but now thought better of it. The doctor had informed her that the whole eating-for-two thing was, unfortunately, not true. A svelte figure seemed to be expected in this family. She wasn't sure pregnancy would be an excuse to lose hers.

Chloe leaned on the far end of the island and sipped the coffee Cookie had poured her. She took it black. Willow made a mental note.

Perhaps she'd try to learn to like black coffee when she could drink it again. "Is Gerry feeling any better?" she asked.

Chloe gave a small shake of her head. "It seems to come in waves. She'll be better for a bit, then watch out." She looked at the wall clock in the kitchen. "I should probably go up again."

Willow cleared her throat. "I could take a shift."

Chloe turned a cool, blue-green gaze on her. "That's sweet of you, but Dun will take over after her swim. I think Mother only wants family around her right now."

That smarted, but Willow tried to tell herself no one knew she was part of the family yet. Well, no one but Ms. Dunfrey and Cookie and whoever else Ms. Dunfrey told.

Chloe left the room, and Ophelia's shoulders appeared to relax. "I don't know how Dun does it."

"Does what?" Willow asked.

"Swims every morning, regardless of the weather. I hate the water." Ophelia stood and moved toward the door. "Take care of yourself, Willow," she shot over her shoulder.

That sounded more like a warning than a parting comment. There was obviously no love lost between Ophelia and Chloe. Willow would have to tread carefully. She was too new to the family to get in the middle of old drama. "I'd love another half of a bun, Cookie." Compromise seemed best until she got the lay of the land.

6.2.3

JONATHAN WAS awake when Willow returned to the room to dress. He yawned and stretched. "Where've you been?"

"I was in the kitchen having breakfast. I met Cookie."

"And what gourmet delight did he whip up for you?"

"Hot cross buns, but he didn't make them for me. He made them for your mother."

"She loves them." Jonathan scooted himself up and leaned against the headboard. "But I doubt he'll get her to eat anything this morning."

Willow opened the closet, removed a pair of jeans from a hanger—whoever heard of putting jeans on a hanger?—then leafed through her tops. What to wear for apartment hunting? She wanted to look nice, but not like she was trying too hard. She pulled out a white oxford that still covered her growing bump without straining at the buttons.

Jonathan eyed the clothes with a scowl and reached for her hand. "Come back to bed."

"I thought we'd go look at apartments today."

He drew her down next to him. "What's the rush?"

She kissed him, but visions of the Dana Point condo from her dreams played against her closed eyelids. She pulled away. "Come on. Get up."

He groaned.

"Seriously. Your mom is ill. She doesn't need a new daughter-in-law banging around the house."

"She loves having us here. She told me that between barfing sessions last night."

That may be, but Willow didn't love being here. Sunset House was beautiful and extravagant, but it wasn't home. She wanted a place of their own where she could hang her inexpensive prints on the walls, curl up on the couch with popcorn and a movie, and walk around in her underwear if she was in the mood. "That's nice of her, but... "

Jonathan threw off the covers and crossed the room in his boxers, the morning chill raising goosebumps on his well-muscled arms. His abs could be on the cover of a steamy romance novel. For a moment she regretted not going back to bed.

She returned her gaze to her clothes. They could lay around in bed all day when they had their own place. The thought of staying in their room until lunch time then facing Dun's and Chloe's knowing looks, made her cheeks burn.

Twenty minutes later, she and Jonathan descended the stairs. When they reached the bottom, he turned toward her and took her hands. "Before we go apartment hunting, I want to show you something."

A small knot formed in her stomach. What was it now? Every time she brought up getting their own place, he grew quiet or changed the subject. "Okay." She said the word slowly.

He made a left, walked past the great room to the foyer, but didn't leave the house through the big double doors. Instead, he made a right leading her down a hallway that was the mirror image of the one they'd left. This must be the left wing of the house, a place Willow had never been.

Jonathan strode with purpose to the far end of the corridor and threw open a door. Light flooded the dim hallway. He ushered Willow through the doorway ahead of him.

She crossed the threshold and skidded to a stop. The space that opened before her was under construction. Even in its unfinished state, it was stunning. Her gaze traveled across paint-speckled drop clothes to a pair of tall windows that looked out onto a green lawn. The lawn ended in a stand of tall palms, a patch of blue visible between them.

To the left of the large room was an unfinished half wall. On the other side of that was what she assumed was to become a kitchen and dining area. Heavy-duty electrical wiring jutted from holes in exposed wallboard.

"What do you think?" Jonathan's face was bright and shining.

A lump formed in Willow's chest. She couldn't speak. He'd lied to her. He'd said they could go house hunting today. He'd never said he was planning to live here at Sunset House.

"There's more." He tugged her toward a stairway on their right. At the top of the stairs was a loft with two doors leading from it. "We could use this area for a home office." He drew an arc with his hand. "I always end up bringing work home no matter how hard I try not to."

He pushed open the farthest door. "Check out this view." The room had a similar vantage as the living room downstairs but, because it was on the second floor, the ocean view was epic.

"This is the master bedroom. Mom ordered a double Jacuzzi tub and a walk-in shower for the bathroom, but if you don't like that layout, we could change it." Willow followed him across more dropcloths into a bathroom that was bigger than the bedroom she'd had growing up.

"And… " He left the bedroom, walked onto the landing and placed a hand on the other door. "For the baby." He gave it a shove and stepped back. The space was half as big as the master bedroom but still a good size. It was the only room in the apartment in which the walls had been painted. They were a lovely soft yellow. It was also the only room that had any furniture in it. In its center was an old, wooden cradle. It looked scuffed and used, and she loved it.

Jonathan must have told Gerry about the baby. It was the only explanation. This was her gift. A beautiful, incredible gift, but it was ruined by the sense of betrayal that lay like a brick on her chest. She couldn't speak, couldn't shove words past the tightness in her throat.

Jonathan's grin faded. "We can change the color, and we don't have to use the cradle."

"Was it yours?" She managed to say.

A tentative smile tugged at the edges of his mouth. "Yes. Chloe and I had matching cradles. This one was mine. Mom took the blue bumpers off it before she had the workmen bring it up."

"She knows about the baby." It wasn't a question. Willow knew the answer.

His gaze dropped to his shoes. "She and Dad guessed."

"Because we got engaged so quickly?"

He nodded.

"Why didn't you tell me? Why make me think we had to keep it secret until the perfect moment?"

"I didn't know."

"So this," she waved at the rooms around them. "This wasn't your idea?"

His chin jerked forward. "No. I wouldn't do all this without talking to you about it."

Willow walked to the cradle and stroked the wood. She loved its simplicity. "Whose idea was it then?"

"Dad's. He started renovations when I bought the ring. He wanted to give it to us as a wedding present."

"When did you find out?"

"Last week. Right before we left for the Central Coast. I was going to tell you, but I thought it would be better if I showed it to you."

The heaviness in her chest loosened a little. He hadn't known about the apartment when he'd asked her to elope. He hadn't lied when he'd said they could get their own place. No wonder he'd grown quiet every time she mentioned house hunting on their wedding trip.

She turned to face him. "It's beautiful." There was hesitation in her voice.

"But... "

"It's not ours. It's your mother's."

Jonathan threw open his arms. "Someday everything will be ours."

"That day could be a long way off."

"Yes, but why get something else when we have all this?" He gestured toward the master bedroom on the other side of the wall. "I can't afford that view on my paycheck."

"Then we don't get that view. We get what we can afford."

A muscle twitched in his jaw. "I don't understand you, Willow. This apartment is perfect. Mom even held off on tile, paint, and appliances because she wants you to pick out what you want. If we rent something in town, it won't belong to us either."

That was true. They weren't in a position to buy anything at the moment, not at Orange County prices. Jonathan's family may be wealthy, but he wouldn't receive anything other than his trust fund until his mother died. And he'd told her he had that wrapped up in investments.

Jonathan stepped toward her and placed his hands on her shoulders. "Would it make you feel better if we paid rent?"

It would make her feel better if they weren't living on his parents' property under his mother's nose. "Maybe. But I don't like the idea of having to walk through someone else's house every time I want to go somewhere."

He brightened. "This has its own entrance. Didn't you see it?"

He dragged her down the stairs, through the kitchen, through a glass-paned door, and down a short flight of stone steps into a garden. Willow blinked. The garden was like something from a children's book. The circular space was covered in bright green grass and lined with a horseshoe of jasmine, affording it privacy from the main grounds. In its center was a citrus tree heavy with blossoms. Rose bushes covered with pink buds, hanging fuchsia baskets, and purple and yellow pansies decorated the scene with color.

The horseshoe's opening led to a paved area overlooking the ocean on which wicker chairs were cozied around an outdoor fireplace. To the right of that was a redwood dining set and a grill. If Willow were to design a yard, this would be it.

An image of a baby sleeping in a playpen set in the shade of the tree, she and Jonathan reclining on lawn chairs nearby with books, morning papers, and coffee blossomed in her mind. The only thing missing was a white picket fence.

"We can use the south-facing garage, the small one Dad kept his classic cars in. Mom is going to sell them. Then you can come and go as privately as you please."

"The rent on a place like this would be huge," she said.

He inhaled and exhaled slowly, probably counting to ten. "Mom wouldn't rent it to anyone else. Hell, she doesn't even want to rent it to us. She wants to *give* it to us."

A breeze ruffled the branches of the citrus tree, and the scent of its blossoms tickled her nose. "What if I did the library work for free." Jonathan opened his mouth, but she held up a hand. "I couldn't imagine charging the family anything anyway, especially not after this. I know it's not equitable, but I think I'd feel better. Like I was contributing, anyway."

He dropped his arms to his sides and adopted a New York accent. "If that's what it takes to get you into this apartment today, Missy, I'm sure I can work something out with the boss."

Willow felt the tension in her chest ease. This was fairy tale land. She should relax and enjoy it. "I can't wait to show my mom. She'll be a real help with the kitchen." A pinch of stress returned. She pivoted to face Jonathan. "That's okay, isn't it? I mean, my mom knows appliances. I'm a total dweeb when it comes to cooking."

She hadn't needed to worry. Jonathan was beaming. "Are you kidding? My mom would pay your mom to advise us on the kitchen."

"She doesn't need to do that."

"I know, but my point is—"

Willow never heard his point. Her imagination took her six months into the future, to the day they brought their child home from the hospital. As they made their way through the apartment again, colors and furniture appeared before her eyes. A distressed leather couch sat in the living room. Moss green walls turned to taupe and back to moss. The three black-and-white photos of violins she'd framed for her San Diego apartment were hung over the fireplace.

Jonathan, still talking about whatever he was talking about, opened the door that adjoined the apartment to the rest of Sunset House. The fairy tale popped like a soap bubble.

6.2.4

THE NEXT MORNING when Willow woke, Jonathan wasn't in bed beside her. A note rested on his pillow.

> *Had to run to the office. Should be home by lunch.*
> *Left keys to the library on the dresser in case you want*
> *to look around.*
> *XXXOOO,*
> *Me*

Disappointment washed over her. She lay staring at the ceiling for several long seconds. Jonathan had said he'd take the week off. Even if there hadn't been a big ceremony or honeymoon, it *was* the first week of their marriage. She'd counted on spending it together, finding an apartment, moving her things in, shopping for the extras, building their life.

Of course, most of that was off the table now that they were planning to live here at Sunset House. There really wasn't any reason he shouldn't go to the office.

She threw off the blankets and walked to the window. She was being ungrateful. Most people would give their right arm to live here, and she was pouting because she didn't have to spend money she didn't have on an apartment she didn't need.

She pushed the curtains aside to view the weather. Fog rolled across the pool like low moving clouds blurring its surface. She shivered. The world looked cold and unappealing. It would have been a terrible day to go house hunting anyway.

She was about to turn when movement caught her eye. She stared. Disembodied legs and arms writhed in the water. She took a step backward, and threw a hand over her mouth to stifle a yelp. She wanted to look away, but her gaze was fastened to scene.

Then all at once the arms and legs folded and a blue bottom flashed into the air before submerging again.

Relief was followed by laughter. It had been Ms. Dunfrey's blue bottom. Her suit matched its surroundings so closely Willow had only seen the woman's appendages.

She watched her swim a moment or two longer. Ms. Dunfrey was certainly dedicated, which was more than Willow could say about herself. She couldn't imagine jumping in the pool on a day like today. Eighty degrees and sunny, that was swimming weather. A day like today was for sleeping in and reading books in front of a fire.

When the weather warmed up, however, swimming would be good for Willow. She hadn't exercised since her fall in the karate class, and her clothes seemed to grow tighter every day. She knew the pregnancy was to blame for her spreading middle, but extra padding had recently appeared on her hips and thighs as well.

She didn't like swimming, but wanted to be active during her pregnancy. And, added bonus, swimming was safe. If she fell into the pool, the baby would be fine. However, when she'd left San Diego, she'd told her parents she was moving into a very small place with a girlfriend in Irvine and stowed the bulk of her things at their house. Her swimsuits were packed in boxes in her parent's garage. Swimming was a moot point.

She walked away from the window, slid open the closet doors, and stared at her neatly hung clothes. She'd worn the same six outfits for the past two weeks. She was sick of it all.

That's what she should do today—head to Laguna Niguel and get the rest of her wardrobe. After she got the lay of the land in the library, she'd go see her mother. She couldn't move the furniture from her parents' garage until the apartment in the left wing was ready, but she and Jonathan did need to break the news about their marriage.

She selected jeans and a green t-shirt and carried them to the bed. Would Gerry give them a shopping budget for the new place? Willow didn't have enough in savings to outfit it in the style it deserved, and she didn't think Jonathan did either.

A terrible thought stopped with her hand on a hanger. Would she have to decorate with a bunch of stuffy antiques? Gerry probably had a ton of stuff squirreled away in the attic, expensive stuff. Would Willow seem ungrateful if she wanted to pick out her own things?

She wanted their first place to be comfortable and cozy and Sunset House was neither. It was beautiful and dramatic, but it was more like a museum than a home.

Stress feathered over skin as she dressed. She grabbed the library keys from the dresser and headed downstairs. She'd talk to Jonathan about it after lunch, maybe drag him to her parents so they could sort through her IKEA furniture to see if any of it was usable.

After drinking a cup of herbal tea and eating a piece of toast in the kitchen with Cookie, she exited the house through the French doors in the great room the way Jonathan and she had done the night of the funeral. Fog filled the garden and shrouded the hedges. They made her think of children dressed as Halloween ghosts. Even the ocean vista was obscured by a wall of white. Willow shuddered in the damp chill.

She hurried across the grass, wishing she'd worn sneakers instead of sandals. Damp blades clung to her feet. The scents of roses and jasmine she'd relished the other night were gone, scrubbed from the air by the heavy dew. The morning smelled soggy.

She moved through the far hedge and onto the path of paving stones beyond it. A minute later, the library seemed to appear out of nowhere. She'd remembered it being a longer walk, perhaps because there had been more to look at. That night, the sky had been magenta and gold. It had illuminated everything on the ground in sunset hues. The relentless absence of color this morning was as cheerless as that had been magical.

She was so happy to reach the library, she didn't care that its windows were dark. She fumbled with the keys, trying several before she found the one that opened the door. On her way through the hall, she flipped on every switch she passed. She craved light and color this morning like some women in her condition craved pickles and ice cream.

The warm brown and green tones of the library were a balm. She eyed the mammoth fireplace. Could she light a fire? It would be so cozy on a day like today. There were logs on the grate, but she didn't see matches or a lighter. As she approached it, she noticed a remote control on the coffee table. She picked it up and pushed the button labeled *on*. A fire leapt to life behind the tempered glass screen. She laughed. Of course, Hamish Lauder would have a gas fire in this temperature-controlled room. It created ambiance without giving off much heat.

Willow gazed around her. Where to start? She wandered to the desk to look for a pad and pencil. Lists were always a good place to begin. Willow was an expert list maker.

She made lists of everything, from the usual grocery store items to less common things, like the unique advantages of every karate dojo within a five-mile radius of her old apartment. Reasons why she should, or shouldn't, befriend Michael, the sixth-grade teacher at Cranston. And her favorite meals at the six restaurants she frequented regularly in San Diego. She never knew when she'd have to order in a hurry.

She'd even made a list of pros and cons about marrying Jonathan before he'd proposed. She'd said yes because the pros column was longer. And, of course, because she loved him. That was the first thing she'd written on the pro side of the paper.

She rounded the desk, sat in the rolling chair behind it, and pulled herself forward. She'd create a list of the various categories of books, then ask Jonathan and Gerry how she should prioritize. She folded her hands on the kelly-green blotter and surveyed the room. What would it be like to be the owner of this domain?

When she was a girl, she'd been given an illustrated copy of *Beauty and the Beast*. It wasn't the typical Disney cartoon version of the story. The pictures in it were done in an Art Nouveau style that was both captivating and disturbing. She felt a bit like Beauty now, wandering alone in a surreal castle so different than her humble home. Loss and longing mingled inside her.

Willow yanked open the center desk drawer. It was divided into compartments that contained pens, pencils, paper clips, rubber bands, a small stapler, a box of staples, a staple remover, and a glass dish with a dry sponge in it. She selected a mechanical pencil and closed the drawer again.

On either side of the desk were three-drawer towers. She opened the top drawer on the right. It was filled with letters, some sealed, some unsealed. She pulled one off the top of the pile. It was from a law firm and looked as though it had never been opened. Was someone taking care of his correspondence?

She worried over that, but set it down after a moment. It wasn't her business. She was there to catalogue Ham's collection, not read his mail.

She closed that drawer and opened the one beneath. Here, she found a stack of legal pads. The one on top was covered with writing, a precise hand she assumed had been Hamish's. She didn't stop to read, but reached for the next pad and the next before she finally found a clean one. As she lifted it out, she noticed a picture frame shoved into the far reaches of the drawer. She tugged it out as well.

The frame was ordinary, the kind sold in drug stores and hobby shops. It was plain silver with a cardboard wedge attached to the back that could be popped out to create a stand. She flipped it over.

The photo was old, the colors slightly faded. It showed a family—husband, wife, and young daughter. For a moment, she thought it was Jonathan's Uncle Cob, his wife Marianne and a little Ophelia, but the child was too dark to be Ophelia and the man too short to be Cob.

She peered more closely. The woman wasn't Marianne either. She looked more like Gerry, but instead of gray hair and a thin patrician face, the woman in the picture was dark-haired and her face was plump with youth. Willow tilted the frame toward the desk lamp.

Her curiosity was piqued. Why would Hamish hide a family portrait in his desk? Were they close relatives he'd been estranged from? Or maybe he liked them, but Gerry didn't? The little girl looked familiar, but Willow couldn't place her. A long moment later, she gave up, placed the photo in the drawer, and stacked the legal pads in front of it again.

She pushed herself from the desk and stood. Taking the pad and pencil with her, she walked to the bookcase immediately to the right of the door. It was filled with history books and alphabetized by year rather than author. She wrote *History, seven shelves, 1,000 CE through Middle Ages* and began logging titles. Her plan was to circle the room making notes.

She worked her way into the seventeenth century, just short of the fireplace and came to a stop near the violin resting in front of the tall window. She'd been at this for at least an hour. She deserved a break.

She lifted the violin, settled the chin rest under her chin, and drew the bow over the strings. She closed her eyes and tried to remember Anthony Way's *Cradle Song*. After a couple of false starts, her fingers found it. When the last note faded, she opened her eyes again.

"Lovely," a voice behind her said.

Willow whirled around. She'd been so lost in the music she hadn't heard anyone enter.

The woman took a step toward Willow and looked as if she were about to offer her hand but crossed thin arms over her chest instead. "I didn't mean to scare you. I'm Sophie. Sophie Vara."

Willow recognized her immediately. She was the hollow-eyed woman who had cried at Hamish's funeral. "I'm Willow. Jonathan's—"

"Fiancée." Sophie supplied the word. "I know. I saw you at the funeral."

Willow placed the violin on the stand with careful precision. "I'm supposed to be cataloging the books and music, but it's hard to resist this."

"Don't let me stop you. I'm only here for the mail." Willow raised her eyebrows in question. "I was Hamish's personal assistant. My job at the moment is to let his business connections know about his—" Sophie's words caught in her throat. She must have been very fond of him. Willow hadn't seen anyone else shed a tear, including Jonathan.

Speaking of Jonathan... Her gaze traveled to the mantel clock. It was almost noon. "I was about to leave anyway. Do you have keys? Can you lock up?" Sophie pulled a key chain from a sweater pocket and dangled it in front of her.

Willow felt a small niggle of concern as she collected her things. She had opened the library. Didn't that mean she ought to lock it up again? "Do you work here? In the library, I mean?"

"My office is down the hall next to the kitchen. Hamish liked his own space, but he wanted me close." Her face clouded with emotion, and she turned away.

Willow watched her stride toward the desk in the corner of the room. Her shoulders and hips were narrow, her bone structure as delicate as a young girl's. *A young girl's.* Willow suddenly knew why the child in the photo had looked familiar. She was Sophie.

MOLLY: Sunset House is shrouded in small mysteries. What is Sophie's connection to Hamish and his family? And, although Willow isn't aware of the journal yet, we'd love to know who the writer is.

Here is another entry. This one is both odd and horrifying. And it creates more questions than it answers.

JUNE 5

The sting of the black sea nettle is always painful, but rarely fatal. It wasn't fatal in my case, obviously, but I've been advised to avoid them in the future. I laughed out loud when the doctor said that. I am one of the lucky few who has an allergic reaction to their venom, an experience I never want to repeat.

Because of what happened that day, they say I'm a danger to myself. It's untrue. I was in danger, but not from myself. I would never have gone into the ocean if I'd known there were black jellyfish in it. They're rare. I'd not only never seen one before, I'd never even heard of them.

The most terrifying thing about the nettles is their size. The one that wrapped itself around me was three feet in diameter, but its long, grasping arms were twice that. The color is the next most horrifying thing about them. They're a deep, deep purple, almost black. The color of old, dried blood. Then, of course, there is the pain. A million points of stabbing agony that penetrated to my core.

Thankfully, I don't remember much about that day. I do remember being pulled from the sea and throwing up salty brine onto the sand. I also remember the smell of hot urine showering over me. Peeing on jellyfish stings as a cure is an old surfer tale. It has no basis in fact. I speak from experience when I say it's ineffective, unpleasant, and humiliating. Someone, a lifeguard maybe, rolled me in the sand to remove the black jelly, and then I must have passed out.

I spent the next three days in bed with a raging fever, tossing and turning with nightmares about a purple monster that enveloped me in its gelatinous arms, spewed its poison into my blood stream, and dragged me down and down into an airless world. When I finally woke on day four, I had welts the size of saucers all over me.

I told everyone how I ended up in the ocean jostling for space with a bloom of black sea nettles as soon as I was alert enough to do it. It wasn't the story they'd heard, which was no surprise. What was a surprise was what happened next. For one short day, I think my parents believed that I believed my story. They may have thought I was misremembering or exaggerating, but certainly not lying. On the fifth day, however, nobody believed a word I said.

MOLLY: I, for one, hope I never see one of those jellyfish outside of an aquarium. The ocean, for all its majestic beauty, is populated by a world of creatures even Dr. Moreau couldn't have thought up.

Willow, at this point, seems to be settling into her new life nicely. While there are things she's concerned about—family relationships, where they're going to live, what she's going to do for a career—they're pretty ordinary problems.

We know because of the journal entries that something bad has happened in the past. However, like Willow, we're unaware of any danger lurking around the corner in the present.

On that note, let's get back to her narrative.

6.2.5

BY THE TIME Willow left the library, most of the morning fog had burned off, leaving the sky the pastel blue of a baby romper. She saw Jonathan from a distance and waved. They met on the grass between the walls of shrubbery. "You ready?" he said.

She lifted onto tiptoes to kiss him. "For what?"

"I'm taking you shopping."

The news made her grin. She wouldn't have to furnish her new home with moldy old antiques after all. "Have you been to the design place in Laguna Niguel? It's amazing. They have such nice furniture, window coverings, tile. They have everything."

One of Jonathan's eyebrows rose. "That's not the kind of shopping I was talking about."

Her grin faded. "Oh."

"Mom swears she's recovered, and she wants to have the celebration we were supposed to have had last Sunday tonight."

Willow took his arm, and they walked toward the house. "Do you think she's up to it?"

"It doesn't really matter what I think. Mom is going to do what Mom is going to do. Besides, she's not like your mother. She won't be cooking, or cleaning, or any of that. All she has to do is bark a few orders, then spend the afternoon deciding what to wear."

Willow glanced at Jonathan. The reference to the difference in their mothers' economic status stung. Had he meant to sound condescending? His eyes were wide and clear, his lips turned up at the corners. No, his body language said, *I'm oblivious*. She let it go. "So what are we shopping for?"

"Clothes for you."

"Me?"

He untangled his arm from hers. "It's an early wedding present, or a late engagement present, from Mom."

Willow stopped walking. "She doesn't have to do that."

"She wants to."

"But—"

He put an arm around her shoulders and propelled her forward again. "You need some new things, maternity stuff or whatever pregnant women buy these days."

Willow swayed from one hip to another in an exaggerated wiggle, dropped her voice a half an octave, and mimicked her mother's Kentucky accent. "Are you saying these jeans make me look fat?"

He dropped his arm to her low back and stuck a thumb inside the waist band of her pants. "Ouch." He yanked it out and shook it.

She laughed. "Stop that."

"You're beautiful, but your clothes are too tight."

He was right. Getting dressed had become a puzzle, and the clothes she had at her parents' house wouldn't solve it. "I guess."

It was amazing how much more fun it was to buy things when there was a seemingly unlimited supply of money. Willow was used to budget stores and sales racks. Today Jonathan sat in a chair outside the dressing room of an upscale boutique in Laguna Beach, sipping champagne while Willow tried on loose dresses, linen pants, flowing silk blouses, and even a bathing suit that would grow with her body. They left the store with bags of things Jonathan wouldn't let her pay for, not that she could have anyway.

Color adorned the sky when they got home. Willow ran up to the room to shower and change into the new celery green dress that Jonathan said looked fantastic with her chestnut brown hair.

After dressing, she sat at the vanity in the bedroom and put in the gold hoop earrings she'd worn every day for the last five days. She had a jade pair her father had given her two Christmases ago that would look beautiful with the dress, but they were—guess where—in a box in his garage.

The fall before she'd gotten them, she and Drake had been fighting —a lot. He was supposed to come for Christmas Eve dinner. At the last minute, he called with a lame excuse about why he wouldn't be able to make it. The breakup handwriting was on the wall, but she'd been too blind to see it.

She was still weepy that Christmas morning. The mood lifted, however, when she opened a small, velvet box and saw the dark green jade earrings nestled inside. She turned to her mother. "Mom, these are—"

Honey interrupted her with a shake of her head. She pointed at Booker. "Your Dad got those. I had nothing to do with them."

A happy ember flared inside Willow and melted the frost that had entered her heart with Drake's phone call the night before. Her Dad had actually picked out a gift for her, and it wasn't a baseball glove, mountain biking shorts, or other gender-neutral thing. He'd bought her jewelry.

Traditionally, Booker picked out Ash's presents, and Honey bought Willow's. There was nothing wrong with that system. Her mother's gifts were almost always exactly right, just what Willow would have gotten for herself. It was, however, another brick in the wall that divided father and daughter.

"You look great," Jonathan said, but he wasn't looking at her when he said it. He was looking at his watch. "We should go down."

Willow tossed a last glance at the mirror and stood. "I'm tired of these earrings."

"You should've bought new ones."

"I have some at my parents' that would be great with this dress."

"We'll get them when we bring the wine by." His words stabbed a sensitive spot. She couldn't believe she hadn't yet told her parents she was married.

Willow heard the crackle of the fire before she reached the bottom of the stairs. The great room was only dimly lit by scattered table lamps, but the hearth blazed and a candlelit table had been pulled close to the fire. Unlike the day of the funeral, it seemed everything had been done to make the huge space feel intimate.

Gerry was seated in an easy chair at the end of the room. The glow from the fire blushed her cheeks and danced on her hair, making it appear more copper than silver.

"Come have a glass of that wonderful wine you brought me," she said when they entered.

A black-suited server who Willow hadn't noticed moved silently from a corner of the room and began pouring drinks. He was so like the mimes she'd seen in Paris on her one and only trip to Europe, she half expected the glasses to be invisible and the wine imaginary. He held out a very real glass of ruby liquid to Willow. She shook her head. "Sparkling water, please."

"Oh, give her a small glass, Anthony." Gerry waved a hand at him. "I drank wine almost every night when I was pregnant with Chloe and Jonathan. It didn't do them any harm."

He poured half a glass and handed that to Willow. She took it, but didn't intend to drink it. Gerry may be able to order the staff around, but Willow was less easily intimidated.

Jonathan and Willow settled onto the couch across from Gerry. From this distance, Willow could see that Gerry's rosy cheeks had come from a jar. Her skin was sallow and puckered with dehydration; her eyes had a yellow cast. She didn't look well.

"You don't have to drink it all," she said as Willow set her wineglass on the coffee table. "But I want to toast my first grandchild when the others get here."

"Others?" Jonathan's eyebrows rose as he took a sip from his own glass.

"Well, Dun and Chloe, of course. And wherever Chloe goes, Mat is sure to follow these days. I also took the liberty of inviting Cob, Marianne, and Ophelia. This is a family occasion."

"Can we tell them we're married before we break the baby news?" There was humor in Jonathan's voice.

"Tell them in any order you want." Gerry reached for a plate of crackers on a table next to her, took one, and nibbled. Willow thought of all the mornings she'd done exactly the same thing before getting out of bed.

Not today, though. She hadn't had morning sickness for at least four or five days, she realized with a start. It was funny how a thing absorbed your attention for so long, then, when it disappeared, you didn't even notice.

A murmur in another part of the house grew, and soon the distinct voices of Mat, Ophelia, Cob, and Marianne could be heard. A moment later they entered the room on a wave of scent. Aftershave and expensive perfume mingled as they walked toward the firelight.

"My poor dear," Marianne said, swooping down to peck Gerry on the cheek. "Mat was just telling us how sick you were."

"There's nothing worse than a stomach bug, except maybe seasickness." Cob plucked a wine glass from Anthony's hand.

Mat stood four or five feet away and surveyed Gerry, arms crossed over his chest. "You look better."

"Is she still contagious?" Ophelia eyed her aunt with narrowed eyes.

Gerry pulled the silk scarf she wore more tightly around her shoulders. "I'm fine. Don't kiss me if you're worried about becoming diseased."

Ophelia threw herself onto the couch next to Willow. "I won't. I hate throwing up."

"I've never had a patient who enjoyed it." Mat availed himself of a glass of wine and leaned a hip against the dining table.

Cob struck a pose by the fire, hands behind his back, stance wide, as if expecting a storm at sea. "Now that the weather is warming up, I'm thinking about taking the *Trade Winds* out for a sail. Catalina maybe. What do you say, Jonathan? Want to be my first mate?"

Ophelia leaned toward Willow and lowered her voice. "This should be good. Jonathan hates sailing." She reclined again and lifted her wine glass to her lips to hide a smile. It wasn't a very nice smile. Before Jonathan came up with an excuse, Chloe drifted into the room.

She wore sheer, white palazzo pants topped with a tailored white shirt tied at the waist. Her outfit was elegant and casual at once. Willow, who had been feeling chic in her new dress, suddenly felt dowdy.

"Are you sure you should be up and about, Mom?" Chloe said.

Mat pushed away from the table and draped a possessive arm around his fiancée. "I think she's fine, Chloe."

"Would you all stop?" Gerry raised her voice, but it didn't have the authoritative ring it usually carried. "I don't want to talk about it anymore. Where is Dun? I have a toast to make."

"I'm here. I'm here." Ms. Dunfrey bustled in through a side door. "I hope you didn't hold anything up for me."

"We did, but it's fine," Gerry said. "I want to make a toast before dinner. But Jonathan has an announcement first."

Jonathan took Willow's hand. "Willow and I were married last weekend."

"Lovely," Marianne said.

Cob hoisted his glass. "Good job."

Mat squeezed Chloe's shoulders and grinned. "They beat us to the punch, love."

The others were silent for so long it became awkward. Were they upset? Did they think Willow wasn't good enough for the Lauder family? Her gaze traveled from face to face. Chloe's was a study in neutrality. Ms. Dunfrey looked pinched. Ophelia's mouth was turned down at the corners. What was going on here?

Ms. Dunfrey broke the tension. She cleared her throat, lifted her glass, and said, "Congratulations," in a voice that was just a little too hearty.

"Congratulations." The rest echoed.

Willow's cheeks burned. Her family might not be rich; they might not globe trot to find *objets d'art* to decorate their homes with; they might buy Haide violins instead of Antoniazzi's; but they were good people.

Her mother had pulled herself out of an impoverished childhood with her own two hands and a skillet. Her brother served his country. Her father was a bona fide hero. She'd always been proud of that last fact despite the pain the event had caused her over the years. And, maybe most importantly, they weren't snobs.

"I have another toast to make." Gerry's voice was calm and even. She shot a glance at Chloe, then fixed Willow with a strong gaze. "My lovely new daughter-in-law is carrying my first grandchild. I couldn't be happier."

Jonathan squeezed Willow's hand before lifting his glass and saying, "I only wish Dad could be here."

Everyone toasted, and the smiles seemed genuine this time. Willow's anger disappeared like the morning fog. She had overreacted, possibly due to her own guilt. With all the changes in her life, she hadn't spent enough time with her family the past few months. Tomorrow she was going home to visit, no matter what surprises life with the Lauders threw into her path.

Gerry placed a hand on the arm of her chair and pushed herself up. "Time for dinner." She stood on shaky legs for a long second, took two steps, tottered, and collapsed to the floor.

6.2.6

JONATHAN AND CHLOE were at Gerry's side in a moment. Their mother pawed at the scarf that had shifted up around her neck, and gasped. "Air."

Chloe tugged at it while the others spoke on top of each other.

"This was too much—"

"Too soon—"

"She should be in bed."

Mat's voice rose above the noise. "Would you all be quiet." He and Jonathan helped Gerry from the floor into her easy chair. "Someone get me a glass of water."

Anthony, who must have anticipated the request, was at his elbow in a second. Mat nodded at a side table. Anthony set it down and moved away, while Mat placed two fingers against Gerry's wrist. A minute later he said, "Your pulse is slow. I'll get my bag and take your blood pressure."

Gerry waved a hand in the air, as if erasing his words. "No, Mat. I was dizzy for a moment, but it passed."

"You don't want a relapse, do you?"

"I don't, and I won't have one. Now, stop fussing."

"In my professional—"

She interrupted him. "Jonathan?"

Jonathan's head jerked toward her. "Yes."

"Will you help me to the table?"

"Really, Mom—"

Her voice lowered almost a full octave. "Help me to the table."

Jonathan avoided Mat's glare as he lifted his mother from the chair and supported her the few yards and dropped her onto a chair.

"There now. Everyone, take your places." She sounded breathless but determined.

Willow hung back, not sure which place was hers. She took the chair that was left after the others had taken theirs. This positioned her between Jonathan and Ophelia and directly across from Marianne. Anthony set plates of fish, rice, and asparagus in front of each of them.

The scents of white wine and nutmeg rose on the steam, and her stomach rumbled. Lunch seemed a long time ago. She lifted her fork, looked around the table and noticed no one else was eating. She set the utensil down again. Everyone's eyes were fixed on Gerry.

Her mother-in-law's face was pale and damp despite the powder she'd patted on. Her eyes were closed. Her breathing appeared shallow and rapid.

"Mom?" Chloe said.

Gerry's eyelids fluttered open. She picked up her fork, smiled regally and poked into her fish. The rest followed suit. Conversation was stilted for several long minutes. Only the occasional phrase flew between the pings of glassware and the clicks of cutlery.

Mealtimes in Willow's family were punctuated with loud bursts of laughter and even louder conversation. Thanks to Honey's cooking, their home had always been a hangout for Ash's ravenous friends during his teen years. And Willow's friends loved her mother's warm acceptance as much as they'd loved her warm chocolate chip cookies.

This was the kind of home Willow wanted for The Peach when he or she was school aged. She couldn't imagine that happening if they still lived at Sunset House. Would neighbor kids be driven in by limo? Would their drivers wait out front while they played?

A coffee klatch of capped chauffeurs appeared in her mind. They leaned against black vehicles, sipping Starbucks and comparing their charges' schedules. "Aiden is doing soccer *and* tennis this year. Really, I have no time for myself."

"Charlotte has gotten the lead in the school play. She has rehearsal every day after classes. If I hear *Tomorrow* one more time... "

"This is a strange world, isn't it, Willow?" Ophelia spoke and the daydream disappeared. Ophelia did seem to have an uncanny way of knowing what people were thinking.

Willow shifted a bit of fish to the inside of her cheek and said, "I, ah..."

"Have you been home to see your parents since you two tied the knot?" Ophelia continued.

Willow swallowed. "We're going tomorrow."

Ophelia's head bobbed up and down several times as if agreeing with Willow's answer. "That's good. It's important to stay close to the people who love you."

The statement was both odd and obvious, and Willow wasn't sure how to respond. Jonathan came to her rescue. "Funny thing. Honey—Willow's mother—loves Red Ravish." He raised his glass to emphasize his point. "The wine played a role in her escape earlier this year."

Cob's fork stopped in midair. "Escape?"

"You know the story, I'm sure. It was in the papers."

Willow squirmed in her seat. She didn't want to talk or think about what had happened this past February. It had been terrifying and, although she'd played a part, it was her mother's story, not hers.

"I read about it. The less said the better," Marianne said.

Willow shot a grateful glance across the table. Marianne returned a small, sympathetic smile. Until that moment, Willow had hardly noticed the woman. She was short, plump, and while not unattractive, not exactly attractive either. In this family of larger-than-life individuals, she'd faded into the background. Willow would make an effort to get to know her in the future.

"You can't do that, you know," Cob said. "You can't throw out a tantalizing morsel and not expect the fish to bite. I want to hear the story."

Marianne placed a warning hand on his arm. "You can read about it on the internet when we get home."

Willow chewed another bite of fish slowly, hoping Cob would stop staring at her with that eager look in his eyes. He didn't. She took a sip of water, then said, "My parents found a corpse while they were hiking in Black Star Canyon this past January."

His eyebrows shot up. "Really?"

"They ended up being dragged into—"

A barking cough from the end of the table interrupted her. Gerry's face had turned a dangerous shade of magenta.

Chloe was on her feet. "I think she's choking."

Mat's chair toppled to the floor, and he ran to her side. "Someone, call an ambulance." Ms. Dunfrey bolted from the room.

The next several minutes were a blur of activity. Mat walked outside, speaking on his cell phone. The twins led Gerry to the couch. Marianne wrung her hands, and Cob repeated encouraging phrases like, "It'll pass," and "Hang in there, old girl," and "Help will be here soon."

Only Willow and Ophelia hung back. Willow assumed Ophelia felt as she did, that the best thing they could do was to stay out of the way. But when Ophelia reached for the wine bottle in the center of the table and poured herself a healthy splash, Willow changed her opinion. It seemed callous to sit and drink Gerry's wine while the woman lay suffering on the couch only feet away. For such a perceptive person, Ophelia wasn't very sensitive. Willow pushed away from the table, distancing herself. Perhaps the crazy cousin jabs were deserved.

Retching echoed from the couch. Chloe ran to the table, reached over Ophelia and grabbed an empty wine bucket. Ophelia's nose wrinkled. She hid it inside her glass.

Willow spun away, strode to the fireplace, and stood next to Marianne. She may not be helping, but at least she wasn't eating and drinking and making merry like Ophelia. A moment later, Ms. Dunfrey returned to the room. "An ambulance is on its way."

Help was coming.

That thought brought both relief and an ache. Willow wished her father was on that emergency vehicle. He may have often been angry and distant when she was growing up, but she wanted him now. Booker made her feel safe.

Most children ran to their mothers when they were hurt or afraid.

Not Willow. She loved her mother. Honey was the most comforting and nurturing person she knew, but in her childish brain, her father had been a superhero. The faraway scream of a siren met her ear again, and another wave of reassurance and longing washed over her.

As the sound grew, so did the sting of vomit in the air. Willow's stomach roiled, and she covered her nose with her hand. The morning sickness may have passed, but she was as sensitive to smells as ever.

She shouldn't be here. What if she threw up and added to the chaos? What if Gerry's sickness was contagious? She had to think of the baby. "I'll let the paramedics know where to go." She mumbled the words and fled the great room.

The hallway was dark and quiet after the commotion by the fire. Willow leaned against the wall, pressed her hot cheek against the cool plaster and took several deep breaths. When her nausea passed, she made her way outside through the double doors. A moment later, a blue and white ambulance screamed up the drive and slid to a stop in front of the house.

Two uniformed paramedics, a man and a woman, leaped from the vehicle. Willow waved them forward. "Here." She led them into the hallway and pointed to the open great room door. They rushed past her. Her work done, she walked outside and sat on the edge of the front stoop where she'd be out of the way.

Booker always said it was the non-professionals, the onlookers, who caused the most problems at accident scenes. He should know. He was almost killed by one.

Willow had been eight when it happened. She'd been excited because Daddy's shift ended at 8:00—a propitious number. He would be home by nine on Christmas Eve. Unfortunately, a house fire started by an old clothes dryer was called in at 7:46. The truck rushed to the home. When they arrived, they saw smoke spewing from the half-sized windows close to the foundation of the building. The family had no idea how long the fire had been smoldering in the basement.

A mother and two young boys, one of them holding onto the collar of a golden retriever, stood on the front lawn with tear-stained faces. Willow had heard and recited the details of the story so many times they formed a movie in her mind.

It was as if she'd been there when the children's father pulled up minutes after the fire truck's arrival, and the mother's face turned to ash when she saw him. "Lacy. Where's Lacy?" she asked.

Confusion furrowed the father's brow. "She's here."

"She went with you!" The mother screamed at him, as if anger would make her words true.

He didn't bother answering her but ran for the front door. Booker tackled him before he reached it. It took two firefighters to hold the father back. Meanwhile, Booker adjusted his face mask and climbed a ladder to the little girl's bedroom.

He found her under her bed, terrified but unharmed. He hauled her to the open window, ready to hand her to the firefighter outside. Before that man could reach him, however, the father raced forward presumably wanting to be the one to take his child from Booker's arms.

The altercation at the foot of the ladder wasted precious seconds. The father was restrained again, and the firefighter climbed to the window. Booker passed the little girl outside to safety, then ran down the main stairway of the house to check for other victims on his way out.

Whether it was the extra minutes spent subduing the little girl's father, or whether it would have happened anyway, no one could say, but Willow's father fell through the foyer floor before reaching the front door.

His department rescued him within minutes, but not before his lungs and parts of his flesh had been scorched in the conflagration in the basement. He spent the next two nights in the hospital. The burns and smoke inhalation didn't cause lasting damage, but the trauma did. Booker was never the same after that incident.

For years Willow thought he'd blamed Lacy, the little girl, for his wounds, and that anger had transferred itself to his little girl, to her.

After months of counseling with one of the university therapists, she now understood it was the father's horror that had been etched into Booker's mind. The idea of losing his own daughter had suddenly seemed a real and living possibility. An obsessive need to keep Willow safe had turned him into a harsh dictator at times.

What had been, and still was, confusing was that the obsession hadn't extended to Ash or Honey. Willow alone received the brunt of his apprehension. This had cemented her childhood belief that her father no longer loved her. Now, intellectually, she knew this was untrue, but their relationship was still mending.

The paramedics jogged outside, retrieved a gurney from the ambulance and carried it indoors. Ten minutes later, they emerged with Gerry strapped to it. Jonathan followed behind them but paused when he saw Willow sitting in the dark. "I'm going with them. You'll be okay?"

He continued forward, not seeing her nod, nor seeming to hear her words, "Of course. Go," she said to his back. She watched the ambulance circle the drive and speed toward the gates. When it was out of sight, she rose, dusted off her new dress and returned to the house.

MOLLY: Generally speaking when people refer to the honeymoon phase of a marriage, they're talking about an idyllic time. If this is Willow and Jonathan's honeymoon phase, I'd hate to see what's coming. There's plenty of trouble in paradise. First, Jonathan's father dies, then Gerry gets sick. Very sick, it would seem.

And this leads me to the question of the week. If you were Willow, would you move into the apartment in the wing of the house? Or would you insist on getting a place of your own? The apartment sounds lovely, and it has a separate entrance. However, Jonathan would be at his mother's beck and call as long as he's on the property. If she's heading into a serious decline, that could take up a lot of his time and attention. Talk to me, people.

Join me next time for more *Murders Under the Sun*.

(cue music)

VO: This episode is brought to you by Home BnB in Big Bear, California. Get 20% off holiday vacation cabins when you use the code MURDERS at check out. *Murders Under the Sun* is edited by Jim Wilbourne, theme music is by Eclectic Blends, and I'm your host, Molly Shure.

part four

MURDERS UNDER THE SUN
SEASON SIX; EPISODE THREE

MOLLY: Welcome back to *Murders Under the Sun*. This is Molly Shure, your host.

I loved the debate on the Facebook page this week. As usual, you were divided on the topic. I asked the question: Would you move into the apartment in the wing of Sunset House, or would you insist on finding a place of your own?

Many of you said, heck yeah, to the apartment. Why wouldn't you move in rent free to an ocean-front home in Southern California?

Others of you pointed out there's no free lunch —or rent—in this case. Some things are more valuable than money, like time and freedom and autonomy. These people said they might feel guilty leaving their ill mother, but not if they weren't going far.

I agree with the second group. It would be difficult for a newly married couple to bond with all that family drama right next door. However, I'm not sure moving ten or fifteen minutes away would help all that much. It's a difficult situation no matter how you cut it.

On another topic, at the end of last season, I told you I learned that the drama students and the film students at CS-Fullerton sometimes worked on projects together. It seemed like a good lead to follow up on, but I hadn't yet had the chance.

Well, Camilla Jimenez, Raphael's mother, emailed me this week. It turns out, Raphael did make a film that several of the drama department students acted in. It won a short film award. She

was very proud of him and was sure we'd be able
to find it if we were interested.

I'd love to see whether it gave us any clue to
what happened to him or not. It might give Abby
and I more insight into who he was, and whether
or not he knew Ariana Blackstone. I'll let you
all know what I find out.

And, speaking of finding things out, we need to
get into today's episode. When we left her, Willow
was watching an ambulance drive away with her
mother-in-law in the back. She's really been thrust
into the middle of Jonathan's family crisis.

This wouldn't be an easy issue for a couple
who'd been together for a decade to navigate. I
don't think Willow and Jonathan have been married
for ten days. Let's see how she's handling
things.

Willow dozed by the fire, waiting for news. Everyone else had driven to
the hospital. She'd pulled on a jacket, intending to go, but Chloe had
said, "Hospitals are petri dishes."

Ms. Dunfrey had said, "Think of the baby."

A vision of a pimply-faced Roger standing over her as she lay on the
floor of the karate dojo had inserted itself in her brain like a bad rerun.
She'd slipped off her jacket and acquiesced. The Peach was her priority.

Anthony had been the last to leave. She'd watched the door close
behind him with a hollow thud. That thud heralded the first time she'd
been alone in Sunset House. It hadn't bothered her at the time. She'd
been so drowsy from the food, the little bit of wine she'd drunk, and the
exhaustion that comes after strong emotion that she'd collapsed on the
couch, pulled up a blanket, and closed her eyes.

Something brought her out of her light sleep. She lay listening to the old, empty house and was now aware of room upon room on either side of her and above her, each filled with furniture older than she was. Each one empty of life. She sat up and pushed the blanket away, feeling suddenly vulnerable. What time was it? The clock on the mantel said 12:15, but that couldn't be right.

She left the great room and headed toward the back stairs. Normally, she kept her cell phone with her, but Gerry disliked phones at the dinner table, so Willow had left it in her room. As she climbed the stairs, every third or fourth riser creaked. She'd never noticed the creaks before, but she'd never wandered alone in the house so late at night before. The setup was classic grade-B horror flick, and her pulse raced by the time she reached her room.

The glow of the bedside table lamps, Jonathan's discarded jeans, and her own cast-off flip-flops were comforting. Everything was the way they'd left it. What had she expected? Did pregnancy cause over-active imagination? She'd had some strange dreams the past month, but she'd chalked them up to all the stress she'd been under. She'd have to ask the doctor on her next visit.

She crossed the room, found her phone on the vanity and flipped it over to check the screen. No calls, which was both a relief and a disappointment. No news was good news, as they say, but she ached to hear the sound of Jonathan's voice.

Her thumb hovered over his number. Hospitals insisted that cell phones be turned off, but maybe he was at the cafeteria or on a walk. She punched his number. The phone rang five times and went to voice mail. She disconnected and stood staring at the dark screen.

There was no point in staying up. When there was news, Jonathan would call. She might as well get ready for bed. She took two steps toward the closet and heard a muffled slam somewhere in the house. Willow spun.

She stared through the bedroom doorway into the dim hall. "Hello?" Her voice sounded reedy.

There was no response. She strained her ears until she began to doubt there'd ever been a noise. She walked to the door to shut it but paused with her hand on the knob. She'd never been the kid who pulled the covers over her head. If there was danger, she wanted to face it head on.

What if it had been this same noise that had woken her when she was downstairs in the great room? What if there was someone else in the house? She'd locked the door behind Anthony, hadn't she? The events of the evening were a blur. She'd walked him to the door, but had she locked it? She couldn't remember.

Her father's face, set in stern lines, appeared in her mind. "Lock the door, Willow. If you're home alone, you have to lock the door." He'd tested her regularly in her growing-up years, leaving her alone ostensibly for the evening but returning minutes later to see if she'd followed his orders. The importance of security had been ingrained in her through repetition in the way a pet owner teaches a dog tricks. She wouldn't be able to rest until she'd checked the front doors.

Front doors. In a place as big as Sunset House there had to be as many as ten doors leading outside. There were two in the great room, one in the kitchen, one in Gerry's morning room, and lord knew how many in the left wing. The enormity of the house overwhelmed her again. She closed her eyes and placed a hand over her heart until the spike of panic receded.

When it did, she took off her wedge-heeled sandals, slid into flip-flops, grabbed her phone, and headed to the stairs. Three risers down, and the slam came again, this time followed by the sound of something heavy being dragged across the floor. She stopped, heart battering her ribcage. There *was* someone in the house.

She had two options. No, three. She could follow the sound and find out who was causing it. She could lock herself in her room and call the police. She could race out of the house, find a car that wasn't locked up in that damn garage, and go home to her parents.

She dismissed the third option immediately. She wasn't a child anymore. She couldn't go running to Mommy and Daddy whenever she was afraid. She was a grown woman with a child of her own on the way.

The second option seemed extreme. To call the police because she heard a sound in a house as big and full of residents as Sunset House was laughable. Having been raised by a first responder, she had a healthy respect for emergency services. Trivial 911 calls cost lives.

Option one it was then. Willow pulled up the emergency call button on her phone, just in case, then ascended the few stairs she'd walked down. The sound had been on this floor, and it had come from the front of the house. She followed the hallway forward.

The only upstairs room she'd been in was hers and Jonathan's, so this was all new territory. Her shoes slapped against her feet. The sound seemed to echo off the ecru walls, and she wished she'd worn slippers.

There were four doors in this section of the hall. She passed her room and stopped at the next door. She placed her ear on the wood and listened for a long moment. Pulse racing, she put a hand on the knob and turned.

The room was black. She felt along the wall to the left of the door and found a switch. She flipped it on, and light filled the space. A queen-sized bed was pressed against the inner wall, flanked by marble-topped bedside tables. A low bureau rested on one wall and a highboy on the other. This room was a mirror image of hers. There were no hidden corners. She could see it was empty, and her nose confirmed it. The air inside was stale and musty. She flicked off the light and walked on.

She didn't bother opening the doors across the hall. She pressed her ear against them for a second or two and was satisfied they were empty as well. Besides, she was fairly certain the sounds she'd heard had come from somewhere up ahead.

The hallway made a sharp right turn and opened into a broader space where the doors were farther apart. This was where the noise had come from. She was sure of it. She tapped on the first door she came to. No one responded, so she turned the knob.

Moonlight illuminated the space enough for her to take it in without switching on lights. It was an apartment, not a single bedroom like Jonathan and she were sharing. She could see a small living room with a fireplace which opened onto a separate sleeping area. Beyond that was a door she assumed led to a bathroom. The room was in use. There were personal items scattered about, a novel on a side table by the fire, a pair of soft slippers peeking out from under an easy chair. Chloe's room, perhaps. Or maybe Ms. Dunfrey's. She pulled the door shut and moved forward.

As she approached the next door, the slam came again. It was more distinct this time. She thought it sounded as if someone had flung a cupboard door closed. Someone looking for something, searching cupboards and not finding what they were seeking perhaps?

All Willow's years of music training had developed her auditory skills. She was convinced the noise came from the room two doors up on the left. As she drew closer, she saw the door was slightly ajar.

She hesitated. The room faced west, which meant it had a panoramic ocean view. The other doors in the hallway were spaced closer to each other than to this door; therefore, it was the biggest apartment. If she was calculating correctly, this was the master suite. It was Gerry's room.

But Gerry wasn't coming home tonight. Willow knew that for a certainty. She stood near the door, blood pulsing in her ears so loudly it drowned out almost all other sound. Should she call out? Throw open the door? Run and call the police?

In the end, she did none of those things. As she deliberated, the door opened wider and the room's light spilled into the hallway. Willow took two quick steps backward.

A second later, Ms. Dunfrey exited and skidded to a stop. "Willow?" Her face blanched. "What are you doing here?"

"I heard something," she said. "I wondered... How's Gerry?"

Ms. Dunfrey lifted an overnight bag in explanation. "I came to get a few things for her. She likes her own nightgown. Those cotton hospital gowns—" Her voice caught.

"She's going to be there for a while then?" Willow asked.

Ms. Dunfrey shrugged her wide swimmer's shoulders. "She's not well."

The tight-jawed look on Jonathan's face at his father's funeral crossed the screen of Willow's mind. Losing a father was a horrible thing. Losing both parents so close together was unthinkable. "What's wrong with her?"

"They're not completely sure yet. It seems her liver is failing." Ms. Dunfrey's gaze dropped to the patterned carpet runner beneath their feet. "I can't understand it."

I drank wine every day when I was pregnant. It didn't do Jonathan and Chloe any harm. Gerry's words from earlier that evening rang in

Willow's head. Could Gerry be an alcoholic? Jonathan had never hinted at that. Some people hid it well, but could a mother hide it from her own child?

"I'd better get back," Ms. Dunfrey said, but she didn't move.

The two women stared at each other for a beat, then Willow realized she was blocking Dunfrey's path. She flattened herself against the wall with an apologetic grunt. Ms. Dunfrey strode past her and disappeared down the central staircase. Willow heard her steps clack across the tile entryway and the front door open, then close. Silence reigned in the empty building again.

Willow pivoted toward her room but stopped. No, she wasn't going through that again. She'd make sure the doors were secured before she got into bed. She trotted after Dunfrey, checked the locks on the heavy front doors, then made a nerve-wracking tour of the rest of the house.

6.3.2

JONATHAN WASN'T next to her when Willow woke up the next morning. He couldn't still be at the hospital, could he? She threw off the blankets and padded to the dressing table where she'd plugged in her phone before going to sleep. She turned it on, then wandered to the window as she waited for it to power up. Not much was visible through the morning fog. She'd seen June gloom plenty of times. Her hometown of Laguna Niguel wasn't far from the beach, but it was far enough that she hadn't been immersed in the relentlessly overcast months the coastal towns often experienced. Day after day of gray depressed her.

When her phone came alive, she checked her missed calls and found there were none. Jonathan must not have come home—a bad sign. She marched to the closet. She wasn't going to let him suffer through this alone, no matter what Chloe said. Petri dish or not, she would go to the hospital and be by her husband's side.

When she reached the downstairs hall, she heard voices. They floated from the kitchen on coffee-scented air. It smelled wonderful. It might be small-minded of her with Gerry's illness overshadowing things, but she had a sudden longing for coffee. Maybe Cookie would make her a cup of decaf.

She pushed open the kitchen door and heard her husband say, "I'm gonna get going. I'll keep you posted."

"Jonathan." She rushed across the checkerboard tiles and into his arms. "When did you get home? Were you at the hospital all night? How's your mother?"

He gave her a quick squeeze. "Which question should I answer first?"

Willow gave him a half smile. "Your mother. What's happening?"

"Her liver is shutting down. They don't know why, not yet. Her only hope is a transplant, but she doesn't have much time." His voice was measured and monotone. He must be keeping his emotions at bay so they wouldn't overwhelm him.

"I'm so sorry," she said.

"Herbal tea, Willow?" Cookie asked.

"Good morning, Cookie." She'd momentarily forgotten his presence. "Do we have any decaf coffee? I can make it myself."

"If you don't mind a single-serve cup." He opened a cupboard embedded in the wall at the corner of the counter. Inside was a lazy Susan filled with small appliances plugged into a central electrical outlet. He spun the platform until a fancy espresso machine appeared. He plugged it with a pod and, a moment later, handed her a cup of coffee. She added cream and sugar, sipped, and sighed. This would become a morning ritual. Decaf had never tasted so good.

Jonathan pushed an empty plate away from him and stood. "As to your other two questions, I came home last night. Chloe and I both did. But I didn't want to wake you. I caught a couple of hours in one of the guest rooms."

"What time? I was up late."

"Not sure. It was after midnight." He leaned toward her and gave her a light kiss on the lips. "I have to get back."

Willow took a big slug of coffee and set the half-filled mug on the counter. "I'm coming with you."

"You don't need to. Chloe and I are just sitting around the waiting room. Waiting. Go see your parents, like we planned."

"You shouldn't be—" She was going to say *alone at a time like this,* but he wasn't alone. He'd just told her he had Chloe. A dark spider of jealousy crawled up the back of her neck. How could she compete with a twin?

Twins were famous for thinking the same thoughts, having the same dreams, speaking a language no one else understood. She and Jonathan didn't understand each other half the time when they were both speaking English.

As if on cue, the kitchen door swung open, and Chloe appeared. "Ready?" She looked beautiful, as usual. The dark circles under her eyes, which would have made anyone else look like a zombie, made her look like one of those French, waif-like models.

Jonathan put his hands on Willow's shoulders and pulled her in for a second kiss. "Really. Go see your Mom and Dad. Take them the wine. There's nothing you can do at the hospital."

As he walked away, she remembered the impossible garage. "Oh."

He turned, and she thought she saw the briefest shadow of annoyance on his face before he said, "Yes?"

"My car. I don't have a garage door opener."

His shoulders seemed to relax. "I'll tell Mike to park it outside on our way out."

She wished he'd offered to set her up with the app, but he had a lot on his mind. She'd ask another time. "Thanks. Keep me posted." She stared at the kitchen door as it closed behind him, a lump forming in her throat.

A long beat later, Cookie said, "Eggs? Toast? You gotta feed that baby."

She forced a smile. "Better stick to toast. My mother will be insulted if I don't eat whatever she makes for lunch."

He laughed. It was the deep, round sound of a double bass. "I am the same way. If I make you a special meal, you'd better eat it if we're going to stay friends."

The laugh resonated inside her, and her smile became genuine. "I'll remember that."

She wanted to ask Cookie about the Lauder family, about the relationships, the alliances, and the enmities. Jonathan said he'd been with them for years. He must have a unique perspective, but how to start the conversation? That was the question. She took a bite of a perfectly toasted, buttered slice of sourdough bread.

"It's not easy joining another family, learning their rules, understanding why they do the things they do," Cookie said as if reading her thoughts.

Willow washed the toast down with coffee. "Am I that transparent?"

"I was married once. I know the drill."

"I'm sure it'll get better. We've only been married a few days."

He nodded. "It will."

"It's just the whole twin thing. It seems like they can read each other's mind. I'm close with Ash—that's my brother—but it's not like that. We fought like crazy until he turned seventeen."

"Oh, don't think those two haven't had their share of fights. They're very competitive. There were times when they were in their teens, I thought they were going to kill each other."

Willow pivoted on her stool to face him. "Really? They seem so, I don't know, in sync. I can't imagine that."

Cookie walked to the refrigerator, pulled out an armful of vegetables, and dumped them in the sink. "They worked it out eventually, like you and your brother." He raised his voice over the shush of water from the tap. "When they're getting along, it's like watching people who've been dancing together for years. They seem to know what the other is going to do before they do it."

The spark of contentedness she'd felt when he'd laughed fizzled. She knew that kind of synchronization. She'd played in a string quartet for extra cash while she was in college. At first, they sounded—as her roommate had said when she walked into an early practice—like cats in heat. After a year of playing together, however, it was just as Cookie had described. She knew what each would do before they did it. She and Jonathan were still at the cats-in-heat phase.

Cookie placed the dripping produce on a clean dishtowel and began drying it. "But when they are not getting along, ooh-ooh, watch out, baby. It gets messy." He laughed again and this time Willow joined her treble notes to his bass ones. There was a mean, discordant twang in her own laugh, however, and she cut it short.

She finished breakfast, thanked Cookie, and headed out to find her car. Why was she being like this? She should be glad Jonathan and Chloe were close, but she wasn't. She wished Chloe would marry her pediatrician and move away. Or, better yet, that she and Jonathan would move. She felt like an interloper at Sunset House. Maybe the apartment in the left wing would fix the problem, but she was afraid it wouldn't.

6.3.3

THE SOLIDITY of Sunset House evaporated like mist in the sun as Willow drove north on the 5 Freeway. By the time she pulled into her parent's driveway, it might have been the set of a movie she'd fallen asleep while watching. This, the house where she grew up, this was the real world. The one behind her felt like someone else's dream.

It was no dream, however. She pulled herself from the car, already needing the additional help of her arms due to her compromised abdominal muscles and loosening joints. The Peach was incontrovertible evidence of her current situation.

She trotted up the walkway and pushed open the front door. "Mom." A black bundle of fur slid across the floor and collided with her shins. "Hey, Fury. Hey, baby." She picked up the writhing dog and hugged him while doing her best to avoid his darting tongue.

Her mother came around the corner, wiping her hands on her apron. "Hello there, Dumplin'." She kissed Willow's cheek. "Come keep me company in the kitchen."

Willow followed the trail of her mother's conversation through the front hall and the family room. "Where's Jonathan? I'm making grilled cheese and bacon sandwiches. Didn't you tell me he loved them? But don't worry, I also made quinoa salad. We can't be too decadent. I've been playing around with quinoa lately. It's very versatile. I've got savory quinoa recipes, sweet quinoa—"

Honey prattled on without giving Willow a chance to get in a word. She bustled around the kitchen, pulling bread from the cupboard, condiments and cheese from the fridge. Then, seeming to realize her original question was still hanging out there, she said, "So, where is he?"

"Gerry is in the hospital."

Honey stopped moving and turned her gaze on Willow. "Oh, no. Again? Is it serious?"

"I think so." Willow's throat threatened to shut down. Why? She didn't understand her emotions. She wasn't close to Gerry. "She's got liver failure. Jonathan said something about a transplant." Her voice cracked on the word transplant.

"Oh, sweetheart." Honey's arms were around her in a second. Willow dropped her forehead onto her mother's shoulder, breathed in the flour and vanilla scent of her, and—to her mortification—broke into tears.

Many pats and coos later, Willow pulled herself out of her mother's embrace and walked to the bathroom for a handful of tissues. "I don't know what's wrong with me," she said when she returned.

Honey was busying herself with the tea kettle now. "I'm making tea." Coffee was her beverage of choice, but she knew Willow couldn't drink it. Her thoughtfulness threatened to bring on another volley of tears.

"I didn't realize you and Gerry were that close," Honey said as she placed tea bags into mugs.

Willow blew her nose. "We're not. It's not that." She waved a dismissive hand. "I mean, I'm upset, of course. Jonathan is distraught." He hadn't actually seemed distraught that morning. Controlled was a better word, but she wasn't sure her mother would understand that. Emotions weren't hidden in her house, not the way they were in Sunset House. "I think I'm hormonal."

As soon as those words left her lips, Willow felt like a fraud. She *was* hormonal. She was pregnant, for goodness' sake. Hormones weren't the reason for her upset, though. The problem was, she had to tell her parents she was married.

She'd imagined doing that with Jonathan. Having his support as they navigated the mixed response they were sure to get. What should have been a joyful occasion was now stressful.

It seemed she did more things alone since she'd been married than she'd done when she was single. She would wait until her father got home, though. No sense going through it twice.

"Let's have tea in the yard. Your dad should be home in half an hour. We can eat then. Unless you're starving?" Honey said.

"I had toast before I left."

They settled into wicker chairs, and Willow launched into a description of Hamish's library, the violin, his collections, and her plans to catalog it all. By the time Booker came banging through the front door, she had her emotions in check.

"There she is," he said and planted a kiss on the top of Willow's head. "Where's Jonathan?"

"He's with his mother," Honey said before Willow could answer. "Gerry's very ill. She's in the hospital."

"What's going on?" Booker asked.

Honey spoke for her and filled him in quickly, perhaps fearing Willow would break down again, then said, "Why don't you tell your dad about the library? I'll get lunch going."

"Can you wait, just a minute?" Willow asked.

Honey, who'd risen part way from her chair thumped down again. "Sure. What's up?"

"Jonathan and I wanted to tell you this together—" Her voice shook. She cleared her throat. Best to get directly to the point. "We got married last weekend."

Silence reigned for a long moment. Honey spoke first. "That's wonderful, darlin'."

"Congratulations," Booker said without the heartiness she'd hoped for.

"We're going to have a big reception, maybe even renew our vows, after the baby comes, but we wanted to be official. You know, like you said Mom, so the baby is—"

"Born on the right side of the sheets." Booker's gaze turned skyward as he quoted his wife. "I hope you didn't rush into things because of us."

"No, no, Dad. It wasn't that. When I fell in that karate class, I suddenly realized the baby is a person, a little person who needs her Mommy and Daddy."

Honey's chin shot up. "It's a girl?"

Willow waved a dismissive hand. "No, I don't know yet. It could be a boy. He or she needs their Mommy and Daddy."

"As long as you're happy." Booker's brow furrowed. "You are happy?"

"Yes." Willow's exclamation was a bit too bright. She toned herself down. "I wish we could have done the big event. You know I've been planning my wedding since I was ten and had a crush on Leonardo DiCaprio." She laughed. "But it was beautiful. Oh, and I brought you something. It's in the car."

"Us?" Honey said. "Aren't we supposed to be giving you gifts?"

"You're not going to believe this, but the Lauders know the vintner who makes Red Ravish. We got married at his vineyard. Jonathan insisted we bring a case for you guys and one for Gerry."

Whether it was the mention of the wine, or the fact that Willow didn't have to pretend to be happy when she told them about the wedding, the mood lightened. Honey was grinning by the time she headed to the kitchen to fix lunch.

When she disappeared, Booker said, "So, what's this about Hamish Lauder's library?"

Willow told him the same story she'd told her mother.

"Why are they having you do it? Why not hire somebody who does that for a living, an *Antiques Roadshow* kind of guy?" he said when she was done.

"They think I *am* a bit of an expert, about the music anyway." She couldn't keep the tension from her voice. Why was it everybody on the planet saw her as a competent adult but her father?

"You do know about music, but it sounds like there's a lot of other stuff there besides."

"It was his office, Dad. It's filled with his private things. The family probably doesn't want a stranger messing around in there."

"Hmm."

"Hmm?" Her skin itched with irritation.

"Like what kind of private things?"

"Like letters, bills, photographs."

Booker leaned into his seat and tipped his head to the side. "Photographs are private? What, are they risqué or something?"

"Of course not. I found an old family photograph of a husband and wife and little girl. The girl is, or was, his private assistant. I'm not sure what the connection is." Willow paused. Why had she brought that up? "What I'm trying to say is the business is all tied up with family, you know?"

Booker inspected his fingernails. "You mean like the Mafia."

Willow's jaw tightened. "The point is there are private things in his office as well as professional, and outside people are nosy. It's different for wealthy people."

Booker looked into the distance and bit the inside of his cheek. "Oh, I don't know about that. None of us likes having our dirty laundry aired."

Willow silently cursed herself. Their family had some dirty laundry aired publicly earlier that year. It had been difficult for Booker, a man who prized integrity and whose reputation had no price tag.

They sat in awkward silence for a beat, then both spoke at once. "Dad—"

"Will—"

Willow shut her mouth, allowing him to speak first.

"Will, I don't mean to upset you. I guess I'm not used to having my daughter belong to another family. I feel like it's my job to figure out who these people are, and if they're going to be good to you. Things are moving a bit fast."

Her irritation blew away. She reached out a hand and put it over his. "They're good people, Dad. You don't have to worry about me."

Honey emerged through the sliding glass door into the yard with a tray full of sandwiches. Booker rose from his chair. "I certainly hope so, pumpkin."

They kept the conversation light during lunch. Willow told them about her shopping trip, the green dress and how well it would go with the jade earrings. Honey shared her latest mountain biking adventures. Booker made Dad jokes. It was nice. Willow hadn't felt this relaxed in weeks.

Honey pushed away from the table first. "You want to go through some of those boxes in the garage?"

"I can do it on my own," Willow said.

"You shouldn't be lifting anything heavy," Booker said.

She sighed. He was probably right, but something about his tone of voice made her want to grab a barbell and do a set of sumo squats. "I guess it would be good to have someone else's opinion. I'm not sure what to keep and what to get rid of."

Honey began clearing the table. "I wouldn't make too many decisions until you find a place to live."

Willow rose to help her. "I forgot to tell you—we have one."

"Really?" Her mother sounded excited, but Willow was fairly certain she wouldn't be once she learned where it was.

"Before Hamish died, he started renovating a section of the left wing of Sunset House for us as a wedding present."

Honey lowered the pile of plates she'd been holding onto the table with a thump. "Will." Her voice was stern. "Do you really think that's a good idea?"

"I'm not sure I have a choice. It was a gift from Hamish and Gerry, a very generous one. How do you say no to a recently deceased man and his sickly widow without looking unappreciative?"

"You say, I'm touched, I'm grateful, but if we're going to bond as a couple, we need some privacy."

"It's pretty private." Her words sounded unconvincing, even to her.

Honey lifted the plates and carried them to the kitchen with angry strides. "But it's not neutral territory."

Willow felt her cheeks grow hot. If Jonathan had been here, her mother would've been more diplomatic. Since he wasn't, Willow was getting the full force of her mother's misgivings. She opened her mouth to defend their decision, but Booker spoke first.

"She's a married woman now, Hon. She and Jonathan have to make their own decisions, and we can't be second guessing them all the time."

Willow looked at him with both surprise and gratitude. He hadn't been that diplomatic about her taking on the library job.

Honey's voice carried through the kitchen window into the yard. "Well, whatever. I'm sorry." But it didn't sound like she was.

"It's okay, Mom." Willow wanted to tell her mother she understood, that she had many of the same concerns, that she would always be their kid even if her last name was Lauder, but she didn't. She'd show her. She'd spend more time at home, include her in everything. Honey would see. It would be okay.

Willow rose and began clearing dishes. "Jonathan and Gerry want your help picking out appliances for the kitchen."

Honey's face was composed when Willow entered the kitchen. "I could do that," she said.

Willow set down the dishes, crossed to her mother and pulled her into a hug. "I love you, Mom."

Honey tightened her embrace in answer, and Willow's eyes stung with salt again. What was her problem? She'd never been this emotional. As she pulled away, her phone rang inside her purse. She turned to get it before Honey could see the tears threatening to drop.

She found the cell and checked the screen. It was Jonathan. He must have news.

6.3.4

WILLOW SAW Jonathan as soon as she entered the ICU. He leaned against the wall, his forehead resting in his hand. She ran past the nurse's station, past the windows of rooms filled with the sick and dying, past the beeping, blinking monitors. "Baby, I'm so sorry."

He wrapped his arms around her and rested his cheek on her hair. She didn't ask the questions swirling in her mind, there would be time for that later. Her job was to be there. To love him. To offer comfort. It was a profound moment, the first great difficulty faced as husband and wife, as a family.

They stood locked in embrace for several seconds before he pulled away and wiped his eyes. "Thanks for coming."

Thanks for coming?

Where else would she be?

That was the kind of thing someone said to a neighbor or a distant relative, not a wife. "Sure." She hoped her voice didn't betray her hurt feelings.

He led the way to a room at the end of the corridor without speaking. Inside, Ms. Dunfrey, Chloe, Marianne, and Cob crowded around a form so white that it appeared to be a yellowed spot on the otherwise pristine sheets. Gerry's gray hair was splayed across the pillow, her eyes closed, her face expressionless.

"Whoever heard of death by acetaminophen?" Cob said to no one in particular.

"They're not sure that's what it was," Ms. Dunfrey said.

Marianne looked from one to the other, confusion wrinkling her nose and making her look more like a rabbit than ever. "I thought it was a heart attack."

"Yes, but what caused the heart attack? That's the question." Cob's voice was laced with irritation.

"Not acetaminophen," Ms. Dunfrey said. "I know that. I kept track of her medications."

"Do we have to talk about this now?" Chloe snapped. "They'll be here to get her soon. Can't we have a quiet minute to say goodbye?"

The room grew silent, but Willow's mind raced. Her greatest question had been answered—Gerry had died of a heart attack—but several others erupted to take its place. She knew acetaminophen could kill if someone took an overdose, but wouldn't that take a lot of pills? A person couldn't swallow a handful of pills accidentally.

A nurse in white scrubs covered with cartoon-character cats stood in the doorway, a blue-scrubbed man behind her. "We need to take her now." Her tone was apologetic.

A choked sob sounded behind Willow. She glanced over her shoulder and saw Marianne press a tissue to her mouth. Cob stepped closer to his wife and draped an arm over her shoulders. Where was Ophelia? Willow had just noticed she was missing.

The nurses pushed past Chloe and Jonathan, who both wore stoic expressions. They pulled up metal slats along the sides of the bed and steered it toward the door. Before they reached the hallway, the woman decorated in cartoon cats spread the sheet over Gerry's face.

It is finished. Willow watched her mother-in-law disappear. What's going to happen to us now? The thought was followed by guilt. How could she be thinking about herself, about her position in the household, about the beginning of her new life with Jonathan as Gerry was being wheeled away?

Jonathan spoke into the quiet that followed. "I don't want an—"

"Autopsy?" Chloe's gaze shifted to him. "That's not an option. You heard what the doctor said. They have to—"

"Determine cause of death." Jonathan interrupted her. "I know, but can't we do something about it? Call a lawyer?" The words were uttered in such a harsh tone, the untrained scratch of a bow on too taut strings. Willow's head snapped toward him. "I don't want them cutting her."

Ms. Dunfrey's eyes were wet. "She'd want it, Johnny. It's the only way to prove she didn't try to kill herself."

Chloe gave her a pointed look. "Who said anything about suicide?" She spun on her heel and left the room.

Suicide? Gerry had seemed so excited about the baby, but the family were professionals when it came to masking their emotions. Had she been grieving more over Hamish's death than anyone had realized?

"I was in charge of her medications, and I can promise you she was only given what the doctor said she should take," Ms. Dunfrey said to Chloe's retreating form.

"Nobody's blaming you, Dun," Jonathan said in a weary voice.

Two or three beats passed before anyone moved, then Cob took his wife's arm. "We'd best go find Ophelia. I think she's in the cafeteria."

Jonathan glanced from Willow to Ms. Dunfrey and back. "We should go, too."

As they reached the elevator, the doors opened, revealing a disheveled Ophelia clutching a disposable cup. "You're leaving?"

"No reason to stay now," Jonathan answered.

They piled into the small space. Ophelia withdrew into a corner like they all carried a contagion. "She's gone?"

Cob pushed the button for the lobby. "We'll talk about it later." His tone carried a reprimand, and Willow felt a sudden camaraderie for the girl. She knew what it was like to be the least important member of a family.

The sun was sinking toward the horizon when they reached the parking lot. "We're this way." Cob tipped his head to the left.

Jonathan nodded, took Willow's hand and walked in the other direction. "It doesn't seem real," he said when they reached her car.

"It'll take a while to sink in," she said. "It's only been... " She let her words fade away hoping he'd finish her sentence. She didn't know when Gerry had died.

"An hour," he said.

"I didn't know your mother had heart problems."

"She didn't. That's what's so strange about it. Her organs just started shutting down. First her liver, then her heart."

"And the doctor thinks that could be from an overdose of acetaminophen?"

Jonathan ran a hand over his head. "The symptoms are consistent with what's called a staggered overdose."

"What's that?"

"It's when you take a little too much over a period of time. It builds up in your system. Apparently, it happens more often than you'd think. The ER doctor had a case last week. Somebody takes cough medicine that has acetaminophen in it, and they take the maximum dose in pill form at the same time. Do that for a week, then throw a couple of glasses of wine on top of it, and you have a pretty lethal situation."

The conversation answered Willow's questions, but it also worried her. When he'd called her, Jonathan had sounded like an emotional wreck. Now he recited the information clinically, like it wasn't his mother they were discussing. Were mood swings normal when grieving? She didn't know. She'd have to look it up. She wanted to do this right, to be the support person he needed, whatever that took.

He leaned in for a kiss. "I'll see you at home."

"Are you sure you're okay to drive?"

"I'm fine." He gave her a weak smile and headed across the parking lot.

Sunset House lived up to its name that evening. As Willow pulled through the gates, she saw a blaze of color on the horizon. It seemed the sky was paying tribute to the dead woman. The last time the colors were as vibrant was the night of Hamish's funeral. Was that only a month ago? It seemed an eternity. Something heavy dropped onto Willow's shoulders. How would Chloe and Jonathan cope, both parents gone in so short a time?

Jonathan must have reached home and parked before Willow

arrived. She didn't see his car, and the big garage door was closed. She parked on the side of the building. She would ask Jonathan to get her an opener or the app, but not tonight. Tonight, she walked slowly toward Sunset House in no hurry to get there.

When she arrived in the great room, Chloe was already standing by the fire, sipping something amber from a tumbler, whiskey maybe. Willow had a sudden longing for a glass of wine but, unlike Gerry, she didn't believe wine and pregnancy were a good mix.

Jonathan stood by the bar in the far corner of the room. He glanced at her as he poured himself a couple fingers of whiskey, then pulled a glass from under the counter and poured a sparkling water for Willow.

Jonathan handed her the glass on his way to the couch. Willow skirted the easy chair Gerry had sat in the evening before and moved to the one on the opposite side of the fireplace.

"Dun is getting older," Jonathan said.

"What does that have to do with anything?" Chloe's voice was dull.

"She could've made an error. She could've forgotten she'd given Mom her pills and given them to her again. She could've read the label wrong."

Chloe pursed her lips. "She's not that old. What is she, sixty-eight, sixty-nine?"

Jonathan swirled the liquid in his glass. "She's seventy next month."

"Okay, seventy. That's the new sixty. Seventy is nothing."

"She's very fit." Willow inserted herself into the conversation. The twins' heads swiveled toward her, identical bland expressions on their faces. "I've watched her swim." Neither responded, and their eyes returned to their drinks. Willow's cheeks flushed.

"If it is acetaminophen," Jonathan spoke as if she hadn't. "We should consider—"

"What?" Chloe interrupted him. "Calling the police? Throwing her under the bus at the funeral? Publicly humiliating her?" Her voice was shrill.

"Who?" A lower timbre chimed in. The woman in question stood in the doorway of the great room. "Who are you talking about?"

"No one," Jonathan said.

Ms. Dunfrey approached the group at the fire. "Don't lie to me,

Johnny. You want to blame me for your mother's death. I understand, you're upset. We're all upset." She stopped speaking abruptly and swallowed hard. "I can only repeat what I said at the hospital. I can't believe that simple over-the-counter medicine was the cause of her death. We should wait to hear the results of the autopsy."

"You're right," Chloe said without conviction. "We shouldn't jump to conclusions. He's—" She waved her drink at Jonathan. "You're not thinking clearly. You're in shock."

Dunfrey stepped toward him and placed a hand on Jonathan's arm, which lay along the back of the couch. "This is a sad, sad time, and those of us who are left need each other more than ever."

The two remained still, each locked in their own distress. Jonathan's face was carved in angry, tight lines, Ms. Dunfrey's molded by love and pain. The tableau could have been a work of art named *Grief*, or *Mourning*. The first violin line of Bach's *Mass in D minor* burst into Willow's mind. Her fingers itched to play it on Hamish's violin.

6.3.5

THREE DAYS LATER, Jonathan stormed into the library where Willow had been adding to her list of titles. "He was right." He slapped the back of the leather couch.

Willow looked up from her yellow pad. "Who was right about what?"

"That doctor, the one who ordered the autopsy. Mom died from a staggered overdose of acetaminophen."

She didn't know what to say, but didn't have time to say anything anyway. Jonathan was in a rage. "I told Chloe more than once, before all this, that I thought Dun was starting to slip. It was little things, you know?" His blue eyes flashed like a stormy sea. Willow nodded.

"Mom missed a hair appointment because Dun confused the dates. She forgot to order the silent auction basket for the benefit dinner for the Santa Ana literacy program. Nothing huge. Nothing life-threatening—" his mouth snapped shut. "Until now."

Willow set her pad on the desk, crossed to him, and put her arms around him. "I'm so sorry." Insufficient words, but the only ones she had. He loved Dun almost as much as he'd loved his mother. The thought that one had killed the other, even inadvertently, must be excruciating. "What are you going to do?"

"I don't know." He shook his head. "We have to let her go. She was Mom's secretary, Mom is gone. There's no reason for her to stay, but... "

"But?"

"Mom left provision for Dun in her will. Under the circumstances, I don't think she should get it."

Willow dropped her arms and stepped away from Jonathan. "Even if she did give your mother more medicine than she should have had, which we don't know is true, it would have been an accident. You said yourself she was getting older, maybe confused." *And, Gerry's refusal to give up her nightly wine must have added to the problem.* She didn't dare voice that thought.

"Right." He glared at her. "What's your point?"

"My point is, she doesn't deserve to be punished for this. Certainly not before we know she was culpable."

His eyes narrowed. "How are we going to prove that one way or the other?"

"Exactly." Willow's jaw tightened, and the two stared at each other. *Was this their first fight?* The thought whispered in a corner of her mind. Did defending a woman she hardly knew reach the level of importance to warrant a first fight? Shouldn't that occasion be reserved for something more intimate? Something about them, their marriage, their future?

"I thought I heard voices." Sophie stood in the doorway. The electric tension between Jonathan and Willow broke as if a switch had been flipped. "Jonathan, I wanted to offer my condolences. I'm so sorry to hear about Gerry."

Jonathan turned slowly. "Thanks, Sophie."

"I was planning to come up to the house today. I hope it's not too soon, but I have a couple of questions. Gerry and I had been going over things weekly—"

"Right," Jonathan said. "You'll have to bring me up to speed."

"I have the paperwork in my office." She glanced toward the hallway behind her.

Jonathan took Willow's hand and squeezed it. "Let's talk about this later. I'm not going to do anything immediately."

"Okay." She watched him disappear before returning to the desk to collect her notepad. When she got back to work, her mind wouldn't cooperate. It ran in circles, running the conversation she and Jonathan had before Sophie appeared. Why had it bothered her so much? She hardly knew Ms. Dunfrey. Jonathan had a long history with her. She'd worked with Gerry before Hamish sold the software program, before the family had become so wealthy.

Chloe had mentioned that Dun worked for Gerry when Chloe and Jonathan were small, and Gerry was still in business. Gerry had owned her own corporate event-planning organization. It had been a small company, just she and Dun. When Hamish made his millions, she retired but kept Dun on to manage her social calendar and help with the kids.

Maybe what was bothering Willow was the callous manner in which Jonathan was able to dismiss someone who'd become a member of the family. What would Ms. Dunfrey do if he cut her off? Did she have enough in savings to live out her days? She couldn't get another job at seventy, even if it was the new sixty.

Willow flipped the page on her legal pad and found cardboard. It was full. She walked to the desk, opened the second drawer down on the right, and searched beneath the used pads for a clean one. There wasn't one.

She sighed. She'd only been at it for a half hour today. She'd wanted to finish the bookshelves so she could start on the music cabinet. She'd been saving that like a child saves the cherry on top of a sundae. Best for last.

Maybe there were clean sheets of paper under the used legal pads. She lifted the first pad, planning to flip pages, but something black fluttered out. It was a business card made from heavy stock and embossed with gold lettering. It read Radcliffe and Sons, Estate and Trust Law.

She flipped the card over and noted a pen or pencil had dug into the thick paper but she couldn't read the marks. She held it up to the light and managed to make out a date scrawled in dark blue pen: Tuesday, June 10th.

Hamish had never made that appointment. He'd died the week before. A small hope wiggled to life inside her. Maybe there would be problems with the will. Maybe the estate would be tied up in probate for years, and she and Jonathan would have to move out and find a place of their own until it was all sorted.

She tucked the card inside the pad with a sigh. Not likely. A man as rich as Hamish must have put his affairs in order years ago, but suddenly she wanted to know more about this family she was now a part of.

Her hand snaked into the back of the drawer almost of its own accord. She pulled out the picture she'd found there weeks ago and examined it.

The girl was Sophie, that was clear. But who was Sophie's father, and why would Hamish have this family portrait in his desk drawer instead of sitting out on a shelf or on top of the desk? And why weren't Sophie's parents at his funeral? Why had no one ever mentioned them?

Maybe there were other pictures that would answer her questions. She pulled open the bottom drawer in the right-hand tower, but it was filled with files. She searched the left-hand tower and found stacks of opened envelopes rubber-banded together in the top drawer, and books of spreadsheets in the second. In the third she found what she was looking for. Nestled amongst leather-bound business diaries were two photo albums.

She pulled out the first, a green, fabric volume peeling along the edges of the spine. The first page was filled with an eight-by-ten family photo. It wasn't as professional as the ones she'd seen in the game room at the main house. Those were staged before the fireplace, or on the cliffs, airbrushed and elegant. This looked like something taken in a small studio or at a department store.

Gerry, Hamish, Jonathan, and Chloe were dressed in their Sunday best and seated in front of a blue screen. The twins looked to be about five. All of them smiled widely. Willow turned the page, and it was Christmas. Jonathan held a train set in a box as big as he was. He was a beautiful child, and his grin made her grin. Chloe was also beautiful. She hugged an American Girl doll. The next section showed the twins blowing out birthday candles on matching cakes.

Willow set that album down and reached for the next. This one appeared to be business-related photos. A smiling forty-something Hamish held up a plaque proudly. Another showed Hamish behind a large desk, a window behind him.

She was about to set this album aside but noticed a man's arm in the corner of the photo. She turned the page and was rewarded with a picture of the same scene from a different angle. Two men filled the frame this time. Hamish sat behind the desk; the second man leaned against it. He was the man in the picture with Sophie.

She leafed through this album rapidly. It told a story. Sophie's father must have been Hamish's business partner. There were photos of the two men outside an office building flanking a sign that read *Transportation Solutions*. Another picture showed the men cutting the ribbon outside the same building.

Willow set the album on the desk and drummed her fingers on it. Hamish and Sophie's father had been partners. That explained a few things, like why he'd hired her as his assistant and kept her on long after his retirement. It may even explain her grief at the funeral. Hamish had been much more than a boss. He'd been a kind of uncle, her father's friend and partner.

It didn't explain why no one had mentioned the fact that Hamish had been in business with her father.

"Hey." Jonathan stuck his head through the doorway, startling her. "Come to the house. Time for lunch."

She smiled at him, wanting to say *come take a look at this*. She'd like nothing more than to ask all the questions running through her mind, but he had so much on his. There were enough dark and depressing things to think about without dredging up the past. "I'll be along in a minute."

She replaced the photo albums in the bottom drawer and the legal pad in its drawer. This kind of prying wasn't what she was here to do.

MOLLY: So, two parents down, none to go. I'd never heard of a staggered overdose of acetaminophen before. So, I did a little research and apparently it's not uncommon. People don't realize how potent over-the-counter drugs can be.

Having said that, doesn't it seem odd that both
Hamish and Gerry died within a month or so of
each other? I know it's said that in close
marriages when one dies the other often follows
quickly. However, I don't think those two were
particularly close.

Before I pose the question of the week,
however, let's get into another installment from
our journal writer. This one is disturbing. If
you have young children or sensitive individuals
around, I suggest putting on a headset.

JUNE 6

When I woke on the fifth day after what has come to be known in the family as "the jellyfish incident," the first thing I noticed was a stain on the sheets. I screamed. I know that sounds like an overreaction, but the stain was long and thin and a deep, dark purple-black. I thought one of the monsters had found its way into my room. I was partially right. A monster had found its way into my room, but the monster wasn't a black sea nettle.

I sat up quickly. My head spun. Nausea climbed up my throat. I would have thrown up if I'd had anything in my system. I realized later I must have been given an extra dose or two of the sedative the doctor had prescribed for me. It was the only explanation for my grogginess and the fact that I'd slept like the dead. I pushed myself from bed and stood, holding onto my bedside table for support. My sheets were covered in a crisscrossing pattern of dark lines.

Everyone came running when they heard the scream. They burst into the room, confusion creasing their faces. What had happened? I didn't know. I was just as much in the dark as they were.

My mother was the first to see the problem. She gasped and covered her mouth with her hand. I followed her gaze and gasped as well. The insides of my arms were a road map of tiny, oozing cuts.

As soon as I saw them, I felt them. It was as if my brain couldn't make the connection between the wounds and its pain center until my eyes got involved. Then they began to sting and burn almost as badly as the black sea nettle's pricks had.

"What did you do?" my mother said.

What did I do? I didn't do anything. I said that so many times I lost count, but no one believed me. When they found the bloody razor in my makeup bag, that was that. They decided it was a cry for attention, that I was a danger to myself. Which is why I'm here in this stupid room locked away from the world, only allowed out with supervision.

I've told anyone and everyone who would listen to me the truth, but they only smile, their faces dripping with sympathy. I don't want their sympathy. I don't want their kindness, or their offers of help, or their understanding. I don't want their nice food, or their anti-anxiety medicines, or sleep aids. I want their faces to reflect the horror of what's been done to me. I want them to believe me.

MOLLY: This is like my worst nightmare. I can't imagine someone cutting me while I slept. Then, not only being doubted when I denied doing it myself but also being locked up as a danger to myself. It's horrendous.

I'm sure you're wondering how this story dovetails into Willow's, and all I can say is you'll find out. Patience is a virtue, especially in investigative journalism. Facts take a long time to sift through, and even longer to connect.

And this leads me to the question of the week: Do you think Gerry's death is connected to Hamish's? Once he died, she was the only thing standing between the family and their inheritance. Was someone tempted to take her out?

Jonathan believed Ms. Dunfrey's incompetence was the cause, but she also had an inheritance coming. For that matter, so did Jonathan, Chloe, and any number of extended family members. Wealth can be dangerous, people. This story is helping me embrace my poverty.

Let's talk about it on the Facebook page. Join me next time for more *Murders Under the Sun.*

(cue music)

VO: If you enjoyed this episode, please leave

us a five-star review on your favorite podcast service—it really helps. *Murders Under the Sun* is edited by Jim Wilbourne, theme music is by Eclectic Blends, and I'm your host, Molly Shure.

part five

MURDERS UNDER THE SUN
SEASON SIX; EPISODE FOUR

MOLLY: Welcome back to *Murders Under the Sun*. This is Molly Shure, your host.

The plot thickens today, people. I'm not going to give anything away, but it's about to get very tense.

First, however, a quick update on our missing students mystery. I spoke with the Dean of the Drama Department at Cal State-Fullerton this week. She remembered Ariana Blackstone, whom she called a very promising talent. She also remembered the film Raphael Jimenez made because he'd recruited a number of her students for it, including Ariana.

The ten-minute art film that was his take on *The Picture of Dorian Gray*—a book by Oscar Wilde. She said it was really unique, deserving of the award it won. She also thought it must be on a private YouTube channel owned by the college and would see if she could get me the link. I'm not sure if viewing it will yield any clues, as I said before, but I'd love to see it anyway.

Now on to our main topic—the happenings at Sunset House. Thanks to those who commented in the group. It was pretty unanimous for a change. You all believed Gerry's death was no coincidence. You rightly said this is a true crime podcast. Why would we be talking about this case if no crime was involved?

However, in my defense, you don't know what's coming. Sunset House is the scene of much nefarious activity. I'm not going to spill, though.

You'll just have to wait and see how Gerry's
death fits in the scheme of things.
    So, without further ado, let's get into this
week's episode.

"What are you doing?" Jonathan watched her from the bed, hands behind his head.

"Going swimming." Willow spun toward him holding up her new swim suit.

"Where?"

"There." She pointed out the window at the pool. "Where else?"

"I thought you might be thinking about the ocean."

"No, I'm sure it's still too cold." It occurred to her that she'd never seen anyone walk down the steep stairs to the public beach below. "Why doesn't anyone ever go to the beach?"

Jonathan threw back the covers and swung his legs over the side of the bed. He yawned and scrubbed at his hair like he was shampooing it. "We used to go all the time when we were kids. I'll take you sometime."

Willow pulled her suit over her ever-increasing bump and turned to survey the results in the vanity mirror. It seemed she got bigger every day. "I wonder if I'm having twins."

"Are there any in your family?"

"On my mother's side, and there's also you and Chloe."

He stood and padded toward the bathroom. "Whether we have twins or not depends on you. Some women have the gene that tells them to release two eggs at a time, some don't. If we have a daughter, I could give her that gene, but hanging around me isn't going to make you release two eggs at once."

Willow heard the shower turn on. She grabbed her robe from the closet and followed Jonathan into the bathroom. "What about identical twins? That's only one egg."

"Yeah," he raised his voice over the sound of splashing. "That's not genetic. Identical twins are random. Only fraternal twins are genetic.

Chloe has a pretty good chance of having twins if she ever gets pregnant."

"I'm jealous." Willow took her toothbrush from the holder and began brushing.

"Why? You want twins?"

She spit. "Well, I want more than one child. If we had twins, I'd only have to be pregnant once, only have to do diapers and toddlers once. Our kids would have a built-in playmate. Seems convenient."

A snort that sounded like a whale blowing water echoed from the shower stall. "You do not know what you're asking for."

Willow sat on the closed toilet seat and rubbed sunscreen on her legs. "Why? It seems like you and Chloe are pretty close. Didn't you like growing up with a twin?" Cookie's comments about the fights they had when they were young tripped into her mind. Perhaps their relationship wasn't as idyllic as it seemed.

The water shut off, the door slid open a few inches, and Jonathan's hand emerged, fingers grabbing for the towel rack on the wall. Willow pulled a towel free and handed it to him. "Chloe is six minutes older than me," he said. "A fact she never let me forget. She was a bit of a bully, until I got bigger than her."

"I guess that's a big sister thing. Ash says I bullied him when we were little. That's how he justified picking on me once he outweighed me. I don't remember it that way. I might have been bossy, but I wasn't a bully."

Jonathan stepped from the shower and wrapped the towel around his waist. He was a beautiful man. How had she gotten so lucky? "Chloe definitely bullied me. Ask her. She'll admit it." His tone was lighthearted, not bitter, as if he found the memory funny.

"What are you doing today?" As soon as the words left Willow's lips, she regretted them. Her husband's shoulders slumped visibly. For a moment, they'd both forgotten the tragedies that had struck the family. For a moment, they'd been newlyweds, relaxed and happy in each other's company and excited about the new life they'd made together.

"I'm meeting with Mom and Dad's lawyers this morning, then this afternoon, Chloe and I are going to the mortuary." The words fell from his lips like stones, all lightheartedness gone.

Jonathan dressed in silence, and they walked down the back stairs together. "What made you decide to go swimming?" he said when they reached the bottom.

"It's finally sunny. This May gray, June gloom thing takes some getting used to. I haven't been able to make myself get in the pool until today."

He turned to face her. "Is it doctor-approved?"

"Of course. I'm not ill. I'm pregnant."

"I know, it's just the karate thing..."

"It won't hurt Junior if I fall in the pool."

Jonathan placed his hands on her shoulders and gave her a light kiss. "Just take care of yourself, okay?"

He sounded like her father. Why were men always telling her to take care of herself? Did she seem that fragile? Or stupid?

He made a right toward the kitchen. Willow went left. She exited the house through the sliding doors in the great room and made her way through the garden.

As she strolled toward the pool, she raised her face to the sun. This break from the gray warmed more than her body. When the sun was out, the shadows that made problems seem larger than life retreated.

She rounded the building and the pool glimmered before her, a turquoise jewel set in green velvet. Ms. Dunfrey sliced through the water, leaving a thin trail of bubbles in her wake. Willow slowed her pace.

She'd been hoping Dunfrey would be done with her morning swim before she got there. There were ten lap lanes so space wasn't the problem. The truth was, she was embarrassed. Willow hadn't swum laps in years, not since high school. She'd rather not be watched by such an experienced swimmer her first time in.

She moved to a deckchair, dropped her bathrobe, and pulled on a pair of goggles she'd remembered to pick up on one of her trips to town. Ms. Dunfrey never looked up, not even when Willow lowered herself into the shallow end of the pool and pushed off the side.

It took half a lap to find her breathing rhythm, three strokes, breathe, three strokes breathe. By the time she completed a full lap, she was in a groove. Swimming was just like riding a bike apparently.

Five laps later, she stopped for a breather. When she lifted her goggles to clear the water, she saw Dunfrey standing on the side, wrapped in a large towel. "Good morning." Willow lifted her hand in a wave.

"Nice form," Dunfrey said.

"Thanks. It's been a while, but it feels good to be back in the water."

"It's my sanity."

"I see you every morning, gloomy and cold, or bright and sunny. You're dedicated."

"The water is always the same temperature, eighty-one degrees."

Willow spit in her goggles, rotated the saliva then swished them clean in the pool. "There's something to be said for the constants in life."

"Yes." Dunfrey nodded her head slowly. "I'll miss this one." Willow glanced at her, raising her eyebrows in question. "I'll be leaving after Gerry's funeral."

Willow wanted to protest, to say that it wasn't necessary, that she was sure Jonathan and Chloe could still use her help to run the household, but she didn't. Jonathan's face, tight-lipped and angry, appeared in her mind. He thought Dunfrey was responsible for his mother's death. He wanted her to leave. She adjusted her goggles and said, "I'd better keep moving."

Ms. Dunfrey stuck her feet into a pair of rubber sandals and walked toward the house, her feet squelching with each step. Willow placed her own feet against the wall of the pool, readying herself for another push, but the squelching stopped. She peered over the pool deck. Dunfrey faced her again.

"I didn't give Gerry too much acetaminophen," she said. "I know that's what Johnny thinks, but I didn't. Someone might have, though."

Willow's heart took an extra beat. "What do you mean?"

"Exactly what I said." Dunfrey's eyes were wide and unblinking. "The night before she died, when I saw you in the hallway—"

The woman paused, seeming to expect a response, so Willow nodded.

"I looked for the medicine. I wanted to take it to the doctors, so they could see it for themselves. I wanted to show them the instructions on the label. Tell them I gave it to her exactly as it said. It was gone."

"Gone?" Willow parroted the word.

"I searched the whole room, the bathroom, everywhere. I even moved furniture in case it had fallen behind the dresser or bedside table. It wasn't anywhere."

"Maybe someone had a headache?" The suggestion sounded far-fetched, even to herself.

Dunfrey's wide gaze narrowed, and disbelief clouded her eyes. "The thought crossed my mind at the time. Now I don't think so."

"Why would someone take the pills?"

"That's the 64-thousand-dollar question, isn't it?" She turned and walked to the house.

Sixty-four thousand? Or was it more? How much did Hamish and Gerry leave Dunfrey as a stipend? How much money was at stake? Willow planned to ask Jonathan this evening. If she was a part of the family now, she would act like one.

Whatever had happened, she was sure Ms. Dunfrey hadn't harmed Gerry purposely. What possible motive could she have had? She was a creature of habit. She depended on the constants in life. All of that had been upended by Gerry's death. No, Dunfrey hadn't wanted her employer and friend to die, but it sounded as if she believed someone had.

AFTER HER SWIM, a shower, and some lunch, Willow headed to the library. She only had a couple of shelves left to catalog, but she wanted to look through Hamish's desk again. Perhaps she'd find information there to help Ms. Dunfrey's cause. A sense of injustice had filled her after their talk at the pool. She didn't believe the person who took the pills had killed Gerry, but perhaps they'd wanted to cast suspicion on Dunfrey, wanted her out of the way.

There was so much money in this estate, Willow couldn't imagine why anyone would want to take the little bit Dunfrey had coming to her. There was plenty enough to go around, but greed did strange things to people. Strange things had happened in her own family earlier this year because of greed.

The library door was unlocked when she reached it. She pushed in the heavy, wood door and called out, "Hello?" Her voice echoed down the long corridor.

A moment later, Sophie's brown head popped from a doorway. "Hi, Willow."

A thought entered Willow's mind. Why shouldn't she ask Sophie about the picture and the photo albums? Now that Willow was part of the family, didn't she deserve to understand its politics? If anyone would know what it all meant, it would be Sophie. "Do you have time for a chat?"

Surprise flashed across Sophie's face. "Sure. Actually, I just made a pot of coffee. Want me to bring some into Hamish's office?"

Willow paused. She couldn't drink coffee, but she wanted to bond with Sophie, to create an atmosphere that might encourage her to open up. "I can help," she said. A sip or two wouldn't hurt. "You know, I've never seen the kitchen."

"Oh, it's great."

Willow pushed through the door at the end of the hall and entered a room straight out of the 1940s. White subway tiles covered the bottom half of the walls, the top half green. The laminate counters were a matching green, and the floor was the same checkerboard tile as the kitchen in the main house. Even the appliances appeared old, with their rounded edges and aluminum handles. A drip coffee maker the same color as the counter spit its last drops into the carafe. Sophie pulled a carton of half and half from the fridge, and a milk-glass sugar bowl from a cupboard.

After pouring their coffee, Sophie opened a screen door in the back wall and walked outside. Willow followed her down a flight of three steps into a small rose garden bordered by Italian cypress. In its center was a white wrought iron table surrounded by chairs of the same.

"This is charming," Willow said.

"Isn't it? The big house is grand and elegant and all of that, but this cottage is my favorite place on the property."

"How many rooms are there?"

"Three down and three up, with two bathrooms. I believe it was once the original caretaker's house. He lived here with a wife and two children."

"I've only been in Hamish's office." Willow placed a hand on her stomach and smiled. "And the bathroom."

Sophie returned the smile. "I'll give you the tour when we're done. The upstairs rooms are currently being used for storage, but you can see the architecture. It's really lovely. Hamish's office was the living room, and mine the dining room."

A bird trilled in the bushes and an ocean breeze swayed the cypress trees. Willow closed her eyes against the sunlight and allowed its fingers to warm her face. She hadn't felt this peaceful since... Since, when? Since she and Jonathan were up in the Central Coast. Since she'd been married. She hated to break the spell, but she needed information.

"Sophie," she said. Sophie gazed at her over the rim of her coffee cup. "I found some things in Hamish's office, things I don't understand."

"If it has to do with the collection, don't ask me. I don't know anything about book and manuscript collecting."

"It's not that. I was looking through the desk." She paused, hoping it wouldn't sound like she'd been snooping. "I needed paper." Sophie's soft smile hadn't changed, so Willow continued. "I found a picture. There were three people in it. I'm pretty sure one of them was you."

Sophie's smile grew. "Was I about ten or eleven?"

"Yes, and you were with a man and a woman."

"Those were my parents. I wondered what happened to that picture."

"Were your parents? They're both deceased?"

"Yes. Mom died first. Dad some years later."

"How sad. How old were you when your mother died?" Willow said.

"Thirteen. It was terrible. I was an only child, and we were extremely close. She was my best friend."

"How?"

"Breast cancer. She fought it for a year, but it won. I think her death killed Dad in the end, as well. I was orphaned at sixteen."

"What did he die of?"

"Stroke, same as Hamish. After Dad died, I went to live with my grandparents in Texas, on the gulf. They loved me, but it was a lonely time."

Sympathy for this woman filled Willow. There seemed to be a curse on this household. Jonathan, Chloe, Sophie, all without their parents. A desire to see her own filled her. They'd always been there for her and Ash, and she took it for granted they always would be. But nothing was sure, not even the constants Ms. Dunfrey relied on.

Sophie set her cup on the table. "What else did you find?"

"What else?" Willow asked.

"You said you found some *things*, plural."

Willow shoved her chair away from the table. "Oh, right. It would be easier to show you."

They walked through the kitchen to Hamish's office, and Willow went straight to the desk. She wanted to show Sophie the lawyer's card with the appointment time etched on the back. As his personal assistant, Sophie may be able to tell her why Hamish would have an appointment with an estate planning attorney.

Willow opened the drawer that held the legal pads and stared. They were all gone except for the one she'd filled with book data. Maybe she'd put them away in the wrong drawer? She pulled open the bottom drawer, they weren't there. She moved to the left side of the desk and searched those drawers. The photo albums were still in place, but there were no legal pads. "Did you take anything from the desk?"

Sophie crossed her arms over her chest. "Only the mail from the top drawer. I've been busy in my office."

"Did you see anyone else in here?"

"Well, Jonathan, but you were both here."

"Nobody after that?"

"I don't think so, but I go home in the afternoon when I'm done with work."

Willow circled the desk and leaned against it. "I'll have to ask him about it."

"What's missing?"

Willow opened her mouth and shut it again. She couldn't remember the name of the attorney or the law firm. It was meaningless to say she'd found an estate lawyer's card with an appointment etched on the back. A man with as much wealth as Hamish must have had a team of lawyers. "Never mind," she finally said.

"Want that tour now?"

"Sure."

The upper story was just as Sophie had described, three bedrooms, one slightly larger than the others, filled with antiques, lamps, and boxes. Willow was surprised to see some nice pieces, less formal things than the main house was filled with. Although she'd been concerned about getting stuck with the Lauders' old furniture, she was having second thoughts. Maybe she should browse here for their apartment.

Their apartment. The thought struck her like a slap. What were they going to do about the apartment now? Would the estate be sold and the money divided between the heirs? Would Chloe move into one wing while she and Jonathan inhabited the other? The weight of all Hamish's wealth settled onto her shoulders. It was suffocating.

As they headed down the stairs again, Willow noticed stacks of file boxes along one of the hallway walls. "What are these?"

"That's my job. I'm going through Hamish's old records from the firm."

"I thought he sold the business years ago?" Willow said.

"Actually, he sold a software program that brought him so much money he no longer needed to keep the business operational. Now the corporation only exists to protect assets and make investments."

"It sounds like unraveling all this is going to be a nightmare."

"Not really. He had good estate lawyers, and I have a handle on the company monies."

Willow held the railing as she walked down the stairs. The pregnancy had shifted her center of gravity, and her balance seemed to be getting worse. "I hope Chloe and Jonathan plan to keep you on. We need someone who knows what's going on."

"I doubt that." Sophie's voice was somber. "When Jonathan and I spoke, he mentioned he was planning to move the investments once we get it sorted out."

Willow stopped in the doorway of the library; Sophie's tear-stained face the day of the funeral in her mind. It seemed Jonathan was going to dismiss all his family's trusted help. It bothered her that he felt no loyalty.

His anger at Ms. Dunfrey might be misplaced, but at least she understood it. Why get rid of Sophie? Surely it would be helpful to have someone overseeing the family's business concerns? She added another item to her growing mental list of things to discuss with her husband.

"One more thing," she said before leaving the building. "I saw a picture of your father—"

"Fred," Sophie said.

"Fred," Willow repeated, "and Hamish cutting a ribbon in front of an office building. Were they partners?"

"Yes. They met at Gigasoft then started their own business. My dad was brilliant at software development, a complete nerd. Hamish was the salesman. Together they were unstoppable."

"I thought Hamish wrote the program that made the millions?"

"He did, after my father died. They were both engineers. I was speaking more of their personalities."

"How did you end up working for Hamish?"

"He contacted me right after I got my MBA. I was working at a small accounting firm, and he called out of the blue. *Sophie, how much are they paying you?*" The last line was delivered with in a comical imitation of Hamish. "I told him. He said he'd double it, and that was that."

"He made you an offer you couldn't refuse," Willow said. Her thoughts drifted to Jonathan's proposal, how he'd dropped on one knee and pulled a square-cut diamond from his jacket pocket.

"Hamish was good at that."

"I think it runs in the family."

Sophie gave her a half smile. "Yes, it does." After Sophie disappeared into her office, Willow decided to make an actual—not just mental—list of all the things she needed to discuss with Jonathan that evening. First, she needed paper.

She opened the drawer that had contained the legal pads and looked through it one more time as if the yellow pages might magically reappear. They didn't. It was as empty as the last time she'd looked inside.

She opened and shut drawers, not finding any other blank paper. Maybe there was a notebook in the drawer with the photo albums? Those stood with their spines facing up, so a notebook could be hidden among them.

She pawed through the leather volumes and, sure enough, deeper inside the drawer was a Moleskine journal. She lifted it out. Its cover was stained and dirty. It had obviously been used, but maybe there were blank pages at the end. She opened the book.

MOLLY: Willow has finally found the diary. She's going to learn what we already know, and she'll have the same questions we already have.

Moving forward, I won't break into the narrative to introduce the entries. I'll let Willow do it for me. We'll be learning about the diary writer along with her.

I've finally found someone who seems to believe me. Dr. P asked me loads of questions about my relationship with my father and my mother. She took copious notes and furrowed her forehead while I answered. Unlike the others, she seemed confused, like she didn't believe my childhood would have caused the problems everyone says I have.

I behave myself when I'm with her. I want her to see there's nothing wrong with me. And I've begged to see my parents, told her how much I love them.

That's a stretch, I know. I'm not overly happy with them at the moment, but they're not bad people. They've never abused me or neglected me. The problem is they've been bamboozled by the monster. The monster is very persuasive. Dragons are known for their silken tongues, and for their greed.

Did you know some scientists believe there is a gene that controls greed? It's called arginine vasopressin receptor. These receptors are in the brain and in other organs like the liver and the kidneys. I read all about it. As you can imagine, it is a topic of interest to me.

Anyway, in people, this gene is located on Chromosome 12. There are three different types. Your level of greediness depends on which ones and how many you have. Really greedy people—if you can even call them people—have a short version of the gene. Another name for this version is the "ruthless" gene.

So, you see, science backs me up. It's what I've been trying to tell everyone all along. The monster only looks human, but genetics tells a different story.

I haven't told Dr. P about the greed gene. It's a bit controversial in the psychiatric world, and I'm not sure what her position is. I need to proceed carefully, handle this relationship gently. I don't want to scare her off like I did the others. I need her if I'm ever going to get out of this room.

WILLOW STARED at the open page before her. What a strange entry. Who was this person who believed in genetic mutants that appeared human? She flipped to the beginning of the journal.

The story it told was a bizarre one. A girl locked in a room, seemingly for psychiatric reasons, who had been stung by jellyfish and cut her arms with a razor. There was no name on the front cover or in the back of the book. Willow had no idea who she was or why the journal was in Hamish's desk.

"Willow." Sophie's head and shoulders appeared through the doorway. "I'm leaving. Just wanted you to know you're here alone."

Alone. It seemed a constant state these days. Willow held back a sigh. "Great. See you tomorrow maybe?" She liked having Sophie there, just across the hallway.

"I'll be here." Sophie raised a hand and disappeared as quickly as she'd appeared.

Willow gazed at the empty doorway and chewed her lip. Could Sophie be the author of the journal? It was nestled in with the photo albums of Fred and Hamish's early business years. She would've had to have written it before she turned thirteen, because that was when her mother died, and the journal girl's parents were alive.

The vocabulary seemed advanced for a thirteen-year-old, but Sophie was a thoughtful, bookish kind of person. It wouldn't surprise Willow if she'd been a reader as a child, a reader with a very active imagination.

Finding the notebook in Hamish's things seemed strange, but based on what Sophie had told Willow, Hamish had fatherly feelings for her. He'd hired her as soon as she'd graduated. He had pictures of her as a child in his desk. He'd been partners with her father. He may have thought of himself as an adoptive uncle. Maybe Fred had given the journal to Hamish before he'd died and asked him to watch out for his daughter?

The grandfather clock in the hallway chimed four times. Jonathan had said he'd take her down to the beach for a walk when he got home, and she wanted to change and put on a little makeup first. She'd better get going.

Willow opened the drawer to put the notebook back where she'd found it but changed her mind. She'd take it to her room and finish reading. Curiosity overcame her squeamishness about being nosy. There may be a clue to the identity of the writer in some of the later installments. She wanted to know who it was. She stuck the book into the tote bag she'd brought with her, locked up the building and headed toward the big house.

Jonathan was already home when she arrived. "Where have you been?" he said as soon as he saw her.

"The library," she said.

"How's the job coming?"

"Almost done. I need to get more legal pads though. I'll tell you about it on our walk."

Willow ran to their room, threw the tote bag under the vanity, grabbed a sweatshirt, changed into flip-flops, and ran downstairs again. They walked outside through the heavy front doors, across the circular driveway, through the archway in the hedge, and across the lawn to the cliffs.

Jonathan opened a metal gate in the fence that rimmed the property and held it for her. She gazed down at a steep flight of wooden stairs that made a sharp left, then disappeared behind a mound of pink ice plant. A tickle of anxiety brushed her skin.

She wasn't an athlete, but she'd always prided herself on the coordination and balance she'd gained from her karate training. She was clumsier than a toddler now, but she'd said she wanted to see the beach. She wasn't going to chicken out because of a steep set of stairs. She grabbed the railing with strong fingers and began the descent.

The gate clicked shut, and she heard Jonathan's footfalls following her. "Sorry, I'm such a slow poke," she said.

"Take your time. These stairs are a little scary the first time or two."

Willow was surprised at how rickety they were. A family as wealthy as the Lauders could afford to maintain them. The treads were sloped from years of use. In some, nails protruded where the boards had split. She came to the first landing without a problem and began to relax. She made a left and started down the next flight.

"Some of the wood needs to be replaced," Jonathan said from behind her. "And, the whole thing needs to be repainted."

Willow turned to look at him. "Who does—" Her left foot dropped to the next step and found air. She tottered for a moment, gripped the handrail, and it came loose in her hand. Willow felt herself falling. A whoosh of air hollowed out her chest. Panic replaced it. She saw herself tumbling down twenty feet, bouncing off the next landing, and falling another fifteen feet to the sand and rocks below.

A snag.

She jerked to a halt.

Wood groaned as her butt thudded down on it.

"Hey, careful there." Jonathan gripped the back of her sweatshirt. "Maybe I should go first." He helped her to her feet and moved past her. "There are ninety-eight steps. Chloe and I counted them when we were kids."

Willow believed it. The flight seemed to go on and on. For the rest of the descent, her head floated, light and empty above her thundering heart. When her feet hit the sand, her legs almost buckled. She gave a trembling laugh to cover her nervousness. "It's going to be fun climbing back up."

Jonathan perched on a rock and took off his sneakers. "Now you know why we don't come down here very often. Here, give me your shoes." He reached for her flip-flops and hid both pairs of shoes behind the rock.

The tide was low and the ocean glassy. The sun shone a golden path across it all the way to Catalina Island. They held hands and walked into the water, wet sand enveloping their feet with each lapping wave.

Willow wanted to ask about Jonathan's day, but she knew it had been filled with lawyers and mortuaries and things having to do with death, and she was still jumpy from her near mishap. It seemed better to soak in the peace of their surroundings.

A single swell raised its head higher than the others. They ran inland, but not before the bottoms of their pants were soaked. Jonathan laughed. Willow squealed. Something slimy had wrapped itself around her ankle. The black jellyfish she'd read about in the journal slithered into her mind. She did an awkward jig.

"What's wrong now?" Jonathan said.

She glanced down and saw a fat piece of kelp. She exhaled. "Nothing. Just seaweed. I thought… " She leaned over to untangle it.

"Thought what?"

"Thought it might be a jellyfish."

Jonathan took the kelp from her and tossed it onto the sand. "We don't get many jellyfish here."

"No?" She'd assumed the accident in the journal had happened here. Although, it could have been anywhere. Hadn't Sophie said she'd gone to live with her grandparents in Texas? Willow had heard the Gulf of Mexico was rife with dangerous sea creatures.

She wanted to ask Jonathan about the journal but didn't want to seem to be prying into his father's private things. She had been tasked with cataloging the collection. She felt funny about going through the photo albums, never mind reading a diary.

Thinking about the photo albums reminded her of why she'd found the journal in the first place. She'd been looking for paper so she could make a list of the things she wanted to talk to Jonathan about. First up was their living situation. "What's going to happen to our apartment in the left wing? Do you know?"

"The estate lawyers are still pushing things through probate, but when it's all said and done, we can do what we want with it. Finish it and use it for guest quarters. Let Chloe live there until she gets hitched. We don't have to decide right away."

"We're not going to live in it?" Willow asked.

"No, why would we? We'll have the whole place."

"The whole place?" She repeated his words, trying to absorb their meaning. She'd assumed they'd divide up Sunset House somehow and live here with Chloe or sell and split the equity. It didn't sound like that was the plan.

Jonathan kicked a seashell down the beach. "Right. We're inheriting the house."

"What about Chloe?"

"She'll get a share of Dad's investments, but I get the property."

Willow's chest tightened. She struggled to grab a breath. How had she gone from living in a tiny rental to owning a massive, multi-million-dollar estate in San Clemente in less than three months? She'd always imagined herself with a home like the one she'd grown up in, four bedrooms, two-car garage, and a yard. She ought to be excited. Thrilled. She'd won the lotto. But she felt trapped. "Why?" was all she managed to say.

Jonathan stopped and turned her toward him. "Because of you. You and the baby." He gave her a lop-sided grinned.

"Me?"

"The will states that the heir with the oldest grandchild inherits Sunset House. Dad didn't want it broken up or sold. So, we luck out." He pulled her in for a hug.

Willow wished she shared his enthusiasm. "It seems so unfair. Poor Chloe."

Jonathan resumed walking south along the beach. "I think Dad hoped it would be me anyway. Carry on the family name and all that."

Willow, who had lagged behind, jogged to catch up. "What if I hadn't wanted to take the family name? What if I'd wanted to keep Wells? Would we still inherit?"

Jonathan laughed. "Of course. If Chloe had gotten pregnant first, she'd inherit, whatever her name was. Besides, our kids would be Lauders either way."

That was true, but it rankled. Why did children always take the father's last name? Why couldn't they be Wells-Lauder? Or Lauder-Wells? The latter sounded better, more musical. Of course, it probably wasn't practical. Their children would, hopefully, marry one day, and what would they do? Add another surname? Lauder-Wells-Smith? Then would their kids be Lauder-Wells-Smith-Johnson? In a couple of generations everyone would have a string of names as long as an Arabian sheikh's.

"You can hire your own staff," Jonathan said. He'd been talking while Willow pondered the problem of surnames, but she hadn't been paying attention. This caught her up short, however.

"Hire staff?" Her voice tripped up the scale.

"Well, you can't manage that big house by yourself. It's more work than you think. I figured we'd keep Pablo and his team." Pablo was the landscape maintenance man. "And, Mike." Mike was... general maintenance? Willow wasn't sure what Mike did. "And Cookie." Jonathan's eyes shifted toward her. "You want to keep Cookie, don't you? He's kind of a family institution."

"This sounds like a full-time job." Alarm bells jangled in Willow's head. She didn't want to run a staff; she wanted to play music, to teach.

"That's what I'm trying to tell you." Jonathan's smile widened. He was obviously happy about this turn of events. Much happier than she was.

Willow stopped walking. "What if I don't want to?"

He spun to face her. "What do you mean?"

"What if I don't want to run that house? What if I don't want to live there?"

Jonathan's grin faded. "Why wouldn't you? It's one of the only coastal estates left in southern Orange County. It's spectacular."

"Because, I want to... " She spread her fingers wide, palms lifted to the sky, hoping the right words would fall into them.

"You want to what?" His voice was deadpan, his face expressionless.

"Play violin," she finished quietly.

His features softened. "That's it? You want to play violin?"

She nodded.

"You can do that. We'll find another Dun. Someone who manages the household and reports to you. You can even hire a live-in nanny if you want." He took her hand and pulled her along the beach again. "Look, I know this is a lot to take in. It's a big change, but, babe, we can do whatever we want. We have resources now."

"Can I have Ms. Dunfrey?"

He didn't answer her for a long moment. "I think we should hire somebody younger. There are real pros out there, people who have degrees in this stuff. Dun was great for Mom, but you're going to want someone closer to your own age."

"I like—" she hesitated, feeling strange about using the nickname, but if she was going to plead for the woman, she had to sound like they had a relationship, "Dun."

Again, Jonathan didn't answer for a minute. "I don't know, babe.

How about we think about it? Sleep on it? We don't have to make any decisions tonight."

At that, he turned and began to retrace their steps. "What's Cookie got going for dinner?"

Willow told him, and they switched to safer topics for the remainder of the walk. The first point on her list had rocked her world enough for one evening. Life, like the sand beneath her feet, was shifting.

WILLOW SNEAKED out of the bedroom before Jonathan woke the next morning. The world outside was white and wet and dreary, but Dun's proclamation that the pool was a constant eighty-one degrees prodded her on. She had a lot to do today and wanted to get a swim in first.

On her walk with Jonathan the evening before, she'd been shaken to her core at the idea of living in Sunset House forever. The beach stairs had seemed symbolic of her new life. She felt confined, like every plan she'd hatched—whether it was for a career or an apartment somewhere other than Sunset House—had crumbled beneath her.

She woke with an epiphany. She hadn't left the property for days. That was what had made her feel like a prisoner. She could come and go as she pleased, and it was time to go.

Today, she had a shopping trip planned. While she was out, she'd stop by her mother's store, surprise her, and take her out to lunch. She would also start doing research on the local private schools, both academic and music and begin applying for the next school year. If she didn't want another full-time position, it didn't mean she had to stop working altogether. There were part-time jobs out there. She just had to find one.

With all the abrupt changes in her life, she'd been neglecting her music. It was time to put herself on a practice schedule. Hamish's violin deserved to be played. With that instrument under her chin, she might be able to get an orchestra chair if she was on her game. She'd given up that dream her last year of college when she'd learned auditions were prejudiced by the prestige of the instrument played in them. Well, she now had an instrument with prestige.

She marched across the wet grass with determination. Feeling sorry for herself because she'd just become an heiress was about as stupid as feeling sorry for herself if she got first chair in the LA Philharmonic.

Wisps of low-lying fog hung over the pool, turning its brilliant blue a muddy gray. She shivered. "It's eighty-one degrees." She said the words aloud. "Eighty-one," she repeated, trying to convince herself.

At least she wasn't diving into the Pacific. She pulled her goggles from her bathrobe pocket and put them on. The ocean was cold.

Besides, she wouldn't take the beach stairs again until they were completely rebuilt, which she'd told Jonathan as soon as they'd reached the top. They were too dangerous.

She had one shoulder out of her robe when she saw something in the water. She squinted through the foggy plastic covering her eyes. The something was large, as big as a person, as big as Ms. Dunfrey, but it wasn't moving. Willow lifted the goggles and peered again. The morning fog was thick, a pea-souper, as her friend from Boston would say. She took two steps toward the pool deck, trying to get a better look.

A blue bathing suit almost the same color as the water, white legs, white arms, a white bathing cap. It was Dunfrey. Was she taking a breather? Floating as she rested? But who floated on their face for this long?

"Ms. Dunfrey?" Willow's words fell to the concrete, the heavy air saturating sound waves. She stepped closer. "Dun?" she said. The only answer was the slow bobbing of the form in the ripples caused by the pool motor.

Get her out. The words screamed in Willow's head. Quiet confusion became intense action. She dropped her robe on the deck and ran toward the woman, readying herself to spring into the water.

"Willow." A voice cut through the damp, its urgency stopping her. "Willow, wait."

She pivoted, but could see no one.

"Here. I'm up here."

Jonathan's voice came from above her, from their bedroom window. She screamed, "It's Dun. She's in the pool, but she's not moving. Get help. I'm going in."

"No!" Again, the sheer panic in his voice halted her. "Don't get in the water. It might be electrified. Wait there. I'm coming down."

She spun toward the pool again. Electrified? How could that happen? More likely, Dunfrey had a cramp or a heart attack. Willow took a step toward the woman but paused. How could she know for sure?

Dunfrey's nose and mouth were submerged. If she was alive, she'd stopped breathing. Brain damage would occur in minutes. A force greater than logic urged Willow to pull her from the water and begin

CPR. Minutes, seconds, meant the difference between life and death in a drowning. Her father had drilled that into her from childhood.

She searched the deck with her eyes. A long, silver pole peeked out from behind the wall that hid the pool motor. She slipped across the tile and retrieved it. She stared at the net in her hand. Metal conducted electricity, but it seemed she'd read something about aluminum being a poor conductor, and the net itself appeared to be made from some kind of nylon attached to a plastic hoop.

She carried it as close to the body as she could get and knelt. If she didn't touch the water, but only touched Dunfrey, she would be okay. Wouldn't she? She hesitated but only for a second. She couldn't sit there and do nothing. It was impossible.

Carefully, making sure the pole didn't drop below the surface of the water, she slid it along the deck toward Ms. Dunfrey. Willow closed her eyes. "Help, please," she said to her mother's God, opened her eyes, held her breath and touched the body. Nothing happened. She exhaled with relief, then began to steer Dunfrey to the pool edge with the hard plastic end of the net.

"Willow." Jonathan appeared out of the morning mist. "What are you doing? Get away from there."

"But, she's—"

"Wait. I'll turn off the power."

He ran behind the wall, and she heard the hum of the motor die away. He was in the water in a second, lifting and rolling Dunfrey onto the deck. Her face was white, her lips blue.

Willow didn't bother checking her pulse. Dunfrey was so cold and still, Willow was sure she wouldn't find one. She placed her hands over the woman's sternum and began pumping. "Did you call 911?" She barked the words at Jonathan, who stood dripping next to her.

"They're on their way."

Willow paused to see if Dunfrey was breathing. She wasn't. *Where is the ambulance?* Willow quickly resumed chest compressions.

Jonathan placed a hand on her arm. "I think she's gone." Willow shook him off and continued CPR. She pumped and pumped for endless minutes. Fatigue washed over her, but she didn't stop until a siren broke through the veil of wet air and footsteps slapped the deck next to her.

The paramedics moved Dunfrey into the pool house where it was dry, and Willow heard someone yell, "Clear," and the thwack of a defibrillator. Again. And again. It struck her that Jonathan blamed electricity for killing Dunfrey, yet it was now her only hope. He slipped Willow's robe over her shoulders and wrapped an arm around her. She realized she'd been shivering.

They stood that way for so long she lost track of time. At some point a dark-haired, muscular paramedic exited the pool house and gazed at them through sad eyes. He shook his head. Dunfrey was gone. "You said you believe this was an ESD?"

Jonathan's face clouded. "Electric Shock Drowning," the sad-eyed man explained.

Jonathan nodded his understanding. "I think so. Can you tell?"

The paramedic lifted one shoulder. "Her armpits are red. That's consistent with electric shock, but we won't know for sure without an autopsy."

Willow opened her mouth to ask why Jonathan believed it was electrocution, but another siren shattered the morning.

She allowed him to tug her toward the house. Tears and moisture clouded her eyes, making it difficult to see. Droplets hung from her lashes and blinking only added them to the saltwater pooling below.

He walked her all the way up the stairs, into their room, setting her on the bed. "I'll go down, talk to the police. You need to warm up."

He disappeared into the bathroom. A moment later, he pulled her to her feet and steered her toward the shower. The bathroom was wreathed in steam. He helped her out of her robe and suit as if she were a child. She stepped into the stall. Needles of heat stung her cold skin, but it began to revive her.

"Are you okay now?" Jonathan said.

"Yeah." She wasn't okay. She wouldn't be okay for a long while.

"I'll tell Cookie to make you a pot of hot tea and send it up."

She heard Jonathan's footsteps recede and their door slam shut. Willow stayed under the hot stream until she felt her core temperature rise, then shut it off. As she was wrapping a towel around her head, she heard a gentle tap on the door. She pulled on her robe and went to answer it.

Cookie stood in the doorway, a tray in his meaty hands. She'd never seen him away from his kitchen. He looked large and awkward in the small space of her room. "I brought you tea," he said.

She stepped aside to make room for him to enter. "Thank you."

He set the tray on the vanity. "It's a terrible thing, what happened to Dun. Thank the lord, you're okay."

"I never got in—" Her words choked off. Somehow, she hadn't realized until this moment what it would have meant if the water had carried a lethal current and she'd gotten into it. She covered her mouth with her hand and sat down hard on the edge of the bed.

Concern created lines across Cookie's forehead. He seemed to understand the effect his words had. "But you didn't. That's the important thing."

"The baby," she said.

"You didn't get in the water." He repeated the words.

She began to shiver again, but not from the cold this time.

Cookie crossed and uncrossed his arms, obviously at a loss. "You're okay, Willow. The baby is okay."

Tears sprang into her eyes. "Yes, we are, but if Jonathan hadn't called out—"

"He did call out," Cookie interrupted her. "Now, you have some tea. You're shaking like a leaf." He stirred a teaspoon of sugar into the mug. "Milk?"

She nodded. He added a splash from a china pitcher that looked like a piece from a child's tea set in his huge hands and brought it to her. She sipped gratefully, not minding the searing of her tongue. She dropped the mug to her lap and cradled it there. "How did he know?"

"How did who know what?"

"About the electricity? Why did he think that's what killed Dun?"

Cookie's head wagged slowly from side to side. "That's a good question. I don't know the answer. You're going to have to ask him when he comes up."

Her gaze shot to his face. "It's strange, isn't it, Cookie?"

"Not so strange." His tone belied his words. He sounded as if he thought it was very strange indeed. Willow could see the arguments revolving in his mind before they came out of his mouth. "He must have ordered some work done."

Willow nodded. "I guess so."

"That's probably it," Cookie said. "He knew there was something wrong, then when he saw Dun—who's a great swimmer—floating there and not moving, he put two and two together."

"It must be," Willow said.

"What must be?" Jonathan stood in the doorway.

Willow glanced at Cookie to see if he was going to answer, but he stared at the bedpost as if it had just come to life. "We wondered how you knew about the electricity," Willow said.

"What did you decide?" Jonathan asked.

Willow didn't answer immediately, leaving room for Cookie to chime in, but he just continued his examination of the newel. "Cookie thought you must have known something was wrong with the electricity. Then, when you saw Dun, you figured out what happened."

"Cookie was correct. The pool guy mentioned the grounding wires were old when he was here on Monday. He was going to make a special trip out and replace them on Friday. I asked if I should close the pool, but he thought it was okay. He made it sound like it was a maintenance thing." Jonathan's voice broke. "If that's what happened, it's all my fault."

"It's not," Willow said.

"Don't take that on yourself," Cookie said.

Jonathan buried his face in his hand. "What if I hadn't woken up when I did? What if I hadn't looked out the window?"

"We're not even sure the pool was electrified," Willow said, but it was fainthearted comfort. Dun had been healthy and an excellent swimmer. In all likelihood, that was what had killed her.

Cookie crossed the room in two strides and wrapped an arm around Jonathan. Willow's husband was a tall man, but he looked like a youth next to Cookie. The image was reinforced when his shoulders began to heave. "Hey, now. Don't do that," Cookie repeated over and over.

After several long minutes, Jonathan got control of himself, looked up and wiped his wet face with his forearm. "I'm sorry," he said.

Cookie stepped away. "Want me to bring you something? Tea and whiskey?"

Jonathan patted his arm. "No, thanks. I just want to be alone with Willow."

"Okay, then. Call me if you need me." Cookie picked up the tray with the tea things and left.

JONATHAN PERCHED on the edge of the bed next to Willow, but didn't embrace her or speak. They sat that way until his phone buzzed. He answered and his face, which had been blank and staring only a moment before, reanimated. "Yeah, sure." He hung up. "That was Chloe. The police are downstairs. They want to talk to us."

Willow glanced at her lap enfolded in terrycloth. "Can I get dressed first?"

He put a hand on her leg and squeezed. "Sure. I'll go down now."

After he left, Willow pushed herself from the bed. A strange mix of adrenaline and fatigue bubbled inside her. She wanted to lie down, to pull the covers over herself and hide in the oblivion of sleep. She wanted to begin this day over, but those weren't options.

She dressed quickly, ran a hairdryer over her roots, walked to the door, and turned the knob. Nothing happened. There was no click, no movement in the door mechanism. She rattled it and tried again. Nothing.

Willow wiped her hand on her jeans, gripped the knob, and gave it a sharp yank. No movement. She was locked in. She raised her fist, thumped the wood a few times and yelled, "Hello. Anybody out there?"

Nobody responded. She turned to survey the room, hands on hips, looking for something to wedge between the door and the jamb. Her gaze fell on her purse sitting in an easy chair by the window. She retrieved a credit card from her wallet, jimmied it into the space and felt a satisfying click. The bolt retreated, and she pulled the door open. Old houses played pranks, but she had tricks up her sleeve too.

Her first roommate in college was forever locking Willow out of the room. The girl was such a sound sleeper—especially after an evening of partying—that she never heard Willow's thumps on the door. Willow should have carried her key with her, but often she didn't think she'd need it. She'd only been heading to the shower or down the hall to visit a friend. The good thing about a dorm was there was always someone around, always a credit card or ID card to borrow.

She jogged down the stairs, through the hallway and burst into the great room hoping the police wouldn't be annoyed with her for taking so long. Six pairs of eyes swiveled her way. She skidded to a halt. Her entrance was more dramatic than she'd intended.

Jonathan lounged in an easy chair. Chloe perched on its arm. A dark-skinned woman in khakis leaned against the stone fireplace. "Willow?" the dark-skinned woman said.

"Inspector Sylla?" Willow crossed the room quickly and shook the detective's hand. The two had met months before, during her own family's ordeal. "I'm surprised to see you here."

"And, you. When were you married?"

"Three weeks ago? Four? I've lost count."

"Well, congrats. Rotten way to start a marriage, this. Although, it could have been worse. I understand you had quite a close call this morning."

A flush of post-traumatic fear heated Willow's cheeks. She didn't want to think about herself or the baby or what might have happened. "I'm the one who found Ms. Dunfrey," she said, skirting the issue.

"So I heard." The detective's British accent coupled with the grand, old house made the scene surreal, like a PBS murder mystery come to life. Sylla indicated the couch with an upturned hand, and Willow sat. "Can you tell me, in your own words, exactly what transpired this morning?"

Willow recited the events to the best of her ability, although some memories were shrouded in the morning's haze. When she said she'd been about to dive into the water but had been stopped by a voice calling her name, the detective interrupted her. "So your husband, Jonathan, called to you?"

"Yes," Willow said.

"Where was he? I thought you said you'd gone out alone."

"I had. He was in our bedroom, looking out the window."

Sylla's gaze shifted from Willow to Jonathan. "You saw your wife approaching the pool?"

"I did," he said.

"Did you see Ms. Dunfrey in the water?"

Jonathan paused, then said, "Yes. That's why I called out to Willow."

"You could tell Amelia Dunfrey had been electrocuted from your upstairs window?" Sylla's tone was light, maybe too light.

"No," Jonathan said, annoyance lacing the word. "But I could tell something was wrong. She wasn't moving."

"And that led you to believe she'd been electrocuted?" Doubt gilded Sylla's question.

"I already told you this. The pool guy mentioned the wiring for the pool lights was getting old and needed to be replaced. When I saw Dun—"

"Dun?" Sylla asked.

"Amelia Dunfrey, I call her Dun. When I saw Dun just floating there, not moving, I immediately thought about what he'd said."

"You didn't think she'd drowned?"

"No. Dun was an excellent swimmer."

"Hm." Sylla exhaled the syllable with a single nod of her head. "It was certainly unfortunate you didn't have the power to the pool turned off until the wiring was repaired."

It was the same accusation Jonathan had leveled at himself earlier. He'd broken down then, but the only emotion in his voice now was anger. "The pool maintenance man turned off the power to the lights, but we decided to keep the motor running. It keeps the pool clean. I didn't think there was a problem with the motor wiring."

Sylla typed something into her tablet, then looked at Willow. "What did you do when your husband called to you from the window?"

Willow finished her story with no further interruptions.

"I understand"—Sylla checked her tablet—"Geraldine Lauder, died on Sunday night." The shift in topics was startling.

Chloe, who had been sitting quietly during Willow's story, spoke now. "She did. At South Coast Hospital."

Sylla turned her intelligent eyes on Chloe. "And your father, Hamish Lauder, died only last month?"

Chloe nodded slowly. "A stroke."

"You've certainly had more than your share of death recently."

"It has been a very difficult time." Chloe closed her eyes, seemingly unable to continue.

"And what caused Geraldine Lauder's death?"

Jonathan stood. "I'm not sure what that has to do with what happened here this morning."

"Actually, I was on my way here to talk with you about your mother when I heard the call about a possible drowning on the property. Strange coincidence, yeah?"

"Why are you investigating Mother's death?" Chloe sounded genuinely confused.

"Suspicious circumstances."

"There was nothing suspicious about it," Jonathan said.

Sylla tilted her head. "No? What, in your mind, caused it?"

He crossed his arms over his chest and thrust his chin forward. "I assume, since you're here, you already know. It was an overdose of acetaminophen, probably unwittingly administered by Amelia Dunfrey. Now, detective, we are shocked and exhausted and would like to be alone with our grief. Can we wrap this up?"

Willow shot a disbelieving glance at Jonathan. She'd never seen this side of him before. If someone had asked her to describe his personality, she would have said accommodating, charming, easygoing. This was none of those things.

His abruptness didn't seem to faze Inspector Sylla, who shone a benign smile in his direction. "Right. Just one or two more questions."

Jonathan glared at her, but she continued. "An overdose of acetaminophen doesn't seem like something that could be given accidentally. Can you explain?"

Chloe spoke before Jonathan could, her tone more conciliatory. "The doctors believe Mom was given a little too much for several days in a row, and it built up in her system. Apparently, it's fairly common. There are many over the counter drugs that contain acetaminophen. People don't always realize they are taking more than the recommended amount."

"Your mother was taking several drugs containing it, then?"

Jonathan looked at Chloe. "No. She wasn't."

"We're not sure," Chloe said.

Tension stretched between the twins like the strings of a spider's web. Willow felt it. Sylla must have, as well. "Amelia Dunfrey," the detective said, and the strings snapped. Jonathan and his sister turned to her again. "She was the one in charge of your mother's medications?"

"Yes," Jonathan said.

"Was she also in charge of your father's?"

The question made Willow sit up straighter. Hamish? Why were they talking about Hamish?

"No, she wasn't. My mother cared for him." Chloe's words were mild, but Willow heard the strain underlying them. "Our father suffered from hypertension for years. He had a stroke six months ago, and at the time, his physician warned us another was not only possible, but likely. It was tragic, but not unexpected."

Sylla busied herself with her tablet for several minutes, then her head shot up. "I'd like the names of the doctors who attended your parents."

"Why?" The word burst from Jonathan like a gust of wind.

Her eyebrows rose comically. "I'd like to talk to them."

"Doctor-patient confidentiality will inhibit them from answering your questions."

The placid smile Sylla had been wearing since she'd arrived expanded into one that wasn't as pleasant, but she didn't speak.

"Is this a slow season for crime?" Jonathan said. "Are you bored or something? What happened this morning was terrible, but it was an accident. My mother's death was also an accident. My father's was caused by a medical condition. Nothing nefarious is going on here. There is no mystery to solve. I'd appreciate it if you'd leave us in peace." He held out a hand to Willow. "Let's go, babe."

Willow stared at it for a beat. Showing disrespect to an officer of the law, to anyone in a uniform, was out of her comfort zone. She understood how Jonathan felt, at least she imagined she did. She hadn't lost father, mother, and longtime friend, but her parents had their share of difficulties recently. The detective was barking up the wrong family tree, adding to his grief. *Insult to injury* was the adage that came to mind. But—

"Willow," Jonathan said again. This time, she took his hand and stood.

On their way out, Willow heard Chloe say, "I'll get the names for you." Chloe chose to cooperate. It was good someone had.

Jonathan walked so quickly, Willow had to jog to keep up with him. He loped through the front door, made a left, and headed toward the main garage. "Where are we going?" She panted the words.

"To your parents," he said without breaking stride.

"Why?"

"You need to be somewhere safe. Somewhere else," he corrected himself. "And I need to talk to a lawyer."

"Do you think you're in trouble?" She corrected herself. "We're in trouble?"

He pulled out his phone, held it up to a monitor on the side of the long, low building, and the garage door rolled open. "I'm not going to be bullied."

"I'll go with you," she said.

"No. I need to handle this on my own."

As she settled into his blue BMW, she thought about arguing, telling him she was his wife, not a child. They should face whatever music must be faced together, but truth be told, she was tired. Her parents' living room, with its overstuffed furniture, tables piled with cookbooks and magazines, and corners filled with kicked-off shoes, sang a siren song. She wanted—no, longed—to be there in its messy, familiar comfort.

FURY SHOVED his nose under Willow's hand when she stopped petting him and gave it a nudge. She grabbed one of his silky ears and rubbed it between her fingers. Fury's chin sank to her thigh in contentment.

A dog. That's what they needed at Sunset House. Actually, they should have a couple of dogs on the property, big ones, with loud barks. She'd have felt immeasurably safer the night she'd been alone there. The night she'd seen Dun in the hallway.

"I didn't tell you what Dun told me," she called to her mother, who was fixing tea in the kitchen.

Honey entered the living room with two steaming mugs, one in each hand. "What did she tell you?" She set a mug on the coffee table in front of Willow and took the other to a soft, brown chair across from her.

"Let me back up. The night Gerry went to the hospital, I was alone in the house."

"That big house?" Honey shuddered.

"I know. I'm getting a dog or three. Anyway, I heard all this slamming around, so I went to investigate—"

"Haven't you seen enough horror movies to know that is never a good idea?"

Willow shook her head at her mother's bad joke. "It was only Dun, Ms. Dunfrey. She said she was there to pick up a nightgown, but then yesterday—gosh, I can't believe it was only yesterday. So much has happened."

"What did she say? You're making me crazy."

"Sorry. She said she was actually looking for the acetaminophen bottle so she could take it to the hospital and show the doctors. She wanted them to see the instructions on the label, instructions she said she'd followed to the letter."

Honey blew into her mug and took a careful sip. "I don't know what good that would've done, unless she thought someone tampered with the pills."

Willow paused her ear massaging. "I didn't think of that."

"Maybe she did."

"You don't think… I mean… No."

"Good lord, child, would you please finish a sentence? I don't think what?"

Willow waved a hand in the air, and Fury's head shot up. "I was going to say that whoever tampered with the acetaminophen could have tampered with the pool wiring, but that's silly."

"Why is that silly?"

Fury nosed Willow's hand, and she grabbed his ear again. "That would mean that someone purposely killed Gerry and Dun, and we know that didn't happen."

"We do?"

Willow shot her mother an exasperated look. "You have any cookies?"

"I do, but I'm not getting them until you tell me how you know Gerry and Dun weren't murdered."

Murdered. The word was black and ominous, the stuff of dark, popcorn-scented theaters and musty-smelling paperbacks. It wasn't a word she associated with reality, that's how she knew. But it had been a part of Honey's reality not that long ago. Her mother saw possibilities where Willow was blinded. "Mom," was all she managed to say.

Honey rose from her chair and disappeared into the kitchen. She returned a moment later with a plastic container of chocolate chip cookies. "You shouldn't go back there until the police figure this out. When I think about you almost diving in that pool this morning." Honey placed a hand over her heart. "I can't think about it, that's what. I just can't."

Willow understood. She was Honey's baby, just as the child she carried was hers. Whenever she thought about what might have happened, she wanted to throw up. "We're okay, though." She repeated her mantra.

"Thank God for Jonathan," Honey said. "I'm going to hug the stuffing out of him when I see him again."

"I know." A soft smile formed on Willow's lips. Jonathan had been so tender when he brought her to their room after the paramedics left. "He was wonderful." She frowned. "That's why it was so out of line for that investigator to question him the way she did."

"She?" Honey's eyebrows raised over the rim of her cup.

"Detective Sylla."

Honey's mug thumped to the coffee table. "Sylla was there?"

"Yeah."

"Good. Makes me feel better to know she's looking into things."

Willow shrugged. "I don't think there's anything to look into."

"Three deaths in two months. That's odd, sweetheart."

"Two accidents and a stroke."

Mother and daughter stared at each other for a long moment. Willow had inherited her mother's stubbornness, but Honey had practiced the art longer. Willow looked away first. "Well, if she's as good as you say, she'll prove nothing criminal went on."

A breeze blew in through the sliding door from the backyard. It carried the scent of orange blossoms from the blood orange tree that had been in the yard since her childhood. A wave of nostalgia threatened to wash away the years of maturity and reduce her to a young girl, scared and insecure, and needing her mother's comfort.

Willow closed her eyes against the emotions and a vision of the photo from Hamish's study appeared in her mind. Sophie, another young, scared, insecure girl. One whose mother soon wouldn't be there to comfort her.

"I found a journal, a diary, of a young girl who was either sent to a psychiatric hospital or locked up at home because people believed she was a danger to herself. It was in Hamish's office."

Honey nibbled a cookie and waited for her to continue.

"She seems pretty bitter toward the people who had her put away."

"You think the family had something to do with it, and this girl might have taken revenge?"

That's exactly what Willow was thinking, but it sounded far-fetched when it was verbalized. "She's probably a woman now. The journal looks old."

Honey's eyes narrowed. "A minute ago, you were telling me you thought everything was one big coincidence. Now you think it was murder?"

"No. Maybe. I don't know." The journal was ancient history. Most likely, it had nothing to do with current events.

Willow turned her gaze on her mother. "If the journal belonged to who I think it belonged to, she loved Hamish. Maybe she believed Gerry caused his death. Didn't take care of him well enough. Disliked her for other reasons. I don't know."

The front door opened and shut, and Fury bolted off Willow's lap. A moment later, Booker entered the room holding the squirming black bundle of fur. "Hey, Pumpkin. What a nice surprise." He dropped Fury to the floor, leaned over Willow, kissed her forehead then turned and kissed his wife. "To what do we owe the honor?"

"Your daughter had a close call this morning," Honey said.

Booker's grin faded. "What happened?"

Willow told him the same story she'd told so many times now, ending with Detective Sylla's questions and Jonathan dropping her off on his way to his lawyer. By the time she'd finished, her father's expression was grim.

"He did the right thing," he said.

"Who? Jonathan?"

"Yes. You need to stay here for a while. Get out of that house."

"I'm only staying for a couple of hours. He's picking me up on his way home."

"Not a good idea. I'll take you over there myself, and we can pick up your things." Booker stood and retrieved his car keys from the coffee table. "Ready?"

Irritation itched beneath Willow's skin. "Dad, I'm not going anywhere. Jonathan needs me right now."

"He needs you to be somewhere safe. He said so himself. Now, get your purse, and we'll be going."

Her jaw set in a hard line. Willow loved her father, but she hated when he got like this. "I'm safe with Jonathan."

Booker looked at his feet, jaw working, for several seconds. When he gazed up again, his eyes were softer. "Listen, Will, the police don't send out investigators every time there's an overdose, especially when there's no illegal substance in play and the death happens in a hospital."

"So?"

"So, someone must have brought Gerry Lauder's death to their attention, and that someone must have had enough evidence to cause a busy detective to take time out of her day to head over to Sunset House."

"You think someone reported the overdose?"

"It would make sense."

"Who would do that?"

He gave a small shake of his head. "That I don't know, which is why we should go pick up your things and bring you home for a couple of days."

"I am going home with my husband when he comes to get me."

Willow and Booker glared at each other for a long moment. Honey broke the tension. "Tell him about the journal."

Booker stood immovable for a beat, then sat, shoulders slumped. "Tell me."

Willow sighed. She wished she'd never brought up the damn journal, but it was too late. She relayed the story then said, "There's one more thing. It's probably nothing, but it's weird. I found a business card for a Will and Trust attorney in Hamish's desk drawer. There was a date and a time on the back of it."

Booker leaned his elbows on his knees and looked at her intently. She continued, "The appointment was for two days after his death. Yesterday, I wanted to show it to his assistant. See what she knew about it. But it was gone."

Her father didn't react. It was as if he was waiting for the punchline.

"I just thought it was strange," Willow mumbled.

"Did you tell Detective Sylla about all this?" Booker said.

Willow stared at her hands and patted the couch. Fury hopped up, and she began smoothing the fur on his head. "No. It didn't seem relevant."

"I think you need to talk to her." Honey's voice was more gentle than her husband's.

"Not until I talk to Jonathan." Willow raised her eyes. "He might have a simple explanation for all of it."

"Why don't we do it when he gets here," her father said.

"Booker." Honey's tone was sharp. Fury's head shot toward her, and his body tensed. "Willow doesn't need to get involved. She should take it to Sylla and let her do it. This is Lauder clan business."

"She's a Lauder now."

"Married in isn't the same as born in—just ask your mother."

Old injustices die hard. Booker's mother wasn't thrilled with his choice of brides in the early days of their marriage. It was best to head that tussle off at the pass. "It's a moot point. The card isn't in the drawer anymore, and I don't remember the name of the firm," Willow said. She didn't bother telling them the journal was in her bedroom.

She wasn't about to take that to anyone before she'd read the whole thing. It was a slim clue at best. Nothing to do with anything, most probably. Bad press for the family at worst.

Honey put her hands on her thighs and pushed herself out of her chair. "Well, there you go. Jonathan probably knows all about it anyway. Are you two hungry?"

"Always," Booker said.

Three hours later, Jonathan came to get Willow. He refused food and drink, but hugged Honey and tossed a few jokes at Booker as they left. The jocularity faded from his face as soon as they reached the car. "How did it go?" Willow asked.

His profile was tight in the passing streetlights. "It's a mess. This is just the kind of thing lawyers and accountants love to use to prolong probate."

"What kind of thing is that?" Willow couldn't believe he meant Ms. Dunfrey's death. That would be so cold, so unfeeling.

"The police." His hand slammed the steering wheel. "As soon as they start sticking their noses into things, as soon as terms like 'suspicious death' start getting thrown around, everything grinds to a halt."

Willow chewed her lip, not knowing what to say.

He went on, "They're not going to find anything. Mom and Dun both died accidental deaths, but by the time they're done sorting paperwork and questioning everybody who knew them, it could put things off for a year, maybe more."

"But if there was something... " She said in a hesitant voice. "You'd want to know. Wouldn't you?"

He shot a quick glance at her. His face was lit for a brief moment by a passing car then muted in shadow again. "There isn't something."

She exhaled. Should she ask him about the journal? Or the appointment card? It might sound as if she wasn't on his side, as if she doubted him or the family.

"I talked to Sophie the other day." Willow examined his profile, looking for a change in expression. There wasn't one. She forged ahead. "I didn't realize her father was Hamish's business partner."

"Yeah, he and Fred started Transportation Solutions back in the nineties."

"Sounds like she had a pretty rough childhood."

"She did."

She rolled one shoulder forward. "You don't think she could be resentful?"

Jonathan barked a derisive laugh. "You've been watching too much *CSI*."

Willow bristled at the dismissal. "I'm just saying, if there is something suspicious about your mother's death, shouldn't the police know everything there is to know?"

"Sophie had no reason to kill anybody. Dad wrangled her out of a dead-end job, moved her out here, paid her twice what she deserved. She loved him."

"What about your Mom?"

"Oh." He stretched out the exclamation dramatically. "You think it was a love triangle?"

A radiator lit in Willow's gut. Heat flushed her face. "Don't make fun of me."

"Then don't say ridiculous things."

They didn't talk for the rest of the ride.

When they reached the property, the gates opened smoothly. As they closed behind the car, Willow had a sense of unreality. The world she'd always known, the world of friends and family and music classes and cheap restaurants, all of that receded and was locked away on the other side of the wrought iron rails.

Sunset House was dark except for a light shining in an upstairs bedroom. Chloe must be home alone. The idea of being alone in this place set Willow's heart beating. "I don't care if we inherit this property or not." She blurted out the words.

He pulled into the garage and turned off the engine before responding. "It's a legacy, Willow."

"Why? It hasn't been in your family for generations. Your father didn't build it. He bought it fifteen years ago. Why can't we buy something else, something more livable, and call that a legacy?"

Jonathan inhaled and exhaled slowly, probably counting to ten in his head. "If we don't inherit, Chloe will. Chloe is a spendthrift. I don't know if you've noticed her wardrobe?"

Willow nodded, but she wasn't sure if he saw.

"Chloe isn't responsible enough to take care of the place. Money goes through her like crap through a goose. She'd end up losing it to the bank."

"Does she even want Sunset House? Maybe she feels like me, that we should sell it." Willow's voice rose.

He opened the car door and got out. She had to do the same to hear his response. "Trust me. She wants it."

Willow didn't speak again until they stood in front of the massive front doors. "If we're going to live here, I want dogs."

"Dogs?" He smiled for the first time since they'd left her parents' house. "I always wanted a dog when I was growing up, but Mom was allergic."

"So can I get some?"

"Some? Not one?"

"No, I want a pair. Boxers maybe. Something big and scary looking."

Jonathan tipped his head. It was an ambivalent movement. Neither a nod, nor shake.

She thought about pushing for an answer, but as they trudged up the stairs to their room, fatigue dropped on her like a weighted blanket. Willow was too tired to argue anymore.

They got undressed, got into bed, and rolled onto their respective sides in silence. Within minutes, Willow was asleep, but it wasn't restful. She dreamed all night about trying to keep puppies from falling down the stairs that led to the beach and woke exhausted.

MOLLY: How about Willow's close call, people? It gave me goosebumps. Thankfully, Jonathan thought quickly or this whole thing would've ended today in tragedy. I don't blame Booker for wanting Willow to come home for a while. As a parent, I'd have felt the same.

There have been three deaths in two months. If Detective Sylla was suspicious, I'd be suspicious. Even though she's always declined official interviews, I've spoken with her several times when I need clarification on a legal point. She's one smart lady.

She's also a podcast listener. Not sure if you know this, but law enforcement and true crime podcasters don't usually see eye to eye. The fact that Detective Sylla approves of the show is a real compliment.

But the point I want to focus on this week is one Willow made when she learned Jonathan had inherited Sunset House. And I quote, "She ought to be excited. Thrilled. She'd won the lotto. But she felt trapped."

So, here's the question: Is extreme wealth a trap or a blessing or does it depend on circumstances? I know this is more philosophical than our usual questions, but I thought it was a pertinent one. Money—or the love of—seems to be at the center of everything that's happening at Sunset House.

Pop on to the Facebook Group and let's bat that ball around.

Join me next time for more *Murders Under the Sun*.

(cue music)

VO: This episode is brought to you by Don's Diner in Lake Forest, offering free pie every Tuesday night for diners sixty-five and older. *Murders Under the Sun* is edited by Jim Wilbourne, theme music by Eclectic Blends, and I'm your host, Molly Shure.

part six

MURDERS UNDER THE SUN
SEASON SIX; EPISODE FIVE

MOLLY: Welcome back to *Murders Under the Sun*. This is Molly Shure, your host.

We're in for more shocks and surprises today, but before we get to that I want to fill in the listeners who didn't join us on Facebook this week. The discussion was deep. Sometimes true crime junkies get a bad rep for being shallow and gullible, but not you guys. You're truly astute.

So, here's the run down. A segment of you believe wealth is always a blessing—or could be. This group said the first thing they'd spend money on was someone to help them manage their riches wisely. They felt confident they would have the strength of character to use it for good.

Another segment took the exact opposite position. They believe extreme wealth is inherently evil. That no matter how much character they possessed as a less affluent person, it wouldn't be able to stand up to the corrupting influence of riches.

The third group believe money is neutral. They think it's the person's character and their circumstances that dictate whether it would be a blessing or a curse.

I'm simplifying here. There was a lot of back and forth. It got very interesting.

I ended up doing a little research on the topic myself, and here's what I learned. If someone is in poverty, or in a great deal of debt, an increase of money can lead to happiness, or a state of emotional wellbeing. However, having more than enough actually makes people less happy. It brings stress.

At the time the study was done, an income of $75,000 a year was the sweet spot. Based on recent inflation, I'm sure that number would be higher today. But you get the point.

Willow's gut reaction to the news that she and Jonathan had inherited Sunset House was more logical than she gave herself credit for. Managing the property and everything that went with it could be a full-time job, and would definitely mean a big lifestyle change. In her case, looking a gift horse in the mouth was probably a good idea.

Let's get back into the story.

She didn't swim in the morning. Willow wasn't sure she'd ever swim in that pool again. She didn't even do her usual walk to the window to pull back the curtains and check on the world. She didn't want to see the empty blue water, didn't want to see the fog. Instead, she dressed by electric light and headed downstairs.

Cookie was in the kitchen, flipping an omelet expertly in a stainless-steel pan. "Chloe and Jonathan are in the dining room. Why don't you join them? I'll bring you a decaf when I bring out their eggs." Willow would rather perch on one of the stools at the island and talk music or cooking or anything rather than eat in the formal dining room, but she did as he suggested.

She heard Jonathan and Chloe talking before she entered and paused. Why was it she felt like an interloper every time she entered a room they were in together? She was Jonathan's wife, a relationship closer than a sibling relationship. He should be leaving and cleaving, shouldn't he? Willow had. She saw very little of her own family now, and they had almost no influence on her life. She stepped forward boldly.

"How can we set a date when we don't know when the ME is going to release her?" Chloe's voice was a hiss.

Willow halted just outside of the doorway.

"I thought the hospital took samples. What more can the police expect to learn?" Jonathan said.

"Apparently, the hospital sent her directly to the medical examiner."

Willow heard a thump, possibly a mug on the surface of the table. "Why? Why wouldn't the hospital handle it?"

Chloe's answer was so quiet Willow had to lean forward to hear it. "Someone must have gone to the police when Mom died. Detective Sylla—who you should be nicer to, by the way—said as much."

"Who would do that?"

Chloe didn't answer that question. After a long beat, Willow cleared her throat and stepped into the room. The twins' heads swiveled toward her, their blank expressions quickly adjusting to welcoming. It was uncanny how synchronized their reactions were. "Good morning," she said.

"Morning." Chloe returned her gaze to the planner opened before her.

Jonathan pushed the chair next to him away from the table. "Have a seat, babe. Chloe and I were just discussing funeral dates. Do you have any restrictions?"

Willow sat. "No. I don't have anything on the calendar." The words felt strange in her mouth. When was the last time she'd said, *I don't have anything on the calendar*? She couldn't remember. High school, college, working in San Diego, those had all been massively busy years. She'd jiggled social outings into the cracks between obligations like sand running between stones. Now her calendar stretched empty before her. The good thing about wealth was it had given her more free time. The bad thing about wealth was it had given her more free time.

"We're trying to plan Mom's funeral," Jonathan said.

"And Dun's." Chloe looked pointedly at him.

Jonathan lifted a coffee mug to his lips but didn't respond. Willow glanced back and forth between them. There was tension in the air. She wasn't sure what had caused it, but she had an idea. She opened her mouth and closed it several times, trying to think of something to say, but was saved by Cookie.

"Mushroom for you, Chloe, and bacon and spinach for Jonathan." He set steaming plates before them, and a mug of decaf in front of Willow. "Veggie everything?" he asked her.

"Yes, please." She gave him a wide smile. Having meals prepared by someone who cooked as well as her mother was one of the perks of riches she could adjust to.

"There are bagels and pastries on the sideboard." Cookie gestured toward a low wooden cabinet centered under the picture window. Willow rose and walked to the food.

"Let's get everything in place. Then we can pull the trigger when we get the go ahead," Jonathan said.

"Dun was planning to replicate what she'd done for Dad's funeral. I'll go through her files."

"The police took them." Jonathan's tone was flat.

"Her files?" Chloe's was sharp. "Why would they take her files?"

"Why do they do anything?"

Willow chose half of an everything bagel to go with her everything omelet, added a schmear of cream cheese, and returned to the table. "Do you have music planned?"

Chloe's gaze lifted from her organizer. "Do you have something in mind?"

Jonathan slapped the table with both hands. "That's a fabulous idea."

"But, I didn't—"

"Why didn't I think of it? You can play Dad's violin. A mass or something. It would be so moving."

Willow was tongue-tied. She hadn't planned to offer herself as the musician but recruit some of her old string quartet buddies. She wasn't sure how she felt about playing music at her mother-in-law's funeral.

Chloe narrowed her eyes. "I'm not sure that's protocol."

"You haven't heard her play." Jonathan warmed to his idea. "She's amazing, Chloe. More professional than the violinist at the Thurber wedding last year."

"I'm not arguing her ability," Chloe said.

Jonathan's brow hovered like a thundercloud over darkening eyes. "Then what?"

"Decorum, dear brother. Willow is family. Family *should* be grieving at the funeral." She accented the word should. "Grieving people don't perform."

"Musicians emote through their music. Isn't that what separates the true artists from the hacks? Besides, Willow hardly knew Mom."

Chloe set her fork down hard. "If you want me to plan the funeral—"

Willow intervened. "I don't think I'm in any shape to play." She held up her hands and wiggled her fingers. "I've hardly practiced in the past three or four months."

"You sounded wonderful—" Jonathan began.

"She doesn't want to," Chloe interrupted him.

The two glared at each other until Cookie broke their standoff. "Veggie everything," he said, coming through the doorway.

"Thanks." Willow said too enthusiastically. "That looks amazing."

"As good as your mama's?" he asked.

Willow took a bite, closed her eyes and focused on the flavors. She tasted onion, sweet peppers, mushrooms, spinach, feta—all expected ingredients—but there was something surprising in the layers that took her a moment to pinpoint. Her eyes popped open. "Is that basil?"

Cookie tipped his head back and laughed. "You got me."

"If you tell my mother I said this was better than hers, I'll deny it."

"Does that mean it is better?"

"Maybe." Willow forked up another bite and grinned past the food.

Cookie busied himself lifting lids and filling juice glasses before leaving them. The tension that had filled the room earlier seemed to flow out the door with him.

Chloe pushed away from the table. "I'm going to the florist."

"See you tonight." Jonathan turned away from her to face Willow. "What's on your agenda today?"

She dabbed her lips with her napkin. "Not much. The only thing left to catalog in your Dad's office is the music."

He placed a hand on hers. "Why don't you come with me, then?"

Happiness, thin and ephemeral, hardly more than a wisp of cloud, floated into Willow's chest. "Where are you going?"

"I have to see a client in San Diego, your old stomping grounds. I could drop you off in the Gas Lamp district, and you could poke around the shops while I meet with him. Afterwards, I could take you to dinner at the Hotel Del."

He meant the Hotel Del Coronado, one of the oldest, most elegant hotels on the west coast. Willow was very proud of herself. She didn't squeal but took the news in stride. "Maybe Jaiden could meet me for lunch."

"Have I met Jaiden?"

"Yes, silly. The gorgeous fifth grade teacher from Cranston Academy."

"Oh, right." He raised one eyebrow suggestively.

Willow glanced down at her jeans and t-shirt. "I'll have to change."

"You look fine."

"Not for the Hotel Del." She stabbed at the last bite of her eggs. "I'll hurry."

Jonathan rose. "I'll tell Cookie to take the night off."

San Diego was magic. It was as if Willow had gone back in time to the days before their wedding when she and Jonathan were dating. While she shopped, she thought about meeting him later. She tried things on she knew he'd like. The butterflies returned to her stomach, and it wasn't the baby. It was him.

Jaiden couldn't make lunch but said she'd meet for coffee. At 3:00, Willow wandered toward the Starbucks near her old school. It was like going home. She pushed open the glass door, and the familiar aroma of coffee and vanilla and sweets beckoned her in. She didn't see Jaiden but got in line and pondered her options from the overhead board. She couldn't have her usual, too much caffeine.

"Willow?"

She turned to see her friend. Jaiden looked fit and hip in perfectly torn jeans and a white tank top. Her dark hair fell in ringlets to her shoulders. Had Willow ever looked that hip? She didn't think so, not even when she was footloose and single. "Jaiden." She was so glad to see a familiar face, she hugged the woman hard.

Jaiden extracted herself. "What brings you down from the OC?"

"Jonathan is seeing a client. I'm shopping." She lifted a full bag to prove it.

Jaiden checked her watch. It was one of those that answered emails, counted calories, and tracked every breath you took in a day. "I'm so sorry, I only have about a half hour. Next time, give me more warning."

They ordered drinks and found a small metal table in the shade outside the shop. "So tell me everything that's happening at school," Willow said before Jaiden had taken a sip of her latte.

"Oh, you know, same old stuff," Jaiden said and smiled.

Willow primed the pump with a couple of well-placed questions about Craig Hartley, their least-favorite math teacher, and the dam broke. Jaiden caught Willow up on gossip for the next ten minutes. When she paused for a breath, she touched Willow's left hand. "What's with the ring? I thought you two weren't getting married until next year?"

"We eloped. We got married at a winery in Paso Robles."

Jaiden's deep-set eyes grew round. "Romantic." She said the word with relish. After Willow filled her in on the wedding, Jaiden rocked her chair onto two legs and surveyed Willow. "Have you found a job for next school year?"

Willow gave a small shake of her head. "No. I've been doing some work for the Lauder family—cataloging books and music scores."

"Sounds nice," Jaiden said as if she didn't actually think it did.

Willow gave her a sanitized version of the past few weeks, then said, "My father-in-law left behind the most amazing violin." Jaiden listened politely as Willow described it, but she wasn't a musician. Her eyes began to glaze over.

When Willow finished, Jaiden changed the topic to the school's summer basketball camp. Sports had the same effect on Willow the violin had on Jaiden. After a few more conversational stabs, Jaiden said she had to get going. They hugged again, and Willow watched her lithe form slip away through the crowds of tourists strolling the street. An emotion she couldn't name filled her. Wistfulness? Melancholy? Sadness? She wasn't sure, but she missed her old life. She missed the busy days and friend-filled nights.

You are in transition, and transitions are hard. The words that formed in her mind had her mother's slight Kentucky twang. Willow had left a job she loved, moved, married, and experienced three unexpected deaths in under two months. No wonder she was feeling blue. Her phone sang Jonathan's theme song, and she grabbed for it. She would focus on the good things, all she'd gained, not what she'd lost.

"Hi." Her tone was perky and bright.

"Where are you? I'll come get you," he said on the other end.

After they hung up, Willow gathered up her things and walked toward the street. He was coming from the north, so it would be easier for him to pick her up on the opposite side. As she waited for the light to turn, she watched the parade. A Pedicab—San Diego's bicycle carriages—churned by, club music blaring. A ragged-looking man sorted through the trash, looking for cans and bottles.

The light turned green, and Willow entered the crosswalk. A mother pushing a stroller and dragging a preschooler by the hand hurried up the sidewalk on the opposite side. The preschooler tripped on the curb, fell into the street, and started wailing. The mother crouched, comforting and encouraged her as she anxiously glanced at the waiting traffic.

Willow was so focused on the drama taking place in front of her, she never saw the car. She heard the screech of brakes, felt a rush of air, a crush of pain, then darkness.

6.5.2

WHEN THE WORLD came telescoping back, the first thing Willow saw was a Latina face, plump, pretty, and concerned. "Don't move. An ambulance is on the way."

Willow tried to lift herself onto an elbow in direct disobedience and saw the uniform. The Latina face belonged to a cop, who asserted her authority by gently but firmly pressing Willow to the ground again. "I'm okay," Willow said.

"We'll see about that," the policewoman said.

"My husband was coming to get me. He'll be worried." Willow tried again.

"Yeah? He should be. You just got hit by a car."

A bubble of panic burst inside Willow, its poison gas moving into her lungs, making it hard to breathe. "The baby," was all she managed to say.

The furrows in the cop's forehead deepened, and she cursed. "You're pregnant?" Willow nodded. The woman patted her arm. "The paramedics will be here any minute. It'll be okay."

It'll be okay? That was an empty promise if Willow ever heard one. This woman had no idea if she was okay, or if the baby was okay. She had no idea what was going on inside Willow's womb. Willow clutched her stomach and squeezed her eyes shut as if she could hold the baby inside her by sheer willpower. Not again. Not her little Peach. The Lauder curse wasn't going to take her baby. Tears leaked down her cheek and dropped on the dirty street beneath her head.

The policewoman continued to pat her arm, but didn't speak again until the ambulance screamed to a stop in the intersection. "They got you now, honey," she said and was gone.

What seemed hours later, Jonathan stuck his head around the doorway of Willow's hospital room. She couldn't speak but opened her arms, and he filled them. After several snot-filled, sobbing minutes, she hiccupped her story into his chest as he rocked her. When she was done, she released him and reached for the tissue box on the bedside table.

As she blew her nose, she noticed him wiping his face with his shirt sleeve. Her heart squeezed out an extra beat. Was he crying?

"I talked to the doctor," Jonathan said.

"What did he say?" Her voice was a whisper. She was so afraid to ask the question she could hardly get the words out.

"The ultrasound looks good."

Looks good? She wanted to believe him, but what about his tears? "Why are you crying?"

His face clouded with confusion for a brief second, then cleared. "Happy tears," he said.

Willow allowed relief to cascade over her. "I thought... I heard the baby's heartbeat, but I wasn't sure."

"The baby is fine." One half of his mouth slid into a smile. "I know what it is."

"The sex?"

He nodded. "Do you want to know?"

She had to think about that for a moment. "Yes. Yes, I want to know."

"It's a boy."

A jolt of joy shot through her. She laughed and immediately

regretted it. She threw a hand around her rib cage. "I think I broke a rib or two."

"No. You didn't break anything, miraculously. Only soft tissue damage. You're one tough kid. The doctor said you'll be sore for a week or two, have some colorful bruises, but otherwise you and the little guy are okay."

Willow grinned. "A boy." It wasn't that she'd wanted a boy more than a girl. Whichever she had would be perfect, but she'd felt the presence of that tiny being within her since the day in the karate dojo. It had felt boyish somehow. She'd bonded, or believed she'd bonded, with her little Peach, and bonding implies you know the person you've bonded with.

"The doc will be in soon to start the checkout process, but meanwhile there's a police person waiting outside to talk to you. Are you up to it?"

Willow nodded. The news, both that her baby was okay and that he was a he, made her feel up to almost anything. Jonathan disappeared and reappeared a moment later with the same police officer who'd stayed with Willow while they waited for the ambulance.

She wasn't a tall or heavy woman, but there was something substantial, unflappable, about her that filled the room. She walked toward the bed. "How you feeling?"

"Sore," Willow said.

"I never introduced myself. I'm Officer Hannity." The woman held out a hand. Willow took it and wondered at the name. It didn't sound very Latin. Her face must have shown her confusion. "My husband is Irish," Hannity said. "Mind if I ask you a couple of questions?"

"Sure."

Officer Hannity pulled a pad and pen from a pocket, which seemed right for her. Most cops had tablets these days, but Hannity had a warm, old-school vibe that Willow found comforting. "Did you see the car that hit you?"

Willow started to shake her head, felt a pinch in her neck and stopped. She reached up a hand to rub it. "I don't think so. Did anyone else?"

"We have a couple of witnesses."

"What did they say?"

"One says it was a black SUV, someone else says navy blue. Both said it looked new, fancy. Ring any bells?"

"I'm sorry."

Jonathan stepped from the corner of the room, moved to Willow's side, and hovered over her protectively. "I'm sure this was a random hit and run—a drunk businessman afraid of getting another DUI."

Officer Hannity glanced at him. "Most likely, but we have to ask. You know?" Jonathan gave her a reluctant nod, and she returned her gaze to Willow. "So, is there anyone who might wish you harm, Mrs. Lauder? Anyone with a grudge?"

"Of course not," Jonathan said.

Hannity didn't acknowledge his outburst.

"Not that I know of," Willow said. The stress and pain of the past few weeks had grown brick by brick into a load too heavy for her to bear. Gerry and Dunfrey's deaths, her own near escape at the pool, and now this. The idea that the driver was gunning for her wasn't something she could contemplate at the moment. And she didn't want to. She wanted to bask in the happy glow of knowing her little boy was tucked up safe and sound inside her.

The officer withdrew a card from her shirt pocket and handed it to Willow. "If you think of anything, you'll call? We'll do our best to find the perpetrator, but we don't have much to go on. Nobody got the license. The windows were tinted, so no one saw the driver."

Willow promised she would, and Hannity left, passing the doctor in the doorway.

The attendant was young, red-haired, and red-eyed. He looked almost as tired as Willow felt. "Ready to get out of here?" he said.

Forty-five minutes later, they were on their way. Willow curled into a knot in the passenger seat of Jonathan's BMW and was asleep before they hit the 5 Freeway. She never woke until he stopped the car in front of Sunset House.

When the engine died, she opened her eyes and shifted in her seat. She moaned. A deep ache started in her ribs, moved to her hips, then to her neck. Everything hurt.

"Don't move," Jonathan said. "I'll help you." He rushed around the car, opened her door, and lifted her onto the walkway.

She made a half-hearted attempt to push him away. "Go park the car. I can do this."

"Nope. One accident a day is enough."

The truth was she needed his support. He held her close and walked her through the quiet house, up the stairs, and into their room.

Willow glanced around at the mess she'd left in her hurry to leave that morning. Her jeans and t-shirt sat in a tumble by the vanity. The closet doors were flung open. The heavy curtains were parted and a sliver of moon showed through the panes. This wasn't home. It was like a hotel she'd grown accustomed to, but it wasn't home. "Maybe we should move into the wing," she said.

Jonathan led her to the bed, she sat, and he removed her left shoe. "You want to talk about that tonight?"

"The Peach needs a home. Not just a room."

He lifted her right leg and slipped off her shoe. "The Peach?"

"It's my nickname for the baby."

"Well, it's going to be a while before The Peach needs a room of his own. We don't need to make a decision tonight."

Willow lay on the bed and began to wiggle out of her jeans. "What about the library?"

Jonathan grabbed the bottom of her pants and pulled. "What about the library?"

"We could move in there."

He threw her pants into her pile of clothes on the floor and pulled back the bedspread. Willow slipped between the sheets, and he covered her. "I think we should think about this tomorrow."

She yawned a big, earsplitting yawn and closed her eyes. "I like the library."

Jonathan leaned over her and planted a kiss on her forehead. "I'm going to sleep in one of the extra bedrooms."

"Why?"

"You'll be more comfortable without me. I don't want to roll over and hurt you." He turned off the light.

She was going to protest, but didn't have the energy. The last thing she remembered was the sound of the bedroom door closing and the click of the lock.

6.5.3

A RIBBON of sunlight slanted across the covers. Willow's eyes focused on the dust motes floating in it. The tiny specks danced and hovered, and she thought of the baby, her little Peach, dancing inside her.

She'd seen a video once, one of those *What to Expect When You're Expecting* kinds of things. It had fascinated her to watch the progress of life from zygote to infant. A scene that had left an indelible impression on her was one of the baby in the early stages of pregnancy. It hadn't yet filled its mother's womb and still had space to play. It waved its new limbs and turned somersaults, the movements free and joyful.

She placed a hand over her abdomen. "Good morning, Peach." She stayed that way for a moment longer, wishing she didn't have to rise, but she did. Her bladder was about to burst.

She'd forgotten for a split second about the accident the day before, because nothing hurt as she lay still. She was fairly certain that would change as soon as she moved. Her right side, the side that had been hit, was sure to be bruised and painful.

Cautiously, she rolled onto her left. Her body protested, but it wasn't as bad as she'd expected. She dropped her legs over the edge of the bed and raised herself into a seated position. Now, that hurt.

Her abdominals and ribs had taken a beating. She closed her eyes and took several deep breaths, but the image of a dark, metal monster bearing down on her filled her imagination. She opened her eyes again.

Sweat dampened her upper lip and her forehead, and she waited for the pain to subside. When it did, she pushed off the bed like a swimmer pushes off the side of the pool and headed into the bathroom to relieve herself.

Once she was up and walking, she began to feel a bit better. Careful, slow movements greased the wheels. She walked to the closet, pulled a loose cotton dress from a hanger, and carried it to the bed. Dressing was an ordeal, but ten minutes later, she was clothed. Another fifteen and her hair was brushed and her makeup on.

Her stomach rumbled as she walked to the door. When had she eaten last? No dinner. She'd been in the hospital when she should have been in the dining room of the Hotel Del. No lunch because of the big omelet Cookie had made her for breakfast. It had been twenty-four hours since her last meal.

Willow grabbed the doorknob and turned. It stayed still beneath her hand. She tried a second time, and a third. The door was stuck. Again. Why this morning? She was stiff, sore, and starving. She didn't have the patience to play with locks.

She glanced around the room looking for her purse. A credit card would be the quickest way out. Her purse wasn't on the dresser where she usually put it. It wasn't in the closet. She shuffled to the bathroom. Maybe she hadn't noticed it when she'd washed her face. But no. It wasn't in the bathroom. She moved to the vanity and leaned against it. Where was it?

The last place she remembered having it was on the street before the accident. A pulse throbbed at her temple. It would be such a pain to replace everything in it, her driver's license, credit cards... Her phone was in her purse, so she couldn't even call Jonathan to come and let her out. Frustration coursed through her.

She bent forward to sift through the pile of clothes on the floor in the small hope her purse was hiding beneath it and swore under her breath. A twinge in her back had brought tears to her eyes. For nothing. Her purse wasn't there either.

Could it be under the bed? She gazed across the room. A sense of helplessness washed over her. Under the bed was a long way down. She'd have to get on her knees to see under the bed.

The clump of feet sounded in the hallway. Her head snapped toward the sound. "Hello. Who's out there?" She made her way to the doorway as she called out.

The clumping stopped. Willow put her mouth to the crack of the door. "Good morning."

Nobody responded.

"Jonathan? Chloe? Is that you?"

No answer. Maybe it was one of the staff. She hadn't learned all their names yet. That would have to change.

"Please, I'm stuck in here. Could you see if you can unlock the door from that side?"

The silence was so thick, her ears rang with it. Willow sighed and leaned against the cool wood. The footsteps must have come from farther away than she'd thought. Whoever it was hadn't heard her.

Her gaze rested on the window. She could open it and call out to anyone she might see below. Since nobody had gone swimming since Dun's death, it could be a while before anyone came. Her stomach cramped, and she groaned.

As she stepped away from the doorway, she heard the footsteps again, more rapid this time. It sounded as if they ran down the stairs, then faded into the distance. Her mouth dropped open in disbelief. Who would do that? Who would leave her stranded?

Maybe one of the cleaning crew brought their child to work. That was a violation of Gerry's house rules. What day was it? Tuesday? Wednesday? With no job and no appointments, she'd lost track of time.

Willow snorted. Not that it mattered. She had no idea which days which staff came anyway. She knew it was more than once a week, more than twice. She'd seen them moving quietly about their work, slipping from room to room trying to be as unobtrusive as possible. Well, she wished they'd be obtrusive now. She didn't care what rule they'd broken. She just wanted help.

The window it was, then. On the way across the room, she heard the rattle of the knob behind her, a click, and the door swung open.

"I brought you breakfast." Jonathan carried a shiny black tray.

Willow glared at him. "How did you get in?"

"What do you mean, how did I get in?"

"I mean, that door was stuck again. I couldn't get it open."

His chin dropped to his chest. "Stuck?"

"Yes. It happened last week, but I opened it with a credit card. I forgot to tell you about it."

"Strange. I'll talk to Mike. Have him take a look." His face brightened. "Meanwhile, how about breakfast?"

Mike must be the maintenance man. Willow would learn everyone's names and tell the cleaning people they could bring their kids in if they were in a jam. The rules were going to change.

She hesitated, then said, "Sure, thanks."

She'd wanted to go downstairs, sit at the counter, and watch Cookie work. She felt more at home in the kitchen than in any other room of the house. However, Jonathan looked so pleased with himself and so dismayed by the fact that she was up and dressed, she climbed onto the bed.

He plumped the pillows and perched next to her. "You should rest today."

"I wasn't planning to go hiking," she said between mouthfuls of pancake and bacon.

"No, seriously. I want you to stay off your feet. That's what the doctor said."

"When did he say that? I didn't hear anything about staying off my feet."

Jonathan trained his gaze out the window. "Must have been when I talked to him alone, before I came in to see you."

Willow stared at him, but he refused to meet her gaze. Was he lying to her? "I'm fine."

He looked at her now. "You may be fine, but the baby... "

Guilt gripped her. The baby. She wouldn't do anything to endanger the baby. But why hadn't the doctor talked to her, told her to stay in bed? "What did he say?"

Jonathan placed a hand against her cheek and stroked it softly. "He only said it would be best if you stayed off your feet for a couple of days. Make sure everything is okay, you know?"

"What was he worried about? Did he say I might lose—" she couldn't finish the sentence. When had this inconvenient pregnancy turned into someone she was willing to protect with her life, if necessary? The emotions coursing through her were raw and shocking.

Jonathan grabbed her hand. "No. No. He didn't say anything like that. Only that it would be best for both of you if you rested for a day or two."

Willow pushed her tray away, no longer hungry. "Okay. I'll stay in bed if it's best."

"I think it is."

Neither said anything for a long moment. Willow broke the silence. "I can't find my purse. Did we have it when we left the hospital?"

Jonathan's brow furrowed. "I think so. We must have left it in the car. I'll check."

"Thanks."

Jonathan picked up the tray and stood. "Do you need anything else? More tea?'

Willow shook her head. "Just my purse."

"Got it." He moved toward the door.

"And, Jonathan?"

"Yeah?"

"My laptop? I think I left it in the library."

"I'll look." He started to pull the door closed behind him.

"And leave that open?"

He hesitated, shoulders stiff, as if he was about to argue with her, but he didn't. He left the door ajar a few inches and disappeared. Willow listened to his steps as they descended the stairs and faded away.

Now what? What was she going to do with this long day stretching ahead of her? She had no phone, no laptop. All her books were in a box in her parent's garage. There was a TV in the room, but daytime television would spiral her into depression. There was nothing worse than watching commercials for online trade schools, ambulance-chasing law offices, and the latest arthritis meds to make you want to jump off a bridge.

Her gaze traveled the lovely room and landed on the pile of clothes next to the vanity. It was an eyesore. She may have to lie here all day, but she didn't have to look at dirty laundry. A few steps wouldn't hurt anyone. She wasn't an invalid.

Willow eased herself off the bed, placed one hand on the vanity, and squatted. "Lift with your legs," she mumbled. She picked up the t-shirts and jeans and was about to rise when she noticed the tote bag she'd dropped under the vanity.

She'd completely forgotten she'd put her laptop in it the last time she was in the library. She'd sent Jonathan on a wild goose chase. Hopefully he'd bring her purse to her before looking for her laptop. She snatched the handle of the tote bag and stood.

After dumping the clothes in the hamper, Willow climbed onto the bed again. She arranged herself in a half-seated position, pillows leaning against the headboard, reached into the bag, and pulled out the first thing that came to hand. She stared. She'd forgotten about the journal as well.

I read a quote from *The Hobbit* by J.R.R. Tolkien that made me laugh out loud. Bilbo Baggins was talking about Smaug. He likened the dragon to a rich person who flew into a rage because he'd lost something he'd never actually used or wanted. It's such a perfect description of my monster. In fact, the entire scene following Bilbo's theft of the cup that causes all the ruckus is pure gold. No pun intended.

I'm studying greed, trying to understand why I was attacked in such a brutal way, trying to understand why I was a threat at all. I think it's this. The monster had always taken the treasure for granted, had never understood that things could disappear, be stolen, or given away.

I remember when we first heard about the will. We were all seated at the dinner table—the kids at one end, the adults at the other. The word "will" tripped from one to the other of us like an electric shock goes through people who are holding hands. Everyone reacted.

The adults tried to look disinterested. They muttered statements like: "We don't need to discuss that." "I've never given it a thought." Lies.

The kids weren't as disingenuous. The surprise on our faces was undisguised. I don't think any of us had ever thought about where the wealth came from, who actually owned it, or what would become of it in the future. It was a constant. An unalterable thing, like the sunset in the evening. The idea that it might be divided or changed in any way had never occurred to us before.

It settled on us now like a heavy snowfall, cold and quiet. There was something in the knowledge that made me want to curl up with a blanket and dream golden dreams. There was something in the knowledge that made the monster as angry and hot as Bilbo's dragon.

Three days later, the monster asked if I wanted to go to the beach. I should never have gone, but I hadn't been trained in dragon lore. I didn't know you couldn't trust their words. I didn't know what dragons do when their wealth is threatened, that baby dragons, like baby rattlers, could be more lethal than the adults.

What now? That's the question. Now that I know, what am I going to do about it? Until this moment I have been an unwitting sacrifice to greed, but the damsel in distress role chafes. I'm more suited to the part of Saint George, dragon slayer.

I've never been a violent person, but I'm afraid violence will end this thing. Monsters don't change. They may shed their skin, they may encrust themselves in gems like Bilbo's Smaug, but they are always dragons at heart. I'm not going to show this journal entry to Dr. P. I'll never get out of this room if I do.

6.5.4

THE HAIR on Willow's arms stood on end as if the electricity that had traveled the length of the dinner table she'd just been reading about had touched her as well. It seemed as if the writer planned to kill her monster.

Willow slapped the journal shut and slid it into her tote bag, no longer wanting to view even its cover. It felt dirty and dangerous, the rantings of a disturbed mind.

She was the one in charge of your mother's medications? Detective Sylla's voice whispered in Willow's mind. *Was she also in charge of your father's?*

Could Sylla's suspicions be correct, not about Dunfrey but that Gerry and Hamish's deaths weren't accidental? Could it be the girl of the diary had taken matters into her own hands and killed them? But who was she?

Dunfrey couldn't be the author of the journal. She was too old. This writer had been a child or a teen at the time of the writing. A child or a teen who was present when Hamish discussed his will. There were only two women who qualified.

Sophie seemed the obvious choice. Jonathan had never talked about her presence at the house when they were younger, but it would make sense she'd been in and out. She was the daughter of Hamish's business partner and friend. Perhaps this discussion took place before Fred had died.

Willow chewed on the side of her thumb. However, Sophie seemed genuinely fond of Hamish.

It could be Chloe's diary. Willow had a difficult time imagining the cool, calm Chloe penning the cryptic words or being locked away for mental health problems. Willow hadn't known Chloe as a child, though. Maybe she'd been a problematic teen.

If only the journal writer were less cryptic, but she was paranoid. That much was clear from the entries. Paranoid people guard themselves from prying eyes and black helicopters and mind-reading lasers. Writing in code would come naturally to them.

Willow rubbed her forehead. Her mind was spiraling. She didn't know who wrote the journal, who the monster and the dragon were, or if they were even one and the same. Her gaze drifted to the tote bag and its contents. If she read more, she might find the answers. She was tempted and repelled at the same time. It was dark reading, and she really didn't know if it had any relevance to the recent deaths. Reading more might make her as crazy as the writer.

"Knock, knock." A man's voice, deep and friendly, brought her out of her reverie.

"Come in," she said.

A middle-aged man with the red nose of a drinker poked his head through the doorway. "I'm Mike. Jonathan said you've got a problem with the door lock."

Willow started to rise. "Yes, it's gotten stuck twice now."

Mike held up a hand. "Don't get up. Jonathan told me you're supposed to be resting. I'll be out here in the hall."

She leaned into the pillows and smoothed her dress. "Okay, great." The minutes crawled by as she sat looking at her hands in her lap. It was awkward lying there while a strange man fiddled with her bedroom door. She wished she could leave, go for a walk, and come back when he was done.

Mike's huff broke the silence. "Well, this is funny."

Willow glanced toward him. "What's funny?"

"Somebody put the whole mechanism in backwards." She swung

her legs off the bed with a wince and walked to where he crouched. "See this?" He pointed at a lever on the hallway side of the knob. "Flip it down, and the door locks." He demonstrated. "This should be on the inside of a bedroom door."

The skin on her arms prickled again. What if it had been installed that way on purpose? She gave a small shake of her head. She wasn't going to read any more of that journal. It was playing with her mind.

"Unless, you wanted to lock somebody in," Mike said as if reading her thoughts.

"Who wants to lock who in?" Jonathan's head popped above the landing as he climbed the stairs.

"That's the question," Mike said.

"Mike says the door lock was put on backwards." Willow's voice sounded more shrill than she'd intended. She cleared her throat. "I wonder how long it's been like this?"

"Probably forever." Jonathan laughed. "Mike's predecessor was pretty old when Dad finally gave him the sack. It wouldn't surprise me if you found a whole lot of things installed backwards around here." As he approached the bedroom, Willow saw her purse dangling from his hand. Thank goodness. Some of the tension left her shoulders.

Mike stood and put his hands on his ample hips. "I can attest to that."

"But why was it locking?" Willow said, not ready to let it go.

"It's old. The lever flicks down pretty easily. If someone gave the door a good pull, it might rattle into place." Mike slammed the door, and it did just as he said.

He opened it again to reveal a grinning Jonathan. "Mystery solved."

She didn't return the smile but looked at Mike. "Can you fix it?"

"Unfortunately, I'm going to have to get a new mechanism and these are special order. You want it to match the others." He gestured to the door across the hall.

Jonathan waved a hand at him. "No problem. We can wait. We'll just have to be more careful meanwhile."

Willow eyed the door. The thought of getting locked in again made her squeamish. "We could take the knob off."

Jonathan narrowed his eyes. "Then we'd have a hole in the door."

Mike glanced back and forth between them as if waiting to see who would win the contest of wills. When neither of them spoke, he said, "Okay, then." Obviously deciding in favor of Jonathan, he gathered his toolbox, hitched up his jeans, which immediately fell into place under his substantial belly again, and strode toward the stairs. "I'll order that kit today."

"We need our privacy," Jonathan said once Mike disappeared.

Willow wasn't going to argue over something that would be fixed in a day or two. However, if she was going to have a wonky door lock, she would make sure she always had a credit card with her. "Is that my purse?" Her words came out with a bite.

He glanced at the bag dangling from his hand as if it was the first time he'd seen it. "Oh, yeah." He handed it to her. "It was in the car, but I couldn't find your laptop."

"It's in my tote bag." She pointed toward the bed. "I forgot it was here." She didn't apologize. Willow was tired and cranky and unhappy about having to stay in bed. Somehow, all that translated into her being unhappy with Jonathan.

He chewed on the inside of his cheek as if biting something back before saying, "No worries. I had to talk to Sophie anyway." He took her hand. "How about you lie down again?"

Willow allowed him to lead her to the bed. "Need anything else?" he said. "There are some mystery novels in Mom's office. I could grab a couple for you."

"No, I'm good." In truth, Willow wanted to be left alone. Now that she had her phone, she planned to call her mother and fill her in on everything that had happened. Maybe Honey would come visit.

Willow's throat tightened, and she felt tears form behind her eyes. What was it about parents? Just thinking about them could reduce you to eight-years-old again.

Jonathan leaned over and kissed her on the forehead. "Okay. I have to head to the office for a bit, but Cookie said to text him when you want lunch. He's making chicken soup. I told him you didn't have a cold, but he said chicken soup is good for everything."

"Soup sounds good."

She waited until she could no longer hear Jonathan's footsteps before pulling her phone from her bag. It was dead. Of course. It had been left on all that time. She plugged it into the charger on her bedside table and waited as the little battery charging light came on.

Willow lay her head on the mountain of pillows and closed her eyes. It must be the stress of the accident that made her so tired. She would take a short nap while she waited for the phone to charge. When she woke, she'd call Honey. Sleep wrapped her in a cocoon of soft down.

What seemed like only moments later, a sound in the hallway woke her. Footsteps again. The same heavy tread she'd heard earlier, but louder this time. Willow rose and walked quickly to the doorway. She wanted to see who it was, to find out why they hadn't helped her earlier.

She stepped into the hall just in time to see the door across from hers pull closed. "Excuse me," she called. But the door remained shut. Willow stood in indecision, irritation crawling up her arms. Why wouldn't this person help her earlier? Why did they ignore her now? She wanted to go after them, find out who they were, but for a reason she couldn't name, she was suddenly afraid.

She glanced the length of the hallway and realized with a start it had changed. Rather than making a right several rooms up and following the shape of the house, it stopped. She turned her head the other way, where the stairwell should be, and found a solid wall.

The lights in the hall were different too. Instead of the coated-glass sconces she was used to, the bulbs hung bare and cast a yellow hue. The walls were no longer the clean ecru they had been, but were now dirty white and streaked with mold. The shushing of water whispered against them. Fear climbed her throat, strangling her. Where was she? This wasn't Sunset House.

She spun, planning to run into her room, to slam the door, to put something solid between this strange scene and herself, but it was closed. Willow grabbed the knob. It wouldn't turn. She tugged and pulled, but her hands, slick with panic, slipped from the metal.

She turned and rested her back against the door. "Jonathan," she screamed, finding her voice. His name echoed off the filthy walls. The only response was a snicker so quiet she wasn't sure she'd actually heard it.

Get out of the hallway.

Those words rang so loudly in her head, she thought they might actually be audible. But where should she go? Her room was locked behind her. She gazed up and down the corridor, counting doors. There were seven. This, too, was wrong. She was sure this section had only four. She counted again. Seven.

Which door should she choose? Pushing her shoulder against the wall to make herself as small as possible, she slid forward until she reached the entrance to the room next door to hers. She placed a hand on the knob, then snatched it back. The metal was so cold it burned her fingers. She walked quickly to the next room, but before she reached it, she could hear sounds coming from behind the wall. A roar followed by a crash then a growl. A battle raged behind that door.

She scuttled to the door at the far end, pressed her ear against the wood, and heard the howl of a hurricane. She returned along the other side. Each room sent shivers of fear down her spine for one reason or another. One doorknob was too soft and turned to putty in her hand, the next was burning hot.

Finally, she came to the room across the hall. The one the unseen person had disappeared into only moments ago. She put her hand on the knob. All her nerve endings were jangling. Her body thrummed with the desire to flee. She ignored it. Maybe the person inside could give her answers, tell her where she was. Tell her how to get out of the hallway. Willow turned the knob, heard the click of the tongue pull back, and pushed.

6.5.5

"WILLOW."

She jerked awake, her heart thudding. Cookie stood in the doorway, a mug in his hand. "Willow, you okay?"

She placed one hand across her eyes, the other on her chest, and struggled to bring herself into the waking world. It had been a dream. A terrible dream.

Cookie strode toward her, set the mug on the bedside table, and squatted so his face was level with hers. The scents of vanilla and coffee came with him. "Willow, should I call someone? Do you need a doctor?"

Her gaze snapped to meet his. "No. No, I'm okay. I had a nightmare, that's all."

The lines of his face relaxed. "My ex had terrible nightmares when she was pregnant. She dreamed she gave birth to all kinds of things: a litter of puppies, a full-grown man, an alien. The last was after we watched *Mars Attacks!*" Cookie straightened with a grunt. "My knees don't work like that anymore."

Willow propped herself onto an elbow, felt a wave of dizziness and waited for it to pass. "I didn't know you had kids."

"I don't. Marlie miscarried. Three times."

The sadness in his voice acted like caffeine to Willow's system, bringing her out of her stupor and landing her solidly in reality. She sat up. "I'm so sorry."

Cookie gave a quick shake of his head. "Long time ago. How about some chicken soup?"

"Fixes everything, right?"

"Pretty much."

"You are just like my mom."

"I need to meet this woman."

"I'm a little afraid to introduce you." He tipped his massive head to one side, reminding her of an inquisitive Newfoundland. "I think you'll gang up on me."

Cookie laughed his wonderful basso profundo laugh and chased the remaining demons from the room. "I'm going to like her." He patted Willow's shoulder. "I'll bring up the soup."

"No." Willow barked the word.

Cookie stopped, eyes widening in surprise.

"I'm coming down."

"But, Jonathan said—"

"I don't care what Jonathan said. I have to get out of this room." Cookie may have sent the demons away, but she wasn't confident they wouldn't return when he was gone. "I'll be down in a minute."

Cookie's face creased with concern, but he left without argument. She rousted herself and walked to the bathroom. The stiffness in her joints seemed to have lessened, which was a positive sign. Maybe the nap did her good despite the awful dream.

Willow splashed cold water on her face, combed her hair and felt more like herself. She glanced at her phone on the bedside table as she crossed the room. It was fully charged. She'd call her mother right after she had a bowl of Cookie's soup.

When she reached the door, she hesitated. An echo of the dream's anxiety hummed inside her. "Stupid," she said aloud, opened the door, and walked into a brightly lit, cleanly painted hall.

Whether it was the chicken soup or the company, Willow was renewed. She sat at the counter with an empty bowl in front of her, watching Cookie prep dinner. "I'm coming downstairs to eat tonight. I don't care what Jonathan says," she said.

"I don't mind fixing up a tray for you," Cookie said.

"What's the difference? I can sit on the couch with my feet up."

Cookie pulled a knife from the block and began slicing potatoes. "I think it's the walking up and down that's the problem."

Willow waved her spoon in the air. "Maybe I should post up on the couch and stay there. At least I could look out the window, open the French doors, and get a breeze."

Cookie chopped faster.

"Don't you think?"

"Oh, no. I'm not getting in the middle of this. It's between you and Johnny."

Willow slid off the stool. Jonathan would be home soon, and she didn't want to get into another argument with him. At least, not right away. She'd save that for dinner time. "I guess I'll go up, but I am coming down later so don't make a tray."

Cookie pursed his lips as if attempting to stop a grin from stretching across his face.

As soon as Willow reached the top of the stairs, her nightmare rushed down the hall toward her. It had been so real she had to touch the walls to convince herself they weren't damp and moldering. The vividness of the dream made it seem profound, or prophetic. Like something or someone—her subconscious or God—was trying to get through to her. But what had it meant?

She leaned against the door frame of her bedroom, crossed her arms and stared at the corridor. It was quiet, peaceful, perfectly lovely, yet she felt her pulse accelerate. Why? Her gaze traveled to the room across the hall, where she'd seen the door open and close, where the giggle had come from. Her pulse traveled to her throat and picked up speed.

This was ridiculous. She couldn't be afraid of her own house. Like it or not, this was her house now. That thought made her heart race as well.

She unfolded her arms, crossed the hall, and threw open the door in one swift movement. She stopped on the threshold, mouth open in surprise. There was nothing in the least sinister about the space before her.

The layout of the room was a mirror image of the one she and Jonathan slept in, but that was where the similarity ended. Her room had been decorated with a professional eye. This was a hodgepodge of things, most of them from the 1990s.

The walls were a terrible shade of blue. The bed, a full not a queen like the one in her room, had been hastily covered with a plaid spread. The pillows were bunched into a pile, as if someone had slept alone in the center.

She stepped inside and turned in a circle, taking in the details and allowing them to click into logical placement in her mind. This was a boy's room, not a man's, not a female's. The colors were masculine. There were sports trophies—statues of little silver males running with a ball—shoved onto one corner of a bookcase.

She walked to the shelves and perused the reading material above and below the trophies. She saw a stack of *Alfred Hitchcock's Mystery Magazine*, *Moby Dick*, the complete *Lord of the Rings* series, the *Dune* series, and other novels she didn't recognize. She picked up an ancient, dog-eared copy of *The Hobbit*. Funny. She hadn't thought of that book in years, and it was brought to her attention twice in as many days. She tucked the book under her arm, needing something to pass the time. It would be fun to read it again, especially the dragon scenes.

The boy who'd lived in this room must not be a boy any longer. The hodgepodge of hastily tacked up posters were from another decade: *Galaxy Quest, Jumanji,* and the band Nirvana. Jonathan had loved Nirvana. Jonathan had played soccer. This had to have been his room. Dunfrey had implied the room they slept in now was Jonathan's old room, hadn't she? Maybe she hadn't. Maybe Willow had just assumed it was.

She padded across the thick carpet to the closet lining one wall and slid the door to the side. It was packed. She pushed aside a shirt to look at it. Jonathan wore it on the weekends sometimes. She shoved it out of the way and looked at the one behind it—a familiar flannel.

The closet was filled with shirts in various sizes and styles, some still worn, some obviously not worn for years. Did Jonathan keep everything? She had no idea he was such a pack rat.

She walked to the door that should lead to the bathroom, based on her own room, and opened it. She was correct, but again the similarities ended at the layout. This bathroom had the same nineties decor as the room it was attached to.

The fixtures were gold plated, a look that went out of style fifteen years ago, at least. The wallpaper was a navy-blue stripe and the towels mauve and white, another dated look. Unlike the bathroom she and Jonathan shared, this room had another door at its far end.

She passed by a double sink, stood in front of the door, and hesitated. Was she prying? Sticking her nose into her husband's business? He'd said this house was *theirs* now, not *his*. If so, didn't she have the right to walk into any room? *Yes.* That was the logical answer to the question, so why did she feel as if she were trespassing?

Willow clicked open the latch on the doorknob and pushed it open. She was so startled she had no reaction for a long moment, then a mix of emotions she couldn't sort out bubbled up inside her. The room's overall effect was that of a poorly cooked meal: too much of one thing, not enough of another, all coming together to leave a bad taste in her mouth.

It was a girl's version of the room behind her. Pink was the predominant color. The band poster displayed Backstreet Boys, the movie poster, *Titanic*. The books on the white bookshelf had a horse theme —*Black Beauty, Misty of Chincoteague*, and others. The closet was filled with cheerleader uniforms, prom dresses, and boyfriend jeans.

The major difference between the two rooms, aside from an obvious nod to the sexes, was this one hadn't been occupied for ages. A thick layer of dust coated every surface, and the bed, with its bright pink spread and floral pillows, was perfectly made.

Willow backed out of the pink space, the Jack and Jill bathroom, and Jonathan's room swiftly. She crossed the corridor in two quick strides, pushed into her own room, and blinked several times at the late afternoon sunlight pouring through the open window. She felt like a time traveler returning to her own century. What she'd seen didn't fit her paradigm.

The rooms were shrines. Why? The twins were healthy adults. They hadn't died in a terrible accident, leaving behind grieving parents who couldn't bear to part with their things.

Willow's old bedroom in her parents' home had been decorated and redecorated more times than she could count. Today it was a guest room. The only thing left from Willow's tenancy was the dresser, an old tallboy Honey had inherited from an aunt.

She sank onto the chair at the vanity and dropped *The Hobbit* next to her hairbrush. Maybe if she'd grown up in a house as big as Sunset House, she wouldn't feel the need to clear it out regularly. She'd be happy to move from one room to the next as she outgrew them.

No matter how she tried to justify the bedrooms, they felt strange and unhealthy. They reminded her of the Mad Hatter's tea in *Alice in Wonderland* where time stood still, so there was no time to wash the dishes. Consequently, the characters moved around the table from place to place leaving their dirty dishes behind rather than cleaning up and starting fresh.

Her gaze dropped onto her phone, still sitting on the bedside table. She needed to talk to her mother. Honey was nothing if not practical and sane. She'd help Willow sort this new information. She snatched up the phone and made the call.

6.5.6

"**WHY DON'T** you come home for a couple of days?" Honey said after Willow filled her in on the accident, her nightmare, and the *pièce de résistance*, the rooms across the hall.

The suggestion evoked such a sense of longing, Willow immediately began to erect a wall of resistance against it. Her shoulders stiffened. "Mom, I'm a grown woman—"

"Of course you are, sweetheart. But you've also been through a lot in the past few weeks, and you're pregnant. The doctor said you should be resting. Why not rest here where you'll have company? Let me take care of my baby while you take care of yours?"

Honey's logic chipped away at Willow's willpower. "Jonathan is busy," Honey continued. "It sounds like his sister isn't there much, and you two aren't close anyway. Why should you stay alone in that big house all day long when you could be with us?"

"I'm not alone. Cookie is here." Willow's argument was half-hearted at best. She was weakening.

"And I'm sure he's a lovely man, but he's not your mother." Which was true, Willow had to admit. "I can come get you as soon as I close up the shop," Honey said.

"Maybe in the morning instead? Jonathan will be home soon. I can spend the evening with him and pack a few things."

There was silence for a beat, then Honey said, "Works for me. I'll be to you by 9:00. That good?" Her tone had gone from cajoling to businesslike. She'd won but was mature enough not to do a victory dance.

Willow nodded, then realizing Honey couldn't see her said, "Yeah. We can have breakfast with Cookie. I want you to meet him. You guys have a lot in common."

When they hung up, Willow felt a surge of relief followed quickly by guilt. She shouldn't be so happy about leaving Jonathan, but it wasn't Jonathan she was happy about leaving. It was this place, this house. It seemed to hover over her, over all of them, like a raven greedy for baubles. It snapped up the shiny bits of her life and buried them where she couldn't reach.

She couldn't enjoy her new marriage, her growing pregnancy, the Olympic-sized pool, Hamish's violin, or the volumes in the library. She couldn't enjoy having the freedom to work or not to work. These wonderful things were like the beach below Sunset House, visible but inaccessible.

Jonathan's tread on the stairs brought her out of her musings. She painted a smile on her face and prepared herself to deliver the news. She was going to stay with her parents for a few days. She didn't think he'd like it, but he'd understand. She was lonely here.

Instead of turning into their room, Willow heard his footfalls stop, then the door across the hall open and close. Her palms began to sweat. Would he be able to tell she'd been inside? She stood and wiped her hands on her skirt.

She should go after him, ask him about the rooms, just walk in and crack a casual joke. She tried to think of one, a jab at having a shrine in his and Chloe's honor. Nothing that came to mind was even remotely funny.

A lighthearted ribbing, that's how normal wives with normal husbands would react to finding the bedrooms across the hall, but she and Jonathan weren't normal. At least, they hadn't been married long enough to establish what normal was. She could only look at her parents' marriage as an example. Their lives were so different than the one she'd been thrust into, it wasn't much of a comparison.

Some things were universal though. Weren't they? She was Jonathan's wife. This was *their* home. Nobody had said certain rooms were off limits to her. Nobody had said she shouldn't go wherever she pleased. Jonathan hadn't asked for a prenuptial agreement. They'd said the traditional in-richer-or-poorer-and-death-do-us-part vows.

So why did she feel like an interloper in her own house?

She inhaled, then blew the air through her lips. This was her problem, not Jonathan's. She was intimidated by the family wealth and by the sheer size of the house. He'd never done anything to make her feel that way. She'd done it all by herself.

Willow stood. She would go across the hall, greet her husband, and tease him about the bedrooms. Something would come to her. Before she took a step, the door slammed inward and bounced off the wall. Jonathan—face mottled with suppressed emotion—stood on the threshold.

Willow's smile of greeting faded. "What's wrong?" Lord, don't let it be another tragedy. She didn't think she could handle another tragedy.

"Why did you go into my room?"

Willow was so relieved this was the problem, she almost laughed. "I —" she began, but Jonathan interrupted her.

"This house isn't big enough for you?" He waved his arms in large, expansive gestures. "You have to invade my private space?"

He was overreacting. She modulated her voice to calm him. "The house is—"

He cut her off again. "I don't know how it was when you were growing up, but we were taught to respect peoples' personal property."

Defensiveness rose up inside her. He did believe his pedigree was better than hers. He'd as much as said it. "I've always been respectful of other people's things."

Jonathan strode across the room to the vanity and snatched up the paperback she'd taken from his room. "Oh, yeah?" He wagged the book at her. "What about this?"

A low laugh escaped from Willow's lips. "Really? An old paperback? I was only borrowing it."

His voice lowered in volume and timbre. "You didn't ask."

Willow's grew louder. "I didn't think I needed to ask."

Jonathan stared at her, his expression unreadable.

"I assumed you wouldn't mind," she said.

His eyes, filled with disbelief and accusation, bored into her.

"You weren't reading it." Her voice and bravado slipped a notch. It was wrong to borrow a book from someone without asking. She knew that, but these were extenuating circumstances. The someone in question was her husband, and it was obvious he hadn't looked at that book in years.

He turned on his heel and left the room, *The Hobbit* clutched in his hand. Willow didn't move for a beat, then bolted toward the closet. She wrestled her suitcase off the upper shelf, despite the pain in her rib cage, and threw it on the spread. Then she began wrenching clothes from hangers and tossing them into it.

"What are you doing?" She hadn't heard Jonathan return. He leaned against the door jamb, arms folded over his chest.

Willow yanked open a dresser drawer and grabbed a handful of lingerie. "I'm going to visit my parents for a few days." She jammed her underwear into the bag.

"You don't need to do that." His tone was calm and measured now, no trace of the rage of only minutes ago.

"I talked to my mother before you got home. She thought... " Willow paused. "She and I both thought I should stay with them until we know if everything with the baby is okay."

"Why would you do that?"

She spun to face him. "How can you ask me that after everything that's happened? This place scares me. It killed your mother. It killed Dunfrey. It tried to kill me yesterday."

His laugh was mocking. "Really, Willow. The house killed Mom and Dun? And how would it manage to pick up off its foundations and drive down to San Diego to run you over? You're being irrational. The house is just a house."

His words made her feel foolish, but there was something about Sunset House she didn't trust. "You are a different person when you're here."

"I am who I've always been."

"Then I never knew you." She grabbed another handful of clothes from the dresser, stuffed them into her suitcase, and tried to close the lid.

A hand gripped her arm and pulled her away. Jonathan turned her so she faced him. "I'm sorry, babe. It has been a horrible time. I get it. We're both stressed, but we need each other now more than ever. I need you. Please, don't go to your parents."

Willow shook him off. "I don't belong here. You and Chloe have made that abundantly clear."

He took her by the shoulders and pulled her against his chest. "This is my house, not Chloe's. And you do belong here."

Tears pricked the inside of Willow's eyelids. "Then why can't I go in your old bedroom?"

She felt his muscles tighten around her. He spoke slowly. "I shouldn't have gotten angry with you. I guess it's a hangover from when I was a kid. My mom and dad had a very open-door policy. We always had relatives and friends living with us. There were staff around all the time, and they had keys to everything. I became protective of my privacy because I didn't have much of it."

Willow's anger began to drain away. It made sense. She'd only had to contend with Ash, her parents, and the occasional visit from a Kentucky relative. She couldn't imagine what it must have been like to live with a house constantly full of people. "You can't talk to me like that," she mumbled into his shirt. "You can't yell at me and question my upbringing."

He pressed his cheek into her hair. "I know. It was wrong. Can you forgive me?"

"Yes, but I'm still going to my parents tomorrow."

He stepped out of their embrace, a question clouding the clear ocean-blue of his eyes.

"There's nobody here to keep me company," she said. "I can lay around on their couch, and my mother will wait on me hand and foot."

"I'll miss you."

"It'll only be for a few days."

He opened his mouth but shut it again. A moment later, he said, "Can I bring you up a tray?"

"No. I'm coming down for dinner. I already told Cookie."

Jonathan's eyes narrowed, but he must have been tired of arguing. He gave her a weak smile. "See you down there."

Willow listened to his footfalls fade as he descended the stairs, turned to her suitcase and began pulling things out. She'd repack more neatly before dinner.

MOLLY: So, who is after Willow? Or was it just a random drunk driver like Jonathan thought? Speaking of Jonathan, we certainly saw another side of him today. Do you buy the childhood lack of privacy excuse? I personally think keeping his and Chloe's rooms exactly the way they were when they were kids is strange.

There was a lot going on today. The sense of danger is mounting, but where is it coming from? The house itself? Willow's statements about the manor were reminiscent of Gwen's feeling about the house in Season One. Her dream also mirrored the basement in *The Cliff House*, from the seven doors to the dim yellow lights, moldy walls and shushing of water somewhere outside.

The episode raised so many questions, it's difficult for me to settle on just one to tackle on Facebook. How about we do something different? How about you all post your biggest question? It's a free-for-all this week—but no spoilers and no name calling. Keep it civil, people.

And join me next time for more *Murders Under the Sun*.

(cue music)

VO: If you enjoyed this episode, please leave us a five-star review on your favorite podcast service—it really helps. *Murders Under the Sun* is edited by Jim Wilbourne, theme music is by Eclectic Blends, and I'm your host, Molly Shure.

part seven

MURDERS UNDER THE SUN
   SEASON SIX; EPISODE SIX

MOLLY: Welcome back to *Murders Under the Sun*. I'm Molly Shure, your host.

Before we get into your stellar discussion on Facebook, I have news. The Dean of the Drama department from CS-Fullerton got back to me with the link to Raphael's award-winning film. I watched it yesterday.

Wow. That's all I can say. It was amazing.

The plot was a twist on *The Picture of Dorian Gray*, as I mentioned a couple of weeks ago. Instead of a painting, the protagonist—a very hot surfer—finds part of a ship's figurehead in the ocean. Its head, to be precise.

It was covered with barnacles and dried seaweed. As he cleans it, a face emerges. As kind of a twist on the picture in Oscar Wilde's book, the more beautiful the face becomes, the more disfigured his becomes. I won't tell you the punchline, in case you get the chance to view it. It's called *The Disfigured Head*.

Anyway, I got to watch Ariana Blackstone in action. She played the surfer's girlfriend, and she was excellent. Strangely enough, there was another girl in the film, just a walk-on part. She played Ariana's sister. I wondered where they found her. It was startling how much they looked alike. I thought they might actually be sisters, but when I looked into it I found out Ariana was an only child.

I don't think the film gave me any more infor-mation about the mystery than I had before. However, I did feel like I knew Raphael and

Ariana better after I'd watched it. It will be more difficult than ever if we don't get any traction on their case. I'm starting to care just a little too much.

But back to *The Manor*. The Facebook discussion was a free-for-all, as I'd suggested it should be. It was fascinating to see the rabbit trails you all took. For instance, the comments about Jonathan and Chloe's bedrooms became a trip down memory lane. Apparently, decor in teen rooms in the 90s transcended economic boundaries. And, yes, I had a Backstreet Boys poster, too.

You were pretty divided in your sympathies for Jonathan. Some were screaming at Willow to leave him. Others thought he'd been through a lot and was cracking under the strain.

Finally, there was a long thread about Willow's bedroom door that keeps locking. It does seem too coincidental to be a coincidence that the journal girl was also locked in a very nice bedroom with expensive furnishings and second story window looking onto the grounds.

Maybe we'll find out more about that in today's episode. Let's get back to Willow.

Jonathan's side of the bed was empty when Willow opened her eyes the next morning. He'd been so warm and affectionate during dinner the night before—probably to make up for the fuss he'd made over the book—that she'd thought they would make love when they went to bed. He hadn't reached for her. He'd stayed as still as a guard at Buckingham Palace. It had hurt her feelings, but she'd told herself it was because he was worried about the baby.

Willow rolled onto her back and stretched luxuriously in the empty bed. When she got a clean bill of health for herself and The Peach, she'd instigate make-up sex. Funerals and hit-and-runs had a way of taking the romance right out of a relationship. In fact, she'd call her own doctor and make an appointment today.

Today.

Her head pivoted toward the clock on the bedside table. It was 8:00. She'd overslept. Her mother would be there by 9:00. Willow shot out of bed, wincing slightly at the dwindling pain in her side, and hurried to the bathroom. She showered and dressed quickly, threw her sleep shirt into the suitcase along with her cosmetic bag and zipped it.

She hefted the suitcase from the chair. It was heavier than she'd expected it to be, but it had wheels. Jonathan would have told her to call one of the staff to carry it for her, but the thought made her squirm. She had no idea who any of the staff were except for Cookie, Mike the maintenance man, Anthony—who only came for dinner parties—and one cleaning woman whose name started with a vowel. Next week, she'd learn everyone's names, who did what, and when they were there. This week she was going home.

Correction. She was going to her parents'. Sunset House was home. After a good night's sleep, that didn't seem as daunting.

Willow slung her purse over her arm, pulled out the handle of her suitcase and rolled it toward the bedroom door. She stopped by the bedside table to retrieve her phone, which should have been on its charger next to the clock. It wasn't.

She patted the covers and flipped over her pillow. She often listened to audiobooks on her phone before nodding off, so maybe she'd fallen asleep listening. It wasn't under the pillow. She threw the blankets back. No phone. She dropped onto her knees, a painful experience, and peered under the bed. Nothing.

Willow pivoted, sat on the floor, and gazed around the room. It seemed she was constantly losing things these days. Was it a symptom of pregnancy? Her mother said she'd locked her keys in the car four or five times in the two months after she'd had Willow. Honey swore babies sucked up half their mother's brain cells.

Speaking of missing brain cells, Willow couldn't remember if she listened to her audiobook last night or not. She'd been so tired when she'd come upstairs, and she was distracted by the idea that she and Jonathan would amuse each other. Had she left her phone in the living room? Now that Gerry was gone, Willow brought her phone with her to meals.

Using the bed for support, she pushed onto her feet. She'd run downstairs and look. She crossed the bedroom and grabbed the doorknob.

"Oh, come on," Willow said aloud. "I can't believe it." It was locked. She shook and rattled, but the knob wouldn't turn.

At least she had her purse this time. She'd open the door with a credit card, then tell Jonathan she was staying at her parents' house until the lock mechanism was replaced. She lifted her purse from the floor by the bed and felt around inside for her wallet. The familiar shape didn't come to hand. Frustration crawled over her like ants. Why did these things always happen when she was running late?

She dumped the contents of her purse onto the bed. Her makeup bag, two protein bars, five hair clips, a no-tangle hair band, a phone charging cable, a box of rosin for her violin bow, and a mangled grocery list fell onto the blankets. Where the hell was her wallet?

Willow crossed to the door again, kicked it and yelled. Immature and stupid behavior, she knew, but she'd had it with this house.

Nobody came.

She made a fist, banged on the door with the full force of her arm muscles, and yelled. "Hey, will somebody let me out of here. I'm stuck. Again!"

After several minutes of banging and screaming, there was still no response. Willow turned her back to the door and gazed around the stifling room. Her laptop. She could call Jonathan on that if he had his phone on him.

She dropped to her knees, dragged her tote bag out from under the vanity, and stared inside it in disbelief. No laptop. Something struck her then that ought to have struck her right away. Why were both her phone and her wallet missing? One or the other, that could be chalked up to pregnancy ditziness, but both? And now her laptop? Not likely.

A chill breeze seemed to enter the room. She wrapped her arms around herself. Had someone locked her in here on purpose? Had that someone also taken her phone and her wallet so she wouldn't be able to get out or get help?

The only person she'd told about her lock-picking skill was Jonathan. He was also the only other person who'd been in this room for days. But why? Why would Jonathan do this to her?

His face, red and mottled as he waved the paperback at her the night before, played on the screen of her mind. She shivered. The room's chill seeped into her bones.

Was it because she'd taken his book? Was this petty revenge, or a prank? She shook her head and hugged herself tighter. It had to be just a strange confluence of events. The door locked every few days. She was forgetful and scatterbrained. Nothing devious or dastardly was happening here.

She checked the clock. It was five minutes before 9:00. Her mother should be there any minute. When she arrived, someone would come looking for Willow. Everything would be fine.

She sat on the vanity bench, hands folded in her lap like a schoolgirl waiting for lessons to start. Minutes ticked by. Then tens of minutes. Then an hour.

At 10:00, she jumped from the bench and strode to the door. She thumped and yelled, but her heart wasn't in it. Her mother hadn't come. The only thing Willow could think of that would keep her away was if she was told not to come.

It had to have been Jonathan. Willow threw protective arms over her abdomen as if The Peach shared in her grief and confusion.

She wandered to the window and pulled aside the heavy curtains, tears creating a veil of moisture in her eyes that was difficult to see past. Between that and the morning fog curling outside the panes, she could only make out patches of the blue pool. The cold vista echoed the temperature of her heart. She shuddered again.

The belief that Jonathan had locked the bedroom door had opened a different door in her mind. In this closet were all the questionable things that had happened recently, things she'd been doing her best to deny, to stuff into the dark, to ignore.

Jonathan had known the pool was electrified. She couldn't escape that fact or the others that were piling up. He'd blamed Dun for his mother's death. He hadn't wanted to give her a retirement allowance. He'd stopped Willow from jumping into the water, but he hadn't stopped Dun.

Was he planning to get rid of Willow now, too? The idea seemed overly dramatic, but locking her in their room was a dramatic action.

Footsteps.

Grief gave way to fear. Willow ran to the door with new energy. "Help. I need help," she called.

"Got it." Jonathan's voice resonated through the wood.

She scuttled as far from the door as she could and pressed herself into the corner between the window and the wall. The lock clicked. The door opened.

Jonathan stood in the room's entrance with a loaded tray and a wide smile. "Here's breakfast sleepyhead."

Willow gaped at him, at a loss for words.

"Oh, look at you. All dressed. You shouldn't have bothered. I talked to your mom earlier, and we decided it would be best for you to stay here." He set the tray on the vanity table. "Cookie made you a poached egg and toast points. Very Brih-ish, innit?" He laughed at his poor English accent. "Come and eat before it's cold."

Willow didn't move.

Jonathan faced her, placed his fists on his hips and tipped his head to one side. It was a comedic gesture, the expression on his face exaggerated disbelief. "You want to hurt Cookie's feelings? Because he'll be hurt if I take this food back, untouched."

Silence stretched between them for several long moments. Finally, Willow broke it. "Why did you take my phone?"

Jonathan's head tilted from his right shoulder to his left. "I told you, I had to call your mother. I erased her number from my phone by accident, so I borrowed yours." His eyes narrowed and a sly smile played across his lips. "You don't mind people borrowing your things without asking, do you? I wouldn't have taken it if I thought you'd mind, but after our conversation last night... "

The fear that had held her muscles in a state of tension released. Her shoulders slumped; her knees softened. She took a step towards him. "Is that what this is about? You're punishing me for taking an old, dog-eared copy of *The Hobbit* out of your shrine?"

"My shrine?" The humor left his voice.

"That's what it is, isn't it?" Willow took another step. "I've heard about parents doing that kind of thing when a child dies, leaving their room exactly as it had been, never getting rid of their old things. But you and Chloe aren't dead."

"No, we're not." His voice was icy. "Which is why we like our private spaces."

"I get wanting privacy. If you had a man cave, a den, an office, any of those things, I'd understand. But that," she waved a hand toward the open door. "That is just weird."

Jonathan's face hardened and for a moment she thought she'd gone too far, said too much. She backed toward her corner and clenched her fists. He spun on his heel and walked out the door. "Eat your breakfast." He clicked the lock into place.

6.6.2

THE EGGS CONGEALED on the plate. Willow could see Cookie's artistry in the arrangement of pale yellow in the center of the blue floral china, toast triangles jutting from its sides like the rays of a wobbly sun, but she couldn't eat.

She should. It was important for The Peach's growth that she get enough protein. She picked up a fork and poked at the plate. Her stomach lurched. How had her carefully planned life gone so terribly wrong? How had she missed the signs that were so clear now?

Jonathan was polished and charming, but he had been pushy, urging her into things before she was ready. Into bed, into an engagement, into marriage, into living at Sunset House. The trap had been baited by a handsome prince, complete with kingdom, and she'd stepped right into it. He'd gone hunting, bagged the bride, and brought her home.

When she got out of this room—because that was going to happen—she would also find a way out of the marriage. She would be no man's acquisition.

The idea that she should leave Jonathan had been whispering in her mind since Gerry died, but she'd closed her ears to it.

She'd credited his mood fluctuations at his mother's death to the family's tendency to emotional control, but it had bothered her. She hadn't allowed herself to acknowledge how appalled she'd been at his treatment of Dun.

Now that she'd allowed these thoughts access, the knots in her gut began to ease. Her hands unclenched, a tired peace trickling through her veins. Grief would return at a future date, she knew that, but today the confidence that comes with doing the right thing strengthened her.

She stabbed the fork into an egg. Its golden yolk spilled onto the plate. Swallowing a gag, she scooped up a bite and ate. She would need her strength in order to play the part she had to play.

Jonathan returned about ten minutes after she had cleaned her plate. He shut the door behind him and tossed something onto the bed. "Cookie's poached eggs are always perfect," he said and began gathering her breakfast things.

Willow bowed her head in what she hoped was a humble gesture. "Jonathan," she said.

"Yes?"

"I owe you an apology."

He stopped moving.

"I shouldn't have taken your book, or made fun of your room. We all deserve a place of our own. Why is a den any better than a room full of memories?"

He gazed at her, a cautious hopefulness in his eyes. Encouraged, she continued.

"There was a practice room at school I always thought of as *my* practice room. Which was funny, because they were all the same. All eight by eight, all with soundproof walls and doors, all with upright pianos against one wall and two stools to sit on. But I liked room nine. No reason. I just did. If I got there late and someone else had already nabbed nine, I would get angry at them. It wasn't their fault. They didn't know it was my room, but I got angry anyway."

Jonathan nudged Willow to the side of the vanity bench and sat next to her. "I'm glad you understand, although I don't think the analogy is perfect."

"No?"

"No. The practice room wasn't really yours, but my room is mine."

How had she not noticed what a pompous prig her husband was?

She swallowed the bitterness rising in her throat and placed her hand on top of his. "I just want you to know I get it."

"Thanks for trying." He threw an arm around her shoulders and pulled her close.

Willow suppressed the desire to jerk away.

"I'm sorry, too. I shouldn't have gotten so angry. I'm adjusting to the whole husband thing, you know?"

"I'm adjusting to the wife thing." She gave a small laugh.

"So, we're okay?" he asked.

Willow closed her eyes so he couldn't read the deception in them. "We're okay."

"Great." Jonathan stood and picked up the tray in one swift motion, then began to move toward the door.

"Ah," Willow stopped him. "Where's my phone?"

He turned toward her slowly. "Your phone?"

"Yeah."

"It's downstairs. I'll bring it up after you have a nap."

"I'm not sleepy."

"Well, lie down then. Put your feet up. You can have your phone after you rest."

"Jonathan." Willow heard the tension in her own voice and cleared her throat. She tried again. "Jonathan, I really need to call my mom and let her know I'm okay. I won't be able to relax until I talk to her."

A muscle in his cheek twitched. "I told her you were fine."

Willow forced a light tone. "You know Mom, she'll worry if she doesn't hear it straight from the horse's mouth."

He turned to the door again. "She's okay."

Willow stood and followed him. "I wanted to call my doctor, too. Make an appointment."

He tensed. "Why? Is something wrong with the baby?"

"No," she said hastily. "I'm sure he's fine, but I'd like to get the big thumbs up from Dr. Graham."

"You're not cramping? Spotting?"

"No. Nothing like that."

Willow watched his shoulders visibly relax. "We can make an

appointment tomorrow. I can't go today anyway. I have a meeting in Newport this afternoon."

An alarm sounded in her brain. *He* couldn't go today? Why did that matter? He'd never gone to the doctor with her before. "I can go by myself."

"Tomorrow makes more sense." He gave her a tight smile and scooted out the door. The lock clicked into place before she reached it.

Willow's hand flew to her mouth to stifle a scream. What was happening? What did he hope to gain by shutting her up in this room for the day? Was he punishing her? Proving his dominance? She'd had friends with controlling, abusive boyfriends but they'd never been imprisoned. Not physically anyway.

She gripped her hair. Could it be that he really was concerned about The Peach? Worried she wasn't resting enough? Mentioning Dr. Graham was the only thing that had shaken Jonathan's cool.

If so, his plan had backfired. She couldn't rest now if you paid her. Anxiety thrummed through her vibrating her bones. She paced the room, one hand on her head, the other protecting The Peach.

She reached the window, pivoted, and stared at the closed door. He'd told her he would inherit Sunset House if he became a father before Chloe became a mother. It couldn't be...

She began pacing again. He loved her. She was sure of that. He'd told her he would've proposed even if she hadn't gotten pregnant.

She stopped and laughed aloud.

Did she honestly believe a word the man said? *Fool me once, shame on you. Fool me twice, shame on me.* Wasn't that how the expression went?

Jonathan had revealed himself. The man who had proposed to her was the same man who'd had a fit because she'd borrowed a book. The same man who'd locked her in this bedroom. The same man she now suspected of allowing a woman to be electrocuted. Jonathan was unstable and unpredictable.

Willow paused at the window. The sun was burning off the morning fog. He couldn't keep her locked up forever. The staff wandered the hallways. Cookie would wonder how she was and why she wasn't coming downstairs. Her mother would want to talk to her eventually. Even Chloe would ask about her. Jonathan had to know that as soon as she was alone in an exam room with Dr. Graham, she would tell the physician what was happening.

No, she wouldn't be here forever, but there were hours stretching ahead of her now. Willow threw herself on the bed, and her hand struck something hard. The thing Jonathan had tossed onto the covers was a book.

She picked it up, turned it over, and barked a laugh. It was a new hardback copy of *The Hobbit*. She'd lost all interest in reading it, but there was something else she should read. Something that might help her understand what was happening and how to escape from it.

She bounded off the bed, crossed the room in two long strides and dropped to her knees, anxiety acting like an analgesic. She felt underneath the vanity, found her tote bag and brought it to the bed. She'd finish reading the journal.

Willow needed to know who the monster of the story was, although she was afraid she already did. Yesterday she would never have believed Jonathan could lure a girl into jellyfish infested waters, or slice her arms with a razor while she slept, or allow her to be restrained as a mental patient. But that was yesterday.

They gave me soup for lunch every Tuesday. Tomato. I'll never forget the white bowl filled with red liquid the consistency of... Well, never mind that.

On this particular Tuesday, there must have been a new cook in the kitchen because there was no grilled cheese sandwich. I always got a grilled cheese sandwich with my soup, but that day there were crackers and cheese on the tray. Crackers and cheese and a butter knife to cut the cheese with.

I stared at the knife in a state of stupefaction, but only for a second. I corralled my excitement quickly, tore my eyes from the gleaming stainless steel, and forced myself to act nonchalant.

The girl who brought the tray never noticed. She chatted with me as she placed the food on my lap, adjusted the curtains and asked if there was anything else I needed. I assured her I was fine and willed her to leave. It was such a strain not to pocket the knife as soon as I laid eyes on it. I waited a full three minutes after she left just in case she returned unexpectedly, then took the knife from the tray.

I'd noticed a loose piece of moulding in the closet when I'd put away my shoes one day. At the time, I couldn't think how this flaw in an otherwise pristine room would come in handy. Now I knew.

I pulled the board away from the wall, lay the knife down, then pressed the board into place again. It wasn't a perfect fit, but I didn't think anyone would notice.

I ate quickly, put the tray on the dresser, and threw the napkin casually over it. Then I lay down, pulled a blanket on top of myself and closed my eyes.

When the girl returned, I feigned sleep. I don't think she noticed the missing knife. If she did, she decided not to wake me to ask about it. She took the tray and closed the door quietly behind her.

The next few hours were some of the most stressful of my life. Every time I heard a footfall in the hallway outside my door, I was sure it was someone coming for the knife. No one did.

My dinner tray came and went as usual, no knife there. I tried to read until 10:00, my normal bedtime, then turned out the lights.

At midnight, the downstairs lights went out, and the garden below my room darkened. I waited another endless hour to be sure everyone was in bed. At 1:00, I retrieved my knife from its hiding place and took it to the door. Ten minutes of fiddling later, I heard the bolt slide out of place and my door swung open.

In the end, it was my father who believed my story. I told him everything: about the dinner table, the day at the beach, the monster's threats, everything. He'd been away for the month I'd spent in the room and had no idea how I'd been treated. It took some convincing, but I finally succeeded.

I still see Dr. P. She's trying to help me come to grips with what happened. Trying to help me forgive everyone involved. Forgiveness is important. That's what she says. I believe her, but I think justice is even more important.

The monster, Orthrus, Smaug, whatever its name, worries so much about wealth, but wealth is replaceable. Each of the thirty-two days I spent in that room felt like a year. Time is a limited commodity. No one can return that time to me. Justice requires I find a plan to take what is most precious to the monster.

6.6.3

A KNOCK JERKED Willow from her reading. It took her a moment to return to reality. "Yes," she called when she did.

"You decent?" Jonathan didn't wait for her to answer but opened the door. "I brought Mat to check on you."

Willow slid the journal under her pillow and sat up. "I'm fine."

"I'd feel better if he looked you over," Jonathan moved aside and let Mat into the room.

Mat's shoulders slumped, and he gave her an apologetic grin as if he felt as uncomfortable with the arrangement as she did. "Maybe Willow should wait and see her own doctor."

"I should," Willow said. "No offense, Mat, but you're not an OB. I'd rather see Dr. Graham."

"And you will see Dr. Graham, but you know doctors. If you call for an appointment today, it'll be a week before they can get you in. We have our own medical professional in the family—well, almost in the family—we might as well take advantage of him." Jonathan slapped a hand on Mat's back.

Mat squared his shoulders, stepped closer to Willow and looked into her eyes. "Any dizziness? Fatigue?"

"No." Willow slid the word through tight lips.

"How about pain? Muscle aches? Back?"

"I'm still a little sore, but that's to be expected."

"Right. Do you mind lying down?"

She gazed at him with alarm.

Mat smiled. "No pelvic, don't worry. I just want to take a peek at your abdomen."

She reclined slowly, irritation in every inch of submission. She didn't want to cooperate, didn't want to cave in to Jonathan's demands, but perhaps Mat could become an ally. If she could only speak to him alone.

Mat lifted her shirt and palpated her stomach. "Pain?"

"No," she said.

"You've got some pretty colorful bruises," he said.

"Thanks." She tried to relax under his prodding fingers.

Jonathan stood in the corner of the room, arms crossed over his chest. "Is the baby okay?"

That's all he wanted to know. He didn't care about her. How had she ever believed he had?

"I can't be sure without an ultrasound." Mat pulled Willow's shirt over her stomach again. "What did they say in the hospital?"

Willow sat up. "They said the baby was fine."

"And no spotting since?"

She shook her head.

"Then I think you're fine. I'd make an appointment. I'm sure your own doctor would like to see you after everything that's happened, but it doesn't seem like an emergency," Mat said.

"Great." Willow shot a tight smile at Jonathan. "Would you get my phone? I'll call now."

"I'll get it when I walk Mat downstairs," Jonathan said.

Willow stood. "I'll go with you."

Jonathan stepped toward her. "No. You rest. I'll bring it up."

"Actually, I'm going stir crazy in here. I need some fresh air." She slipped her feet into the sandals she'd left near the bed.

"I think you should keep your feet up." His voice held a threat.

"That's not necessary." Mat turned his gaze on her. "I wouldn't run a marathon, but you can be up and around."

Willow gazed at Jonathan through innocent eyes. "You see?"

His jaw clenched, but he didn't argue.

The house seemed even larger after the time in her room. She followed Jonathan and Mat to the great room. Chloe sat by the cold fireplace, a magazine in her hand. She glanced up as they entered. Surprise lit her face. "Willow, what are you doing downstairs?"

Mat crossed to her and planted a kiss on her forehead. "I've pronounced her fit."

Chloe's forehead furrowed. "I thought she was in an accident?"

"She was, but she's tough. She's fine, apart from a few nasty bruises."

"The baby?"

Mat shrugged. "Fine, as far as I can tell."

"What a relief."

"But I did suggest she see her own physician," he said.

"And I will." Willow spun toward Jonathan. "As soon as I have my phone, I'll call for an appointment."

"Right. It's in my office." He left the room.

"*His* office?" Chloe's voice held disbelief. "That didn't take long."

Mat gave a slight shake of his head.

"That office was Mom's until two weeks ago," Chloe spat.

Willow's eyes snapped to Chloe's face. There was something in her tone, a veiled anger that started a cascade of questions in Willow's mind.

Had Willow been looking at this all wrong? She'd assumed that Chloe and Jonathan were close because they were twins. She knew they understood each other well—she'd seen that in their behavior toward one another, the way they often finished each other's sentences and seemed to know what the other was thinking. But understanding and affection were two different things. It struck her now that, sometimes, the better you knew a person, the less you liked them.

"He has a lot of family business to take care of," Mat said. "Why shouldn't he use the office?"

Chloe snapped her magazine shut and stood. "Mom's not even buried yet. It seems wrong."

They were very competitive as kids. Cookie's words echoed in her brain. Perhaps they still were. Perhaps Chloe was the girl from the diary.

If Jonathan were the monster—and Willow was fairly certain he was

—it would make sense. When they'd learned about the terms of the will, that the first of them to have a child would inherit the house, it could have triggered his anger.

Jonathan would have felt at a disadvantage. A woman can get pregnant more easily than a man can find a woman to carry his child, especially a woman as beautiful as Chloe. He might have wanted to take out the competition. Or at least punish her.

The journal had also said the only one to believe her side of the story was her father. Hadn't Chloe and her father had a very close relationship? Jonathan had said she was Hamish's favorite.

If Chloe was the diary girl, she would be an ally. Wouldn't she? Willow would explain that she didn't want any part in the inheritance. All she wanted was to be allowed to take The Peach and go. Chloe could have the house, the money, everything, if she'd only help Willow escape.

Willow shot a look over her shoulder. Jonathan hadn't returned yet. She lowered her voice. "Chloe."

Chloe looked at her.

"I need your help."

"I found your phone, but it's dead. No battery." Jonathan's voice boomed from the doorway. "Why don't you use the landline?"

"With what?" Chloe said in answer to her question.

Willow gave a small shake of her head. Chloe's eyes narrowed, but she didn't say anything else.

"Okay," Willow said. "But I'd like to take my phone upstairs and plug it in."

Jonathan appeared at her side and gripped her elbow. "I've already taken care of that. Let's go make that call."

Willow hesitated for a moment. She didn't want to go anywhere with him, but wondered if now was the time to expose him to Chloe and Mat. What if she was wrong about Chloe? What if Chloe and Mat were in on this with Jonathan? Or what if he'd told them Willow wasn't herself since the accident and was hoping she'd act up in front of them so he had justification for keeping her in her room?

Until Willow knew who she could trust, she'd better play along. She followed Jonathan out of the great room and into the hall. Once they were out of Chloe and Mat's sight, Jonathan pulled her toward the stairs.

Willow stumbled. "Where are we going? I thought we were going to use the landline."

"I told you I'd call Dr. Graham, and I will."

"But I'd like to talk to—"

"You. Need. To. Rest." He punctuated each word with a yank. Willow tripped again, panic and anger rising inside her.

"Jonathan. Willow." A deep voice resonated through the hallway. Cookie stepped out of the shadows.

Jonathan stopped short. "You startled me." His timbre was unusually high.

Willow turned pleading eyes on Cookie. "Just wondering what the missus would like for dinner." His gaze searched hers. "Are you tired of chicken soup yet?"

She was about to say chicken soup would be fine, but hesitated. "A change of pace would be nice," she said slowly.

"Maybe one of your mother's recipes? I always think there's nothing like your mama's cooking when you've got troubles."

Willow's eyes filled with tears. "That would be really nice. I could call—"

"Your soup is what she needs, Cookie," Jonathan said and tugged her toward the stairs.

"I'll see what I can do," Cookie said and turned toward the kitchen.

Hope soared in Willow's chest. Would he call her mother and father? Alert someone as to what was happening? She climbed the stairs with a lighter heart.

After Jonathan locked the door, Willow pulled the journal from under her pillow and leafed to the last entry she'd read. She turned the page, hoping to find more clues, but it was blank. She paged through the rest of the notebook. It was empty.

She leaned against the headboard and stared out the window, seeing the events of the diary rather than the sky. She'd originally thought the writer was Sophie because she'd found the book with the photo albums. However, if Jonathan was the monster described, it made more sense that the author was Chloe.

Hamish wouldn't have written Sophie into his will when she was a teen. He'd probably paid her for her father's share of the business when Fred died and fulfilled any obligations he had toward her. That was before the really big money came in, anyway.

Now that Willow understood who Jonathan was, it seemed obvious that Chloe was the writer of the journal.

Grief flowed over Willow. It was like a death. The man she'd married no longer existed. A tear slipped down her cheek, dripped off her chin, and created a stain on the journal's cover.

The sadness ebbed and flowed. The first waves were for herself. The second set for The Peach who wouldn't have the kind of father she had. The last for Chloe who'd been betrayed by her twin.

6.6.4

JONATHAN DIDN'T COME to bed that night. He brought her a tray of food, waited while she ate, then slipped away. Hours later, Willow heard the door across the hall open and shut. He must be sleeping in his childhood room. That room, filled with things he no longer needed but wouldn't part with, chilled her.

It represented a darkness in his soul she hadn't seen when she'd agreed to marry him. If she'd only seen that hungry hole, she wouldn't have done it, but this train of thought wasn't productive. She had married him.

She lay in the dark, staring at the ceiling, fear settling down on her like snow, leaving her lethargic and cold. Would she and his copy of the *Hobbit* share the same fate? Be hidden away in Jonathan's museum of things once valued, dog-eared and dusty?

A creak of floorboards silenced the voice in her head. She tensed. Someone was outside her room. The clatter of metal in the lock came next. Willow lifted onto her elbows and stared at the door.

Why would he come in now? Her eyes shifted to the clock on the bedside table—3:03. Her heart thudded against her ribs. He wouldn't hurt her, not while she carried the child that was going to win him Sunset House. She told herself that, but wasn't sure she believed it.

A stripe of darkness on the left side of the door began to expand.

She couldn't see the person entering but knew it must be Jonathan. What should she do? Rush him? Plow past him into the hallway?

Willow sat up. She swung her legs over the side of the bed in one smooth motion, adrenaline deadening the stiffness of her limbs. An arm became visible, black against the lighter gray of the door. Willow's leg muscles contracted.

The black shape moved farther into the room. Willow lifted from the bed, crouching, quadriceps twitching with readiness.

The shape took another step toward her.

Willow pushed forward.

"Willow?"

The voice was soft, feminine, and hushed. Not Jonathan's.

Willow fell onto the bed again. "Chloe?"

"You awake?"

"What are you doing here?"

The door shut without a sound. A moment later Chloe sat next to Willow, her eyes gleaming in the moonlight that shone through the window. "I was worried about you."

"Why?" Willow said slowly. How much did Chloe know?

"Your door was locked from the outside. Mat noticed Jonathan unlock it when he came to see you today."

Willow stared at her hands, charcoal against the t-shirt she'd worn to sleep in. "What's wrong with him, Chloe?"

Chloe didn't answer for a long moment, then she said, "He doesn't have empathy. He can't feel your feelings. Can't sympathize."

"He's a sociopath?"

Willow heard Chloe take in a sharp breath. "I didn't say that."

"That's the definition of the term, isn't it? Someone who can't feel the feelings of others?"

Chloe gripped Willow's hand. "I don't know. I'm not here to analyze my brother. I'm here to help you. Do you want to leave, or don't you?"

Willow stood. "My suitcase is packed."

Chloe stood and walked to the bathroom. She returned a second later carrying something. "I'll bring it to you tomorrow. I've seen him when he gets like this. We need to go."

She handed Willow her bathrobe. "Put this on." Willow obeyed and followed Chloe out of the bedroom.

Her eyes crept to Jonathan's door. She couldn't shake the feeling he would break it down and chase her through Sunset House like Jack Nicholson in *The Shining*, but it remained closed.

As they descended the stairs, the wood seemed to shriek in protest. Willow glanced over her shoulder every few seconds, sure he'd heard. When they reached the ground floor, Chloe made a right toward the kitchen. Willow paused. She'd expected to head for the front door.

"Come on," Chloe's whisper was filled with urgency.

Willow hurried after her.

The kitchen's tile and stainless-steel surfaces gleamed in the light coming through the windows. Chloe strode toward the pantry at the far end of the room. Willow remembered the door hidden between the shelves of foodstuffs from her security tour on her one night alone in Sunset House.

Chloe snapped the lock open and yanked on the doorknob, once, twice, three times. The door popped open with a groan. An ocean breeze washed over Willow. The smell of seaweed and salt was so welcome, she had to stifle a sob. She followed Chloe across a grassy lawn toward the barn-like garage.

"I'll take you to your parents," Chloe said.

"I can drive myself," Willow protested.

"Don't be silly. I want to make sure you get there safely." Chloe pulled a phone from her pocket, tapped on the screen a couple of times, and the garage door rolled up. "We'll take my car."

Willow stopped short in front of the opening.

Chloe bustled forward and opened the driver's side door of a dark SUV—a Lexus. A black or navy-blue Lexus with a large dent in the front fender.

A vehicle bearing down on her, the screech of brakes, the pain of impact. All this flashed through Willow's mind. Could it be? *Justice requires I come up with a plan to take what is most precious to the monster.* The last line of the journal. What's most precious to Jonathan? Sunset House, and The Peach that would buy him the key.

Chloe halted, one foot in the vehicle, the other on the ground. "What's wrong?"

Willow couldn't answer. Her throat constricted. Her tongue felt fat.

"Willow, get in the car." Chloe's voice was no longer kind. It had turned cold, like a sudden wind.

Willow took three steps backward. Where would she run? Where could she go?

Chloe disappeared into the car for a brief moment, then emerged with something in her hand. "I said, get in the car."

A gun. She had a gun trained on Willow.

Willow stood in indecision. It was difficult to hit a moving target, especially in the dark. She could run for the stand of shrubs to the right of the garage. But there was The Peach to consider. If she was hit, would he survive? Then again, if Chloe killed her, he hadn't a chance. And that was Chloe's plan, wasn't it?

Willow wanted to live, but not without The Peach. Willow turned her hands palms-up. "Chloe," she said.

Chloe gestured with the gun toward the car. "We can talk while we drive."

"Chloe," Willow repeated. "I don't want the house. All I want is to take my baby and go. I'll apply for a divorce tomorrow."

Chloe laughed. "If only that were possible. You don't know Jonathan very well yet, do you?"

"I have grounds. What's he going to do?"

"Oh, he may divorce you, but he'll never let the baby go. That baby is his golden ticket, the goose that lays the golden eggs, the magic bean."

Something white flitted from the shadows of the garage. Too late, Chloe saw the surprise in Willow's eyes. Before Chloe could turn, a hand slapped the gun to the ground. An arm jutted out and grabbed her around the neck.

"So that's where mother's gun disappeared to." Jonathan pulled Chloe to his chest. "You never could keep your hands off my stuff."

Chloe struggled against him, but Willow didn't stay to watch the battle. She bolted for the bushes. When she reached them, she paused. Where should she go? Where could she hide?

Her first instinct was to run for the gates, head onto the main road, and flag down a passing vehicle. But it was three in the morning. Not many cars were on the road at this time. Jonathan would come looking for her as soon as he'd taken care of Chloe.

Willow shivered.

She could run to the house and call the police, but again, Jonathan would find her before they could arrive.

The library.

The library had a landline. He might not expect her to go there, which would buy her time.

Willow crept along the stand of bushes until she came to the flag-stone path, then she ran.

6.6.5

THE LIBRARY DOOR WAS LOCKED. Willow fell against it and rattled the knob. What had she been thinking? It was locked. She always locked it when she was done with her work, and so did Sophie. How could she have been so stupid?

She rested her forehead against the cool wood. A sob escaped her lips. What would she do now? She couldn't return to the house. She couldn't leave through the front gate. Sunset House, called "a piece of heaven on earth" by *Orange County Lifestyles* magazine, had become hell for her.

A brine-filled onshore breeze wrapped around her. She pivoted and stared at the path behind her—the path that led to the lawn that led to the stairs that led to the beach. The wind came again. It beckoned her forward.

The beach meant freedom. There were public access stairs a little more than a half-mile north on that beach and, above those stairs, a neighborhood filled with sleeping people. Jonathan wouldn't expect her to go to the beach. He knew how afraid she was of the stairs.

She jogged along the flagstones, pausing at the end of the path only long enough to glance right, then left before darting across the exposed grassy area. Her heart thudded in her chest by the time she reached the top of the stairs. She hesitated.

The sensation of empty space nearly buckled her knees. The world spun. She closed her eyes and clung to the gate. She had to do this. The beach was her only escape, but her head swam, and nausea roiled up from her stomach and into her mouth.

She'd go slow. She'd be careful. She'd made it down and up the stairs once before. She could do it again. She swung the gate open and placed a foot on the top step.

Gripping the railing with claw-like hands, she took another step. When she was sure the tread would support her weight, she descended again. It would take her the rest of the night to reach the sand below at this rate, but she couldn't make herself hurry. Step, test, step, test.

What seemed hours later, she came to the first landing. The journey had been excruciatingly slow, but she'd made it. She wiped her sweaty palms on her bathrobe, then untied the belt, allowing the robe to flap open. She was hot now, the hair on her neck wet with sweat.

The next leg of the descent was where she'd fallen. She could see the broken stair from the landing. She gazed away, over the railing to the beach below her. The sand was so far down, dizziness came over her again.

Willow dropped onto her butt and rested her head on her knees. She couldn't stay here. Jonathan would think of the beach eventually. When he couldn't find her anywhere else, he'd think of it. He wouldn't rest until he had her, and the baby.

Her head snapped up. She wasn't a possession, and neither was The Peach. She'd crawl down the damn stairs if she had to. Willow placed both feet firmly on the second step down from the landing and gingerly scooted herself onto the first. It held her. She dropped her feet two steps further and scooted again, holding onto the railing with both hands like a primate. It was slow going, but safe going.

She bypassed the broken tread with her feet, and instead of sitting, she stood. She walked down the last five steps and uttered a shuddering exhale as she reached the second landing.

The waves were loud now. The ground close. She all but ran down the remaining flight of stairs. Relief flowed in the form of cold sweat as soon as her feet touched the earth.

She gazed at the beach ahead of her. The sand glowed in the light of a gibbous moon. It was a lit runway that would advertise her presence from yards and yards away. If Jonathan or Chloe glanced down, they couldn't miss her.

The muzzle of Chloe's gun blossomed in her mind. Willow's gaze shot to the cliffs above her. Chloe would have to be an excellent marksman to hit her from that vantage point. If Chloe had escaped from Jonathan, that was.

Jonathan was taller and stronger than his twin, but it occurred to Willow now that Chloe was cunning. She'd taken Willow in completely.

As her gaze returned to the beach, she noticed a band of black hugging the cliffs. It was narrow and ended at an outcropping of rocks about a quarter of a mile away, but it was something. Willow slid into the shadow and headed north.

She jogged for a minute or two, but the sand here was soft and unstable. Her ankle turned when her foot dropped into a hole, not badly, but enough to scare her. She slowed her pace.

Willow glanced over her shoulder less and less often the farther she got from Sunset House. She was sure she'd see a person following her, even if they hugged the cliffs as she was doing. Her eyes had adjusted well to the dim light. The band of black now appeared gray. There was no one in it.

By the time she reached the outcropping, her nerves were steady. She clambered over the rocks into the moonlight. She'd be around the point in seconds. When she reached the other side, it would be impossible to see her from Sunset House even with binoculars.

She dropped down from the rocks and walked on the hard, wet sand now. It was more important to get where she was going quickly than it was to hide in the shadows on this leg of her escape. If Chloe caught her, Willow had no doubt she'd kill her, even though another death would look incredibly suspicious.

The Lauders were delusional. They seemed to think they were untouchable. How many people had Jonathan killed? Two? Three, if his father's death wasn't from sickness.

Had Chloe been in on those murders, or had she known about them? She and Jonathan seemed to share access to a common brain.

Willow didn't think they could keep secrets from each other. Not for long, anyway.

Perhaps they'd worked together until Chloe found out about Willow's pregnancy. Then Chloe struck out on her own and tried to run Willow down. What would she have done tonight if Jonathan hadn't arrived?

She'd been rescued by her captor, her choices death or imprisonment. A stab of sheer terror ran through Willow. She shut it down. She could fall apart later, when she and her baby were safe.

The moon was lower on the horizon. The sky had lightened from black to midnight blue. There were hours to go before sunrise, but the new day was on its way. That's what she would focus on. A new day. Her first day of freedom.

She plodded on for another quarter of a mile before she saw the stairs. The cliffs were lower on this section of beach, so it was a shorter flight than the one at Sunset House. At its top she could see streetlights and houses lit by outdoor security lights.

She began to jog. She stumbled when her foot hit soft sand, but righted herself and continued on over dried seaweed and up a small incline.

Adrenaline raced through her when she reached the stairs. She bounded up them with renewed strength. When she got to the top, she scanned her surroundings. The stairs opened onto the end of a cul de sac. A viewing bench and a pair of palm trees were on her left, but Willow only gave them a glance.

Instead, she examined the houses along the street. She wanted one with a car in the driveway, a nice, suburban-looking SUV with a bike rack or a car seat in the back. She planned to beat on the front door of that house until someone came.

She'd call the police first. Then she'd call her parents. The thought of sinking into her father's strong embrace, of hearing her mother's voice, made her eyes sting with tears.

Enough of that.

She couldn't break down, not yet.

She chose a two-story, Mediterranean-style house with not one, but two cars in the driveway and stepped off the curb.

"Willow."

Her name dropped like a cleaver. She opened her mouth to scream, too late. A hand clamped over it, another pulled her against a strong chest.

"I wouldn't do that," Jonathan said.

Willow began to struggle.

"Listen to him, Willow." Chloe stepped out from behind the pair of palms, the gun in her hand. "Let's get in the car. Quietly."

MOLLY: Sorry to stop at such a tense, tense moment, but the next episode is just as suspenseful. There are no longer any good places to pause.

Jonathan isn't who Willow thought he was. It isn't uncommon for psychopaths to be very convincing, and based on his behavior it's a pretty good bet he has the gene. They're often really good at reading people. They become who they need to become in order to get what they want. It seems Chloe is cut from the same cloth.

We know there is a genetic component to psychopathy. But most people with the genetic makeup never actually kill anyone. They may be aggressive in business, able to con people or cheat people or cheat on people without remorse, but they're not murderers.

Here's the question, then. We know what Jonathan has done to Willow, but we don't know if he's actually killed anyone. His explanation of Dun's death could've been accurate. What do you think? Is he a murderer? Or just gaslighting Willow until he gets his golden ticket as Chloe called the unborn baby? How much danger is Willow in?

Let me know what you think on Facebook.

Join me next time for more *Murders Under the Sun*.

(cue music)

VO: This episode is brought to you by Randall & Richter, specializing in Family Law. *Murders Under the Sun* is edited by Jim Wilbourne, theme music is by Eclectic Blends, and I'm your host, Molly Shure.

MURDERS UNDER THE SUN
SEASON SIX; EPISODE SEVEN

MOLLY: Welcome back to *Murders Under the Sun*. I'm Molly Shure, your host.

We've arrived at the last week of the season. Today all your questions will be answered. At least, all your questions about *The Manor*. I can't help you with the meaning of life or how to achieve world peace.

This episode is a roller coaster, people. But before we hop on the ride, I want to thank everyone who participated in the Facebook Group. It seems every season we have at least one psychologist or psychiatrist weigh in on the discussion revolving around our villain's behavior.

Thanks to Dr. H for sharing the latest on psychopathy. It's a very rare disorder and even more rare among women. However, according to Dr. H, since Chloe and Jonathan are twins it is possible that she and Jonathan may share that genetic similarity.

However, not everyone who has psychopathic genetic makeup will exhibit the traits we associate with ASPD, or antisocial personality disorder. It's complicated. We don't know the extent to which nature alone will impact a person's behavior. Most likely, nurture will play a role too.

Thing is, Jonathan and Chloe had virtually the same upbringing. So, if Jonathan is what we'd call a psychopath—and it appears he might be—Chloe could be one as well.

I guess we'll have to get into the narrative to
find out.

Willow had lost track of time. It could be two days since her escape, it could be five. Her life had become an endless stream of trays of food she had no appetite for. She'd watched the light peeking through the cracks around the room-darkening curtains grow bright then fade multiple times. How many, she couldn't say.

The door opened and Jonathan appeared with yet another meal. He lowered it onto the vanity table. "Tuna salad a la Cookie," he said. "I don't know how he does it, but it's delicious. I've asked him what the secret ingredient is a hundred times, but he won't tell me."

Willow gazed at him through blurred eyes. What was he blathering on about? She didn't know, didn't care. She would eat a few bites of whatever they gave her, but not for herself. She didn't want anything. She'd eat it for The Peach.

"Sit up," Jonathan said. "I'll put this on your lap."

She did as he'd asked.

"After lunch, you need to take a shower." He wrinkled his nose to emphasize his point.

Willow hadn't showered since they'd brought her back. She hadn't spoken to anyone. She hadn't left the room. She hadn't even gotten out of bed other than to use the restroom. What was the point?

"You can come downstairs for breakfast tomorrow." Jonathan set the tray on her lap and sat at the foot of the bed. "It'll just be me and Chloe. Cookie has the morning off."

Willow lifted a triangle of sandwich from its plate and took a bite. It tasted like cardboard.

"We could take a walk around the grounds afterward. It'd be good for you." Jonathan spoke to her as if she were a child, and not a very intelligent one.

She didn't respond.

"You need to take care of yourself," he said. "For the baby's sake."

She set the sandwich down and took a sip of the herbal tea that had come with it.

"Willow." His voice was sharp. She lifted her gaze and met his eyes. They were as blue as ever, but they no longer appeared beautiful to her. No more did they remind her of a sunny Mediterranean Sea. Now they were cold pools, electric and deadly.

"Don't you think this silent treatment has gone on long enough?'

She barked a single laugh.

His eyes narrowed. "I know you're upset about having to stay in, but it's your own fault."

She swallowed. She hadn't spoken in days and wasn't sure if her mouth still worked. "My fault?" The words were a croak.

"I was trying to protect you from Chloe. If you'd trusted me and stayed put, none of this"—he waved a hand around the room—"would've happened."

"None of this?" Her voice sounded more frog than human.

"Right. Now I have to compromise with Chloe to protect you and the baby. That's not what I wanted." His mouth pursed into a pout.

Willow furrowed her brow. It hurt to think. No, he wouldn't want to compromise. He never wanted to compromise. She opened her mouth to ask what the compromise was, but he spoke again.

"I had to give Chloe the west wing of the house. Permanently. We're writing up the papers with the lawyers next week." Jonathan smoothed the covers with his hand. "We wanted our own place. We didn't want to have to live with the family, remember?" His eyes met hers. "That's no longer possible." His tone was accusing.

Willow was at a loss for words. How could he use words like "our" and "we"? How could he imagine Willow would be willing to live with either him or his murderous sister? As soon as she found a way out of this nightmare, she would tell Inspector Sylla everything, then file for divorce.

"It's not wise for you to go out and about on your own yet, however. Not until the paperwork is signed." He stroked the bedspread as if it was a house pet. "I don't entirely trust my sister. She hates to lose."

Willow sat in silence, digesting his words. Was this a game to him?

To Chloe? A competition in which one twin would emerge the winner and the other the loser? She cleared her throat. "Did you kill your mother?"

She'd wanted to ask him this question for a while but had been afraid to hear the answer. She was no longer afraid. She was numb.

Jonathan's hand stopped moving. "No. Dun did."

Willow stared at him, but he wouldn't meet her eyes. "You switched the pills in the acetaminophen bottle, didn't you? You put something else in there, and Dun didn't know."

"It was acetaminophen."

"Extra strength?"

His eyes jittered to the door and back to the bedspread. "I didn't know Dun would give her the maximum dosage, did I?"

"Dun was a methodical person. She followed protocol."

His head tipped to one side and back again. "I guess."

Willow pushed the tray off her lap. Her stomach was hard and knotted. She couldn't look at the food any longer.

"Chloe started the whole thing." He sounded like a defensive adolescent.

Willow didn't speak.

"She killed Dad."

Something resembling an emotion skittered up Willow's spine. "I thought he had a stroke?"

"He did have a stroke. It was well played. It's not difficult to induce a stroke in someone prone to them. She switched his blood pressure medicine for her antidepressants. Since she'd filled the prescriptions, nobody knew what the pills were supposed to look like."

"Why?" Willow whispered the word.

Jonathan shrugged. "Mat proposed. Chloe wanted Sunset House."

"But I was pregnant."

"She didn't know that. She also didn't think Dad would die as quickly as he did. She was playing a long game."

Willow stood. A wave of dizziness hit her. She placed a hand on the bedside table to steady herself. The fact that he was admitting all this was as terrifying as the information itself. Didn't criminals reveal their identities only when they planned to kill their victims?

Jonathan startled at her sudden movement. "Where are you going?"

Where was she going? Away from him, but she couldn't say that. "The bathroom," she said.

"Well, come right back. We need to talk about next steps."

She stumbled toward the bathroom, stepped inside, and locked the door behind herself. It wasn't much of a barrier, but it was all she had.

Orthrus. That was another name the journal girl had given the monster. A dim memory from a classic literature class returned to Willow now. Orthrus was the two-headed brother of Cerberus, the dog that guarded Hades. She wished the memory had come to her when she'd read the journal. The writer must have been referring to the twins, Jonathan and Chloe.

As children they tricked a girl into swimming with black jellyfish, then sliced her arms and allowed the family to think she was self-harming. As adults they were having a murder competition. And Jonathan was winning. Chloe would want to catch up.

A hand flew to Willow's mouth to stifle a scream.

"Are you coming out of there?" Jonathan called through the door.

"Yes. Yes. Coming." Willow walked to the sink, turned on the tap and splashed her face with cold water. She had to think.

The chill helped. As she blotted her skin with a towel, she decided on a course of action. It wasn't a perfect plan, but it was the best she could come up with in this moment. She would play along with Jonathan. Let him think she was on his side. As repulsive as the idea was, he was her only protection from his other half.

She attempted a smile and opened the bathroom door.

Jonathan's eyes lit when he saw her. "None of this is easy to hear. I get it, babe." He patted the bed next to him.

She suppressed a shudder and sat.

"But you've got to understand, the one percent, we're different. We don't play by the same rules. There's too much at stake."

Willow made a noncommittal sound. He continued. "Mom and Dad did things in their day, too."

Things like murder? she thought but didn't say.

"You know the software program he retired on?"

Willow gave him a quick nod.

"Sophie's father wrote it, but he died before publishing."

"Hamish took the credit?"

"Exactly." Jonathan gave her a broad smile. It was the same smile that used to make her weak. Now it made her sick. "Chloe thinks he killed Fred to get it. I'm not sure though. My money is on Mom. She was the more ruthless of the two."

Willow stiffened. "Did your father tell you about the program?"

Jonathan pulled a face. "No. Mom told Chloe after Dad had his first stroke. His brush with death made him maudlin. He started," Jonathan made air quotes, "*a spreadsheet*. His sins in one column, his good deeds in another. Didn't matter. No way he was getting out of the red."

The lawyer's card with the appointment date penciled on the back popped into her mind. Could it be he'd planned to change his will to include Sophie, and Chloe had found out about it?

Jonathan took Willow's hand and squeezed it. "I'm glad we had this talk. I've wanted to share all this with you, but I wasn't sure how you'd take it."

It was all she could do not to snatch her hand away. She inhaled and exhaled slowly, calming herself as she did before a violin recital. This was going to be the greatest performance of her life. "I'm glad, too."

He brought her hand to his lips and kissed it. "You have to let me protect you. I'm the only one who can manage Chloe. I always have been."

"Okay," Willow said, but couldn't look at him as she did.

He placed her hand on her abdomen and held it there with his. "We have a common interest."

A flutter, the movement of an invisible being, reverberated through Willow's body. The Peach had kicked.

6.7.2

THE PERFORMANCE of Willow's life began the next day. Jonathan let her out of her room, but it didn't bring the relief she'd expected. Chloe watched her like a hungry cat when she entered the dining room, following her every movement with her aqua-green eyes. Jonathan acted as if the past two weeks hadn't happened.

Not only did Willow have no practice in this level of deceit, but it went on and on. The conversation was stilted and false and completely out of tune.

After Chloe left for work, Willow breathed a sigh of relief. Playing along with Jonathan was hard. Playing Chloe's tune was close to impossible. With one twin out of the way, Willow decided to test the parameters of her new freedom. She set down her coffee cup. "I should give Mom a call today."

Jonathan, who'd been reading the news on his tablet, glanced up. "Don't do that. They think we're on Herron."

The Lauders owned an estate on Herron Island in Puget Sound. Willow had never been there but had heard how pristine and remote it was.

"Even so, she'll expect a call."

An annoyed expression crossed his face. "No, she won't. I told her internet and cell reception were sketchy, that the only reliable communication was by sat phone, and we reserved that for emergencies."

Willow's muscles tightened with anxiety, but she forced herself to speak in unconcerned tones. "You told me your father had a satellite dish installed and that the internet was better there than here."

"That's true." He returned his gaze to his tablet, signifying the end of the conversation.

It was also the end of the meal for Willow. Food wasn't going to make it past the tension in her throat. She pushed her plate away and stood. "I think I'll head to the library." This was another test.

He set his tablet on the table with deliberation, then pushed his own chair away. "I have work to do in Dad's office too. I'll come with you." Apparently, he wasn't going to let her out of his sight.

They exited the house through the great room, and Willow turned her face to the sun. She hadn't felt its warmth for days.

Jonathan grabbed her arm and tugged her forward. "If you say anything... That you're unhappy, that you're suspicious about Mom's death, or Dun's, or Dad's, to Cookie or the staff, we will go to Herron."

His statement was uttered with such heavy finality, Willow didn't doubt he meant it. The threat of being taken to a remote island where the only escape was by boat, a boat she didn't know how to operate, was more effective than a ball and chain around her ankle. The idea terrified her.

"I wouldn't," she said with as much indignation as she could muster.

He smiled the absent smile he'd worn through breakfast. "I didn't think so."

They spent the morning together in Hamish's room, Willow cataloguing the last of the books, and Jonathan working on his laptop. Neither mentioned the elephant in the room again.

The next day, Willow and Jonathan walked the perimeter of the property after lunch.

"Fresh air and sunshine are good for you," he said. He'd put on his "loving husband" persona with his shirt and pants that morning.

She stifled a bitter laugh. If he wanted what was good for her, he would let her talk to her mother. Let her make a doctor's appointment. But she'd put on "supportive spouse" when she'd gotten dressed, so she said, "It's a beautiful day."

"Speaking of fresh air and sunshine, I had an idea." Jonathan took her arm and threaded it through his. "Now that Chloe's going to have the apartment, we won't have access to the patio overlooking the beach that you liked so much."

Willow hummed a response. His ability to segment his life into disconnected boxes amazed her. It was a kind of superpower. He threatened her one minute and talked casually about home improvement plans the next.

"What if we built our own patio, complete with outdoor kitchen and fireplace at the top of the beach stairs?" He actually managed to sound enthusiastic.

At the mention of the beach stairs, Willow shuddered. She didn't think she could ever be comfortable on that stretch of ground. There were limits to her supportiveness. "It's so far from the kitchen," she said. "Couldn't we make something closer?"

He nodded thoughtfully. "Maybe you're right. Let's walk around back and see if we can find a better spot." Jonathan veered left past the shrubbery that ran between the gardens and the garage, discussing the merits of paving stone versus tile as they walked.

When they came around the inland side of the house, Willow stopped. The pool glinted in the sunlight just ahead. Jonathan halted mid-sentence and gave her a sidelong glance.

He didn't have to ask. He knew she was remembering the day of Dun's death, remembering her efforts to resurrect the woman because she hadn't realized her heart had long since stopped. Remembering how she almost dove into water that was alive with a deadly current. This wasn't a good train of thought.

Willow began walking again. The pool she'd once thought so beautiful, now seemed as dangerous as a snake pit. She didn't want to go closer, but she had to play her part.

How should a supportive spouse act when confronted by the scene of their partner's crime? Because Willow was now sure Jonathan had killed Ms. Dunfrey.

"If we cut through the trees here," Jonathan pointed to a stand of California Oaks, "we can see the ocean."

Willow followed him wordlessly, happy to leave the pool behind. She and Cookie had looked at the facts the morning that Dun had died. They reviewed them, then she'd stowed them away in the basement of her soul, in a closet where she stored things she didn't want to look at.

She removed them now and examined them one by one. Jonathan had known the pool wiring was defective. He'd known Dun swam every morning. He'd stopped Willow from jumping in to save someone he'd known since childhood.

Why? Because Dun wouldn't quietly take the blame for Gerry's death. She knew she hadn't given Gerry an accidental overdose of acetaminophen. She was digging for the truth and must have gotten too close for comfort. She may have even been the one who'd gone to the police. Booker had said someone from Sunset House must have brought their concerns to Sylla.

At the thought of her father, Willow almost burst into tears. She dodged a tree limb as Jonathan released it, and found herself on a bluff overlooking the Pacific. She blinked away the tears as she stared at the vista before her.

Jonathan spread his arms wide. "This is a fabulous view, and it's much closer to the kitchen. Good thinking, babe."

"It's lovely," Willow said.

"I'm going to call a contractor and see what it would take to build our patio here. We'll have to have the trees removed and a path... "

Willow tuned him out as they returned to the main house. A tiny bubble of hope had popped into her heart. Sylla. She was a bull dog. She wouldn't give up on the investigation into Dun's death. She'd be back.

On the third day of her performance, Ophelia waltzed into the dining room as Willow and the twins were eating dinner. Willow was so surprised, she dropped her fork. It clattered to the floor.

She wasn't sure why their cousin's presence had shocked her. Maybe because she'd begun to think the only people left in the world were the Lauder twins. Willow hadn't seen anyone for days but them, the gardener, and the woman who cleaned.

Jonathan had told her to stay out of the kitchen without explanation. She complied, more for Cookie's sake than her own. She knew what had happened to Dun. She didn't want Cookie to have a similar household accident.

Willow couldn't decide if she was happy to see Ophelia, or not. If she'd bring aid or only more problems. She was a cipher, a question mark. Whose side was she on?

Willow had always sensed animosity between her and Chloe, and there was no love lost between her and Jonathan either. What did she stand to inherit if one or the other got the house? Or did it matter to her? Those were pertinent questions.

Ophelia could be neutral. If so, maybe she could be an ally, but Willow had a hard time trusting her. She was so odd.

"I'll get that." Ophelia bent and picked up the fork. "I was headed to the kitchen to ask Cookie for a place setting. I'll get you another while I'm there."

Chloe raised a cool eyebrow. "Were you invited to dinner?"

"I'm family. Family doesn't need an invite. That's what Uncle Hamish always said." Ophelia disappeared into the hallway and emerged a full minute later with a plate and a handful of silverware. She sat next to Willow and handed her a fork.

"I haven't heard hide nor hair from any of you since Willow's accident. I was worried," she said in an unworried voice.

"Nothing to be concerned about," Jonathan said through tight lips. "She's fine, as you can see."

Ophelia scooped a helping of garlic mashed potatoes onto her white china plate. "And the baby?"

"He's fine too," Jonathan said.

Ophelia paused, the spoon in the air. "He? I didn't know we knew the sex."

"We do." Jonathan took a sip of wine, perhaps to hide the satisfied smile that always spread across his lips when the sex of The Peach was referenced. With all the horrors of Willow's current life, it surprised her that she still found this annoying.

"What have you been up to?" Chloe spoke from her end of the table in a bored voice.

"Oh, this and that. I've been helping Sophie go through the boxes in the library." She nibbled at a bite of food.

Jonathan set his glass down. "Really? What have you found?" He was attempting to sound disinterested, but Willow saw the tension in his jawline.

"So weird, we found an entire box of Fred's things."

"Sophie's father Fred?" Willow asked.

Ophelia turned her pale blue eyes on Willow. "Yes. Strange. Don't you think?"

Chloe sat up an inch higher in her chair. "What kind of things?"

"Business papers. You know, letters, reports... " Ophelia paused again. "A program."

No one said a word. She continued. "Actually it's just a description, not the program itself. It's something you might use for sales purposes. Funny thing is, it sounds an awful lot like the program that made Uncle Hamish his millions."

Jonathan leaned back in his chair. "What are you implying?"

"Me?" Ophelia's eyes widened. "I'm not implying anything. Just thought you'd be interested."

"Where is the paperwork now?" Chloe's voice was low and cold.

"Sophie has it. It's her father's. Seems only right."

Jonathan and Chloe's heads turned toward each other simultaneously as if moved by the same puppet master. Their eyes locked in silent communication. Jonathan said, "Are you almost done Willow?"

Willow glanced at her half-eaten plate of food. She wasn't hungry, but she was interested in the conversation. This was a turn of events she'd never anticipated. She needed to understand what it meant.

If Hamish's will was going to be contested, the proviso about the first grandchild would be null and void, wouldn't it? And if the proviso about the baby was no longer legitimate, she'd be free. Jonathan would have no reason to keep her around. Chloe wouldn't have a reason to kill The Peach. This was good news, wasn't it? "Almost," she said.

"Let the poor girl eat," Ophelia said. "She's too thin for a pregnant person."

Willow chased a half dozen peas around her plate and pondered taking more. Not because she wanted them, but as an excuse to stay and listen.

"I need to talk to Sophie," Jonathan said.

"She'll be here tomorrow, I'm sure," Ophelia said.

Jonathan pushed his chair away from the table. "Tonight."

Again, no one spoke for a long moment. Ophelia broke the silence. "So, go. Who's stopping you?"

"I need to help Willow get settled upstairs."

Ophelia threw her napkin on the table. "Oh, for goodness sake. She's an adult. She can put herself to bed. Besides it's only 7:30."

Jonathan turned a cold, blue glare on Willow, and a chill washed over her. Perhaps this wasn't a good turn of events after all.

She set her fork down. "I'm done. It's okay. I do need Jonathan. The... ah... the accident. You know."

She stood and allowed him to usher her out of the room. The last thing she heard was Ophelia's shrill tones pipe through the open doorway. "Jonathan, the way you boss her around is appalling. You're a monster."

6.7.3

THE MOON SHONE through the window like a beacon. Willow had forgotten to pull the curtains. She lifted her head to look at the clock on the bedside table—10:22. She'd only been in bed for an hour. She flopped onto her pillows again. It was going to be another long night.

She hadn't slept well in weeks. Anxiety and inactivity were an insomnia-producing cocktail. She had nothing to wear her out, to distract her, during the day. Her life used to be full. Now the only thing her days were full of were tension and fear.

She glanced at Jonathan's side of the bed. Empty. He hadn't slept there since San Diego. Whether he was afraid he'd break her or The Peach, or he'd decided to forego the pretense of marriage, she wasn't sure. It didn't matter. She was glad. It was difficult enough playing "supportive spouse" all day. She couldn't have kept it up all night as well.

She wondered what this new turn of events would mean for her. If Sophie had enough evidence to contest the will, would Jonathan and Chloe let her go? More likely, they'd want to tie her up like a loose end. She should be afraid, but her adrenal system had given up the ghost. She couldn't muster up an emotion to save her life. Perhaps she was becoming like her spouse. That happened, didn't it?

Willow threw her legs over the side of the bed and padded to the bathroom. At least she always had something to do during the long nights. How one cup of herbal tea could turn into five trips to the toilet was a feat of chemistry she couldn't fathom.

On her way back to bed, she stopped at the window. The pool shimmered below her. A tendril of fog moved across its surface, wagging side to side like a shark. Or was it a dolphin?

One moved vertically, arching its back up and down. The other horizontally. She was fairly sure the dolphin arched while the shark undulated. She'd look it up in the morning. Another wisp of fog swam across the water, then another. It looked like a school, a school of fog-fish.

Willow yawned. It was early for ground clouds, wasn't it? Or late, depending on how you looked at it. The point was, since she'd moved into Sunset House she hadn't noticed the fog roll in until close to sunrise. There had to be a meteorological reason for this, but she didn't know it. Perhaps that's how she should fill her days, learning about dolphins and sharks and weather patterns.

She shivered. It was chilly in her room. She was about to turn away, to burrow under the covers again, but the pool looked so odd, she stayed a moment longer. A blanket of gray had rolled over the water, almost completely obliterating it from view. And it was rising.

It wasn't just the timing and the amount of fog that held her here, the color was wrong, too. This fog wasn't the pale gray-white of the usual June gloom. It looked dirty, as if someone had mixed red-brown paint into it. It reminded her of the color of the sky during wildfire season.

Her spine snapped straight. Wildfire season. This wasn't fog. It was smoke.

She stood, bursts of adrenaline pumping into her blood stream. What should she do?

Her father's steadying voice spoke in her mind. *Get out, stay out, and call 911.*

Great advice, but none of it was possible.

Check your primary escape route first. If doors are hot, don't open them.

Willow ran to the bedroom door and placed her hand against it. It wasn't hot. She rattled the knob, hoping against hope that Jonathan had forgotten to lock it. He hadn't. She returned to the window, threw it open, and leaned out. The smoke was climbing her wall now, thick and brown and curling. It smelled of chemicals and old campfires. "Fire," she screamed. The only answer was the cry of a gull.

Why hadn't the fire alarms gone off? There must be high tech alarms—the kind that call 911 and spew water from the ceiling—in a house as opulent as Sunset House.

Willow spun away from the window, stared at her door, grabbed her hair with both hands and tugged. "Think, think."

Jonathan must be sleeping in the room across the hall. Maybe she could wake him. She crossed to her door again, balled up both fists and hammered. "Jonathan, wake up. Wake up. Fire."

She banged and hollered until her hands were bruised and her throat raw. Jonathan didn't come.

Willow collapsed against the door and coughed. Her gaze skittered to the open window. Noxious gas crawled over the sill and into the room. She bolted to the window and shut it.

If there is smoke in the room, get low, her father reminded her. Willow dropped to her knees. The air near the floor was cleaner. From this angle, she could see that nothing was coming under the door, which meant the hallway was still a safe escape route.

Her eyes stung. She closed them and imagined the floor plan of the house. The fire must be in the kitchen. Wind off the ocean would send the smoke toward the pool area. It would also fan the flames.

How long would it be before a hungry blaze ate its way through the heavy kitchen door, rushed through the downstairs hallway and began devouring the stairs? How long before the second story lost all support and collapsed into the first?

Willow's eyes shot open. A plan. She needed a plan. Her gaze fell on her tote bag under the vanity.

The girl in the diary had escaped with a butter knife. But Jonathan had taken anything Willow could pick a lock with. If only she'd had the presence of mind to grab the fork she'd dropped at dinner and slip it into her pocket before Ophelia took it.

Ophelia.

You're a monster. Her voice, shrill and clear, rang in Willow's head. She'd called Jonathan a monster.

Willow shook her head. How had she not thought of it before? Ophelia was the diary girl. It made perfect sense.

Ophelia was a blood relative. It was a good chance Cob, Marianne and she were all included in Hamish's will. Jonathan and Chloe called her mentally unstable, said she'd needed psychiatric care. Ophelia had a fear of the water. Why hadn't Willow put the pieces of this puzzle together sooner?

A coughing fit grabbed her by the throat. When it passed, she wiped tears from her eyes and shot a glance at the window. Smoke leaked under the glass.

A thought, a last ditch, hopeless, Hail Mary thought popped into Willow's mind. It was so unlikely she almost ignored it, but she was out of ideas. This crazy thought was all she had.

She pushed onto hands and knees and crawled to the closet. If Ophelia was stung by jellyfish on the beach below Sunset House, perhaps this is where she'd been kept. Perhaps the reason the lock was on the wrong side of the door was because this room had been used to restrain her.

Willow pushed open the closet door and began pulling shoes out. Even if Ophelia had been locked in this room, the knife was most likely gone. Why would she return it to its hiding place once it had done its job?

Willow ran her hands over the moulding on the left wall of the closet. *Because Ophelia might have been afraid she'd be caught and returned to the room.* That thought was so optimistic it scared Willow. "Don't get your hopes up," she said aloud.

The left moulding was intact, nothing there. Willow inhaled through her nose, coughed once and moved to the back wall.

Chances were, Ophelia dropped the knife and ran as soon as the door was open. Willow was on a fool's errand, but what else did she have to do? She could sit and breathe smoke and make her peace with God, or she could search the closet.

She ran her hands along the length of the moulding. She'd make her peace as soon as she was done here, she decided.

A bump.

In the far-right corner of the closet.

Excitement raced through her veins. Her hands trembled as she dug her fingers into the crack at the top of the moulding. It came away from the wall with one tug. Something clattered to the floor.

The butter knife.

Willow stared at the tarnished metal glinting in the dim light of the closet in disbelief. It was there. Ophelia's knife.

She snatched it up as if afraid it truly was a fiction, a mirage, and would disappear as soon as her hand wrapped around it. It didn't.

She backed out of the closet and slid across the room to the door on her rear end. She raised the knife to the door, but her hand shook so hard she dropped it. *Calm down. Calm down.* She inhaled deeply but the noxious air caught in her throat, and she coughed.

She wiped the sweat from her palms on the carpet, picked the knife up, and tried again. She inserted the tip of the blade into the lock mechanism of the door, and pushed forward until it stopped short. She waggled it back and forth like a shark propelling itself through the water, until she felt a click. The bolt popped out of its place, and the door eased open. She barked a laugh and a cough.

Willow pulled herself to her feet and darted into the hallway. *Close all doors and windows. The more oxygen the bigger the blaze,* Booker said. She pulled the door shut obediently, then turned toward the back stairs. A ball of filthy smoke writhed in the stairwell. Not that way.

She jogged toward the front of the house but forced herself to pause at Jonathan's door. He hadn't answered her cries before, so he probably wasn't there, but she couldn't leave without making sure. Willow touched the door. It was cool. Next, she tried the knob. It was also locked. She slammed her hand against the wood. "Jonathan. Jonathan."

No answer.

A vaporous snake wrapped around her ankle and began climbing up her leg. She turned and ran.

Willow didn't stop at the top of the main staircase, but leaped down it, heedless of the charcoal cloud hovering in the air of the first story. Beyond the cloud were the large double doors that led to safety.

She hit the foyer floor and skidded to a stop. She saw her goal, the dusky shape of an open door. She saw the vacuum it created and the dark fingers of smoke racing toward the world outside. She knew this opening would draw the demon that was devouring the house into the foyer. Yet, she paused.

Chloe was silhouetted in the opening.

Her face was unreadable, but there was no mistaking her intentions. The gun was in her hand. "You're not going anywhere, Willow."

The Peach kicked.

Willow had almost forgotten her child. She placed a hand over her abdomen. He kicked again.

"Death by smoke inhalation is less painful than by gunshot," Chloe said.

Willow didn't think that was true. She'd seen her father in the hospital after the accident that changed everything. She'd never seen anyone in such physical and emotional pain, but it didn't matter. She didn't plan to die.

A series of images flickered through her mind like a slideshow: an SUV bearing down on her, the muzzle of the gun on another night, hungry catlike eyes following her movements.

Rage erupted inside her. It was the first emotion she'd felt in a while. It was a hot, consuming flash of anger, and it felt good. She wouldn't be prey and neither would her child.

She strode forward, left hand raised, wrist bent. The strike was so unexpected, Chloe dropped the gun.

Willow pivoted on her rear leg and struck again with all the force her tired core muscles could muster. The second blow made contact with Chloe's nose. Willow felt the crunch of cartilage and bone and the gush of hot blood.

It was strange. She'd performed this movement many times in class. She'd learned the theory behind it, knew why it worked, but until this moment, it had only been a theoretical exercise. She was almost as shocked as Chloe must have been when the woman dropped to the floor in a heap.

Willow didn't stop to examine the full results of her theoretical exercise. She picked up the fallen pistol, stepped over Chloe, and walked out the door.

6.7.4

THE GRAVEL DRIVEWAY hurt Willow's feet, but she didn't mind. Each piercing stone reminded her she was alive. She'd lost pieces of herself in the corners and shadows of Sunset House, but as it burned behind her, it was as if those bits were released by the flames and returned.

She'd thought about pulling Chloe from the doorway, but Willow had heard her moan. She wasn't unconscious. She could drag herself outside. Besides, Willow heard a siren in the distance. A neighbor must have seen the fire and called 911. Help was on the way.

She trudged toward the gate to meet them. As the wrought-iron fence drew closer, she viewed it as if for the first time. Perhaps because she was walking instead of driving, she noticed the decorative post caps on either side of the opening, the curlicues adorning it, its overly ornate construction.

A game show host's voice blared in her brain: *What's behind gate number one, gate number two, or gate number three?* She'd chosen the ostentatious one, and it had shut and locked behind her. Jonathan's wealth had been a well-disguised prison door.

The double swinging gates began to move apart in slow motion, as if an invisible hand had given them a shove. A moment later, Jonathan's BMW pulled through. Willow didn't slow her pace, nor did she hurry.

Jonathan braked when he reached her and leaped from the car, his gaze fixed on the burning house. His features, tinted red by the fire, molded into a horror mask.

Willow didn't stop. The house had been his mistress all along. Let her burn. Let him grieve.

She continued her steady plod toward the gate. The house had exerted a hold on Jonathan, but it had a hold on her as well, and she needed to be free of it.

"Willow." His voice was a scratch of sound.

She didn't answer, didn't pause.

"Willow." He yelled this time.

"What?" She called over her shoulder.

"What happened?"

She shook her head. She didn't know. The sirens were so loud now, she couldn't have answered him if she did. That would be a question for the fire investigators.

Willow didn't stop walking until she was on the public street watching a red engine scream past her. Behind it were three police SUVs. The third pulled up next to her. A young, female, blond-haired officer rolled down the passenger side window. "Were you the one who called in the fire?"

Willow shook her head. "I was in the house."

The officer's eyes widened, and she exited her vehicle. "An ambulance is on the way."

"I'm okay," Willow said, then followed the woman's gaze to where it came to stop at Willow's side. She'd forgotten about the gun. "Oh."

The officer's hands opened in a contradictory gesture. It could have meant she wanted peace, or she could have been readying herself for a shootout.

"Put the gun down, ma'am." Another officer, a middle-aged man, had appeared around the side of the vehicle.

"Yes. Yes, sure." Willow set the gun carefully on the ground and backed away from it. "It's not mine," she said, as if that mattered.

The female officer retrieved the weapon and resumed the concerned demeanor she'd had when she first stopped. "Why don't you get in the car until the ambulance arrives. You must be cold."

Willow realized she was shivering, and obeyed. She sank into the fast-food scented leather seat, leaned her head against the head rest, and asked, "Can I call my parents?"

Two days later a knock sounded on the door to Willow's childhood bedroom. She'd been in the cocoon of her parent's home since the night Sunset House burned.

"Yeah," she answered.

Her father's head appeared in the doorway. "Someone's here to see you."

"What time is it?"

"Three," he said.

Willow's internal clock had been destroyed in the fire along with her external ones. Day and night hadn't yet sorted themselves out. She'd been up at 4:00 that morning and had fallen into a sound sleep after lunch. She was disoriented. "Who is it?"

Booker gave her a tight smile. "Ophelia Lauder."

Willow sat up. "Ophelia?"

"That's what she said."

Willow ran a hand through her tangled hair. "Tell her I'll be down in a minute."

Booker disappeared, but she didn't move. Emotions battled within her. Ophelia had always been the crazy cousin, the black sheep, the unpredictable, unreliable one, but Willow had read her journal. At least, she was fairly certain it was Ophelia's. It was strange how difficult it was for reality to scrub away long-accepted lies. They always seemed to leave a stain.

She shoved herself out of bed and walked down the hall to the bathroom. Five minutes later, she entered the living room somewhat awake and fully dressed.

Ophelia smiled when she saw Willow, but her expression was guarded as if she wasn't sure what her reception would be. "How are you? How is the baby?"

Willow's hand fluttered to her abdomen which had sprouted a full-blown baby bump, seemingly overnight. "Fine. We're fine. How are you?"

"Same."

Willow perched on the armchair across from the couch where Ophelia sat and gazed at the woman. Ophelia wore earth tones today rather than her usual pastels, and it changed her appearance. She'd always seemed amorphous, like the fog that covered the lawns at Sunset House on spring mornings. Today she appeared solid.

"I brought you something." Ophelia lifted a black case from the floor at her feet.

Willow froze. She knew what it was, what it must be. "The Antoniazzi?"

"Yes." Ophelia handed it to her. "If anyone deserves it, you do."

Willow took it from her. "The library?"

"The fire never touched it."

"Good. That's good." And it was good. The library had been the only place on that damnable property that Willow had felt peace. For her, it was a place of objectivity, of lists and values. It was also where the truth had come to light.

"Well, I guess that's it." Ophelia stood and pressed her palms against her thighs. "I just wanted to see if you were okay and give you that."

"Wait," Willow said. Ophelia hesitated, then sat again.

"When I was cataloging Hamish's things, I came across a journal." She glanced at Ophelia to see if there was any reaction. There wasn't. "In it were the writings of a girl who'd been horribly bullied."

A cloud covered Ophelia's face. Willow continued. "Someone had convinced her to go for a swim when a bloom of black jellyfish were in the water."

Ophelia's eyes widened.

"Then those same bullies convinced her family she was mentally unstable, that she needed to be locked up."

Ophelia covered her face with her hands.

"It was you, wasn't it?"

Ophelia was silent for a long time. When she finally raised her head, tears glistened in her eyes. "Uncle Ham knew?"

"He did. The journal was with several photo albums that told another story. A story about Sophie's father, a friendship, and the start of a company. I also found an estate attorney's card with an appointment time scrawled on the back. The date was two days after his death. It could be he planned to change his will to include Sophie and maybe you."

"He was different the last few months of his life."

Willow nodded. "How did he get the journal?"

"I don't know. I left it in the room when I escaped. I assumed it had been thrown out by the cleaning staff."

"Thank God it hadn't been. It saved my life." Ophelia's brow furrowed in confusion. "I found your butter knife."

Ophelia's mouth dropped open, and she laughed. "My butter knife?"

A smile forced its way across Willow's face. "It was still under the moulding in the back of the closet."

"I can't believe it," Ophelia said.

"Believe it, because if it hadn't been there, I wouldn't be sitting here."

Booker, who'd entered the room during their conversation and had hovered in the corner, stepped forward. "I think we owe you a debt of gratitude."

"No. No, I didn't do anything," Ophelia said.

"You did." Willow leaned forward. "Your journal told the truth. Once I figured out who the monster was, I knew I had to escape. Then you gave me the method of escape."

Ophelia shook her head. "It's hard to believe anything good could come from those horrible days."

"What happened to you?" Booker asked.

As Ophelia told the story that Willow had read in the diary, the sun dipped lower in the sky. By the time she'd finished, it shone golden through the windows.

Willow could see the tension in her father's jaw in the warm light. "They're very sick people."

"They are, but no one would believe me." There was a note of sadness in Ophelia's voice. "Oh, my mother did, but she had no pull in the family. Besides, my father wanted us to keep our mouths shut. Hamish bailed him out whenever he made a stupid business deal, or a bad investment, which was often. He didn't want to kill the goose that laid the golden eggs."

"There are a couple of things I don't understand," Willow said. "Why were you so cryptic in the diary? Why didn't you name Jonathan and Chloe instead of making all those references to monsters and dragons? It would have made my life easier."

Ophelia laughed. "You have to remember I was fourteen when the whole thing happened. I was reading *The Hobbit* and *The Lord of the Rings* series and quite taken with that world. It was much more exciting to imagine myself as the captive of evil magical forces than face dull reality. I was also afraid Aunt Gerry would read my entries if she could get her hands on them. I'd rather she thought I was raving mad than naming names."

"Second question," said Willow. "If you left the journal in the room when you escaped, what, ten years ago?"

"Fifteen," Ophelia said.

"Okay, fifteen. Hamish must have known the truth all along. Why didn't he ever do anything about it?"

"Like confront the twins? Or send them to reform school?"

Willow nodded. "Or hire a shrink, at least. He knew what they were, and he allowed it to continue."

Ophelia folded her hands in her lap as if getting ready to recite a well-rehearsed poem. "I didn't even know he had the journal, so I don't know. I can only tell you what I witnessed over the years."

"Please," Booker said, his deep voice startling Willow. She'd almost forgotten he was there.

"Gerry was ruthless," Ophelia continued. "The only things she cared about were money and her progeny. I'm sure she was the one who insisted I was the problem, not her precious children. Hamish went along with it rather than risk inflaming her wrath."

An image of Gerry toasting her new grandchild in the great room at Sunset House ran like an old movie through Willow's mind. She'd thought Gerry was kind and accepting. "I guess I never really knew her."

Ophelia snorted. "You're lucky. She wasn't a nice woman. I suspect she intimidated Hamish into doing a lot of nasty things."

"That came back to bite him, didn't it?" Willow said.

Ophelia's lip twitched in an aborted smile. "Yes, it did. It reminds me of something I once read about dragons. Tolkien said not to leave them out of your calculations if you lived near one."

"Or two," said Willow.

Honey wandered in. "Good Lord, why are y'all sitting in the dark?" It wasn't actually dark. The dying day had turned the room a beautiful shade of violet, but Honey walked from table lamp to table lamp flicking them on.

"That's an incredible story," Booker said.

"It must have been." Honey placed her fists on her hips. "Now how about some dinner? Ophelia, you have to stay. I've made enough stew for an army, and I have biscuits too. I won't take no for an answer."

6.7.5

AS WILLOW WAS MOPPING up the last of the gravy with her biscuit, Booker's phone buzzed. He looked at the screen. "Excuse me for a minute." He pushed away from the table and walked into the living room.

"How about a smidge more, Ophelia?" Honey said.

Ophelia placed a hand on her stomach. "I can't. I'm ready to burst. You'll have to give this recipe to Cookie." Her words ended abruptly, and a look of dismay crossed her face.

"Cookie's out of a job," Willow said, reading her thoughts.

Honey set down her fork. "He called me, you know."

"What?" Willow said.

"The day of the fire. He apologized for not calling sooner, but said it took him a while to get our number. He couldn't remember our last name and didn't want to ask Jonathan or Chloe, for obvious reasons."

"What did he say?" Willow asked.

"He was worried about you. I told him we thought you were out of town. He said that wasn't true. He didn't know what Jonathan was playing at, but he was getting a bad vibe. Booker and I were planning to come get you the next day. We were too late." Her voice broke.

Willow reached a hand across the table and placed it on her mother's. "It's okay now, Mom."

"That was Sylla." Booker reentered the dining room and leaned on his chair back. "Preliminary findings show the fire was incendiary. The arson team found the remains of oil-soaked rags in the kitchen, and the fire alarms had been dismantled."

"Can they say for sure who set it?" Honey asked.

Interesting the way her mother had worded the question. She didn't ask *who had done it*, because they all knew who had.

"They've formally arrested Chloe based on Willow's testimony. Jonathan will be next."

Willow dropped her head into her hand. It was good, and right, but it meant the beginning of a battle she dreaded. The first lurid headlines were already in the news.

Lauder Mansion Burns to the Ground

Heiress Accused of Arson

Dream Wedding Becomes a Nightmare Marriage

The twins had enough money in their trust funds to hire the best legal minds in Orange County. It could go on for years.

She lifted her head. "Why? Why would she do it? Jonathan was going to give her the left wing, and they'd divide the rest of the estate between them. Burning down the house seems a useless gesture."

"You still don't understand them, do you?" Ophelia's eyes were trained on Willow.

"I guess not."

"They can't lose," Ophelia said. "It's that simple. If Jonathan got Sunset House, Chloe would have lost. They've been competing for years. When Jonathan won a surf championship, she took surfing lessons from a pro. She won the women's division the next year. When Chloe got into Yale, Jonathan applied to Harvard. It's the way they roll."

"They both lost this time," Booker said.

"And that's preferable to one or the other winning." Ophelia tapped a finger on the dinner table. "Chloe started the competition by getting engaged to Mat. Waving that diamond in Jonathan's face was like waving a red flag at a bull. Jonathan went out and did her one better. He came home with a pregnant fiancée."

Willow squirmed in her seat. She remembered the night The Peach was conceived. She'd always thought it was odd that she'd gotten pregnant the first time she'd had sex with Jonathan, especially because he'd used a condom. One he'd brought with him. One he must have tampered with. No wonder he was so ecstatic when he discovered she was pregnant.

When she thought of his eyes filling with tears and the way he dropped to his knees, what a loving man she'd believed him to be. What a fool she'd been. It made her want to hide in her room for the rest of her life.

"He told me Chloe killed their father." She blurted out the words.

Ophelia's face didn't register surprise. "I wondered about that when Sophie and I found the information on Fred's software program. It's pretty damning. I guessed one of them had done it."

Willow spread her hands wide. "So Chloe kills her father before he can change the will, but why does Jonathan go after Gerry?"

"He killed his own mother?" Honey looked horrified.

"He all but admitted to me that he switched the acetaminophen in her bottle from regular to extra strength," Willow said. "Gerry might not have died, but it was a good bet she soon would, considering her alcohol consumption."

Ophelia shrugged. "With Uncle Ham gone and a baby on the way, there was only one thing standing between Jonathan and the ultimate prize."

"Gerry," Willow said.

"You got it," Ophelia said. "Jonathan knew Chloe would go after your baby, then try to beat him to the parental punch. The whole thing was a ticking time bomb."

Booker rounded the table and placed his hands on Willow's shoulders and squeezed. "I feel like such an idiot."

She tilted her head to look at him. "You? I think I have the corner on that market."

He shook his head. "I liked him. I thought he was a stand-up guy.

What happened to my radar? I always knew who the bad ones were when you were living here."

"You thought they were all bad," Honey said.

Willow placed a hand on one of his. "We can't always protect the ones we love."

Honey stood and started stacking the dirty dishes. "If there's one thing I learned this year, it's that any of us can be taken in by a charmer, especially when we're feeling a loss." She paused her work and looked Willow in the eye. "You and Drake had just broken up. You were heartsick. Jonathan slid into the void." She picked up the pile of dishes and disappeared into the kitchen.

Ophelia's lips lifted into a small, sad smile. "It took almost getting killed by a jellyfish, having my arms sliced by razor blades, then being locked in a bedroom for five weeks to get it through my head that the twins were evil. I'd always worshipped them."

"You have an excuse. You were a kid," Willow said.

"We don't need excuses." Honey's voice came from the kitchen. "We need to forgive ourselves and place the blame squarely on the shoulders of the perpetrators."

Booker jutted his chin toward the kitchen doorway. "She's still in therapy. Can you tell?"

Ophelia stood. "Speaking of therapy, I'd better get going. I'm supposed to grab a drink with Sophie tonight. We have a lawsuit to plan."

Willow walked her cousin-in-law to the front door. When they reached it, Ophelia turned and hugged her. "I'm so sorry I allowed all that to happen to you. I thought about warning you, but wasn't sure how much you knew. I didn't want to put you in danger by telling tales. Turns out you were already in danger."

"You saved me and… " Willow patted her bump.

She watched Ophelia walk to the curb, get into her car and drive away. There were some things about this terrible time she was grateful for. Ophelia was one of them.

MOLLY: Jonathan and Chloe are evil. I couldn't get Dr. H from our listening audience to make a diagnosis, but in my humble opinion, they are true psychopaths.

However, on a positive note, I love what Honey said, "We don't need excuses. We need to forgive ourselves and place the blame squarely on the shoulders of the perpetrators."

This is one of the reasons I do this podcast. Not only do I want to warn people about the dangers that sometimes come wrapped in attractive packages, but also to help those who've been victimized.

If you've fallen prey to a bad actor, you're not alone. The women I've interviewed for Murders Under the Sun will all tell you that. They'd also tell you to forgive yourself. These perpetrators are often disarming and charming. They can charm the birds right out of the trees, as my grandma used to say.

I love a happy ending, though. So, let's move forward in time and listen to Willow's final installment.

WILLOW COLLAPSED ONTO THE MAT, craned her neck, and eyed the baby carrier in the corner of the bright room. "Why don't babies cry when you want them to?"

Honey uttered a low laugh. "Trust me, this is the best thing for your abs. Completely changed my bike riding."

"One more set," a too-cheerful voice said. Willow groaned.

One set of Hundreds, two sets of Double-Leg Stretches and two of Criss-Crosses later, class was over. The Peach, AKA Forest, slept through the whole thing.

The auburn-haired instructor glided to where Willow lay recovering. "You must be Honey's daughter. I've heard so much about you." She held out a hand.

Willow sat up and took it. "That's me."

"I'm Fiona." The woman released Willow's hand. "I love your mom. She's made so much progress. She's a real inspiration."

"She says you're the inspiration," Willow said.

"He's out like a light." Honey appeared, gripping the carrier with both hands.

"My little guy slept through classes for the first six months, but that was it." Fiona laughed.

Willow eyed her slender form. "You have a baby?"

"He's three and a half. Not a baby anymore."

"So there's hope for me?"

Fiona's eyebrows drew together. "Hope for you?"

"That I'll get my abs back. I used to do karate, but the doctor thought it might be best to ease into my old exercise routine. Mom swears by your Pilates class."

"Ah, yes." Fiona's face cleared. "Plenty of hope. Actually, a lot of martial arts practitioners also do Pilates. The two are a fantastic combo."

A snuffling sound emanated from the car carrier. "Now you wake up," Honey cooed.

"Can I see him?" Fiona said.

Willow loved to show off Forest. He was big for three months, round and pink with a shock of dark hair and a rosebud mouth that broke into a grin whenever she was close.

Willow loved everything about motherhood. She was so in love with her son, she didn't mind dirty diapers, sore breasts, or getting up in the night for feedings. She was spoiled, however.

Unlike many new parents, she didn't have to set an alarm in the morning. She helped out at Sweeter, her mother's shop, but the hours were flexible. And she had plenty of help with Forest, especially when Booker was home from the fire department. These luxuries might be gone soon.

Willow took the carrier from Honey when Fiona was done admiring Forest. "We'd better get going."

"We should." Honey turned her gaze on Fiona. "Willow has an audition this evening."

"Really? What do you do?" Fiona's eyebrows rose.

"I'm—"

Honey cut Willow off. "She's an amazing violinist. Her audition is with the Pacific Symphony."

Annoyance prickled but only for a moment. Mothers brag on their kids. Willow understood that now. She told anyone who'd listen that Forest had learned to roll over at a hair under three months. Most babies didn't master the skill until four or five, and she'd wanted the world to know her progeny was amazing.

She also understood her father better than she ever had. Many times since Forest's birth, Willow had woken in a cold sweat and run to his cradle to make sure he was still alive. She'd stand counting his breaths until she was sure they were frequent enough, but not too frequent. Deep enough, but not too deep.

She checked windows and doors compulsively when Jonathan was released on bail. He hadn't tried to contact her, and he'd signed the divorce papers when they were delivered. She was beginning to relax.

"Congratulations, or break a leg, or a bow, or whatever you're supposed to break," Fiona said.

"Thanks," Willow said.

As Honey opened the door of the Pilates studio, a small, sturdy shape rushed in and careened into Fiona's legs. A gray-haired woman poked her head through the doorway. Willow had seen her in the studio's childcare room on her way into class.

"Here he is," the woman said and disappeared.

Fiona swung the child onto her hip. "My little terror. Caleb, say hi to the nice ladies."

He lifted a chubby hand and waved. "You have a baby."

"I do," Willow said.

"Can I play with him?"

Fiona poked her son in the belly. "You're too big to play with such a little guy."

Caleb doubled over and giggled. "I play with Daddy, and he's way bigger than me."

"Daddy knows how to be careful." Fiona tickled him again. "You don't."

Caleb broke into gales of laughter as his mother lowered him to the floor. She glanced at Willow again. "They get to be more and more fun and more and more work."

Caleb turned a serious gaze on Willow. "Daddy's going to take me sliding."

She smiled. "Sounds like fun."

"He means sledding," Fiona said. "His dad is taking him to the mountains next week."

The little boy jumped to his feet. "There's snow up there. I never seen snow."

Willow tousled his dark blond curls. "You'll love it."

"He will," Fiona said. "I'm the one going through separation anxiety."

"Bye, baby," Caleb called after them as Willow and Honey left the studio.

The chilly air outside hit Willow's damp clothes, and she picked up her pace. "So, none of my business, but is Fiona still married to Caleb's father?"

Honey clicked open her SUV with her key fob before she answered. "Yes. He comes into the studio now and again. Seems like a nice man. Why?"

Willow secured the car seat behind the driver's seat and closed the door. "I don't know. I guess because he's taking Caleb to the mountains and Fiona's not going."

Honey stood with her hand on the driver's door. "Maybe he wanted some alone time with his son?" She got into the car, and Willow walked around to the passenger side.

Alone time with his son. A stab of pain shot through Willow. Forest would never have alone time with his dad. At least, not if she could help it. Chances were, his father would be in prison until Forest was an adult himself, maybe longer.

The trial was slated to begin next month. There would be a media storm. Willow hoped she was strong enough to handle it. She'd met with the prosecuting attorney several times already. He tried to prepare her for the attacks on her character that were sure to come. She was a key witness. The defense would do their best to damage her reputation.

She got into the passenger seat and buckled herself in. Honey started the ignition but placed a hand over Willow's before pulling out of the parking lot. "You're not in this alone. Your Dad, Ash, me, we're all going to be there in the courtroom and beyond."

Willow didn't say anything on the ten-minute drive home. She couldn't. Her throat had constricted, and her eyes stung with tears. Independence was a wonderful thing, but right now she was grateful for her family.

Honey turned into the driveway. "We'll have to work out the babysitting schedule when you start playing for the orchestra."

"If I get in," Willow said.

"You'll get in." Honey got out of the car.

Willow put Forest in the travel crib that had taken up residence in the living room, and Honey headed into the kitchen. "Why don't you go upstairs and get ready for the audition. I've got the baby."

As Willow showered, fixed her hair and put on just a bit more makeup than usual, she ran over the piece she planned to play in her mind, Amy Beach's *Violin Sonata*. It was the first thing she'd played on the Antoniazzi. She hoped it would bring her luck.

Hamish's funeral had only been ten months ago. It felt like ten years. All she'd thought about at the time was molding herself to fit in with Jonathan and his family. She'd been in awe of them, of their wealth, but all of that had gone up in flames, literally and figuratively. Since the fire, she regularly poked through the ashes of her life looking for remnants of that time that were worth saving.

Because of Forest and the trial, she couldn't simply walk away, couldn't close that chapter of her life like a terrible novel she didn't plan to finish. After the court case, she would sue for full and permanent custody, but there were other family members to consider.

She'd developed a tentative friendship with Ophelia, who wanted Forest to call her Auntie when he could talk. Cob and Marianne had come to see her when the baby was born and brought her a beautiful blanket for him. Sophie had also sent well wishes and a gift. None of them had done anything wrong and in many ways were victims of the twins' greed, just as she was.

Cookie was still a part of her life as well. He and her mother had hit it off, just as she'd predicted, and were now working together to expand the home cooking classes that were a growing part of Honey's business.

Willow slipped a black dress over her head and zipped it up. There were many things from the rubble of Sunset House worth saving. When she rebuilt her life, they would make it richer. She slipped on a pair of pumps, picked up the Antoniazzi's case from its place in the corner of her room, and walked out the door.

MOLLY: As I said, I love a happy ending. Willow is doing great these days. She got the job with the symphony, Forest is walking and talking, and she's dating Michael, the guitar-playing teacher from the school she used to work at in San Diego. They're taking things slowly, but she's introduced him to the family and everyone approves, including Forest.

As for the CS-Fullerton student mystery, Abby and I will be heading to the school during the break to visit with the staff who knew Melissa,

Raphael, and Ariana. It may be we'll learn something in a face to face conversation that we wouldn't in a phone call. We shall see. I'll report in next season.

And speaking of next season, we've arrived at the final crime. Before I tell you about what's to come, however, I want to take a moment to talk about the journey thus far.

Season One began with a murder in the house on Cliff Drive. Season Seven revisits that crime. Seven is a significant number. It's the number of completion. There were seven wonders in the ancient world, seven days in the week, and it's the number of deadly sins.

The basement of the house on Cliff Drive, if you remember, had seven doors. In Willow's dream in episode five, she entered a hallway that matched the description of that basement.

In *The Dark Room*, the story that gave rise to this series, Amy had a similar dream. Night after night she found herself in a long hall with dim yellow lighting. She heard the sound of water beating against the walls and noted there were seven doors. Just like Willow, she had the sense that there was danger behind each. (For those who haven't yet read *The Dark Room*, there's a link for a free copy at the end of today's show notes.)

So, what does this mean? I know many of you are diehard realists. You don't believe in angels or demons or anything you can't put in a Petri dish and observe. But, people, this is a crazy coincidence.

I understand why the sense of danger surrounding the number seven was in Amy's subconscious. Someone was drawing scenes from Dante's

Inferno on her walls—one for each of the seven deadly sins. Symbolically, each door may have represented the crimes and punishments associated with them.

But why did Willow have the same dream? Could it be somewhere in her psyche she recognized she was a part of something bigger? I've used many analogies to describe the connection I see between these crimes. We've talked about throwing a pebble in a pond and the ripples that widen and encompass the water around them. We've talked about passing an imaginary baton from one victim-victor to the next.

But what if the location of each crime in this series was a planned stop, a destination on a map written by an unseen and unwholesome hand? What if the events recorded in *The Dark Room* unleashed a presence with an agenda? A being that is following a treasure map from place to place and wreaking havoc at each?

I don't know the answers to these questions, but next season we are about to go further afield than we've ever gone before and yet we're also coming full circle.

Our story will take us to a cabin in Big Bear Lake, a Southern California mountain community popular with tourists seeking snow in the winter, and fishing and hiking in the summer. Our heroes, however, are individuals you met in Season One, *The Cliff House.* REK, aka The Real Estate Killer, returns to haunt Fiona and Devon Randall in *The Cabin.*

Devon takes their almost four-year-old son, Caleb, on a father-son vacation. It's close to Christmas when they leave town. Fiona plans to meet them in the cabin a few days later, after

she closes up shop for the holidays. They'll
celebrate in the snow. It sounds idyllic. And it
would have been, except for the unexpected guest
who arrives at their door.

Join me next season in *The Cabin* for more
Murders Under the Sun.

(cue music)

VO: If you enjoyed this episode, please leave
us a five-star review on your favorite podcast
service—it really helps. *Murders Under the Sun* is
edited by Jim Wilbourne, theme music by Eclectic
Blends, and I'm your host, Molly Shure.

If you haven't picked up your free copy of *The Dark Room*, the origin
story for The Almost True Crime Series, you can grab it here:
https://bookhip.com/ZQMTCLP
You'll also get news about this and Greta Boris's other mystery series
when you do.

If you enjoyed this book, please do one or more of the following:

- Leave a review on your favorite book review site
- Tell a friend about *The Manor: An Almost True Crime Story*
- Ask your local library to put Greta Boris's work on the shelf
- Recommend Fawkes Press books to your local bookstore

VISIT US ONLINE
www.FawkesPress.com
www.GretaBoris.com

FAWKES PRESS

also by greta boris

www.ingramcontent.com/pod-product-compliance
Lightning Source LLC
Chambersburg PA
CBHW061643190726
48289CB00006B/1722